Guide Library

*Hillwood Museum
Washington, D.C.*

SMOKE

THE NOVELS AND STORIES OF IVÁN TURGÉNIEFF

PUBLISHED BY CHARLES SCRIBNER'S SONS

Each 12mo, $1.25 net

SMOKE

BY

IVÁN TURGÉNIEFF

TRANSLATED FROM THE RUSSIAN BY
ISABEL F. HAPGOOD

NEW YORK
CHARLES SCRIBNER'S SONS
1915

SMOKE

(1867)

SMOKE

I

AT four o'clock, on the afternoon of the tenth of August, in the year 1862, a large number of persons were assembled in front of the famous " Conversation " (Hall) in Baden-Baden. The weather continued to be delightful; everything round about—the verdant trees, the bright-hued houses of the comfortable town, the undulating hills—everything lay outspread in festive guise, with lavish hand, beneath the rays of the benignant sun; everything was smiling in a passive, confiding and engaging manner, and the same sort of vague yet amiable smile strayed over the faces of the people, young and old, homely and handsome. Even the dyed and bleached faces of the Parisian courtesans did not destroy the general impression of manifest satisfaction and exultation, but the motley-hued ribbons and feathers, the glints of gold and steel on bonnets and veils, involuntarily suggested to the vision the reanimated gleam and light play of springtide flowers and rainbow-hued wings: but the dry, guttural rattle of French gabble could not take the place of the twittering of the birds, or bear comparison therewith.

However, everything was going on as usual. The orchestra in the pavilion played now a pot-pourri from " La Traviata," again a waltz by Strauss, or *Dites-lui,* or a Russian romance arranged for instruments by the obliging band-master; around the green tables in the gambling-halls thronged the same familiar figures, with the same dull and greedy expression as ever, an expression neither exactly perplexed nor yet irritated, but essentially rapacious, which the gambling fever imparts to all, even to the most aristocratic features; the usual obese landed proprietor from Tambóff, in extremely dandified attire, with the usual incomprehensible, convulsive haste, and eyes protruding, leaning his breast on the table, and paying no heed to the grins of the croupiers, at the moment of uttering the exclamation, *" Rien ne va plus! "* was scattering circles of louis d'or, with perspiring hand, over all the squares of the roulette-board, and thereby depriving himself of all possibility of winning anything, even in the case of luck; which did not in the least prevent him, in the course of that same evening, from humouring with sympathetic wrath Prince Kokó, one of the well-known leaders of the opposition among the gentry, the Prince Kokó who, in Paris, in the drawing-room of Princess Mathilde, in the presence of the Emperor, remarked so truly:

4

SMOKE

"*Madame, le principe de la propriété est profondément ébranlé en Russie.*" According to their wont, our amiable fellow-countrymen and women assembled at the "Russian Tree"—*à l' Arbre Russe;*—they strolled up ostentatiously, carelessly, fashionably, greeted each other majestically, with elegant ease, as is befitting beings who stand at the apex of contemporary culture, but, having met and seated themselves, they positively did not know what to say to one another, and contented themselves with the exchange of empty phrases, or with the threadbare, extremely impudent and extremely insipid sallies of a French ex-literary man, who had long since seen his best days, a jester and chatter-box, with Jewish slippers on his wretched little feet, and with a contemptible little beard on his miserable little phiz. He babbled to them, *à ces princes Russes,* all sorts of stale nonsense out of ancient almanacs of the *Charivari* and *Tintamarre,* . . while they—*ces princes Russes*—burst into grateful laughter, as though involuntarily acknowledging both the overwhelming superiority of foreign wit and their own definitive incapacity to devise anything amusing. And yet there was present almost all the "*fine fleur*" of our society, "all the quality and the models of fashion." There was Count X., our incomparable dilettante, a profound musical nature, who "recites" romances so divinely, and, as a matter of fact, cannot distinguish one

5

note from another without poking his forefinger at random over the keys, and sings somewhat like an indifferently poor gipsy, somewhat like a Parisian hair-dresser; there was also our enchanting Baron Z., that jack of all trades: literary man, administrator, orator and sharper; there was also Prince Y., the friend of religion and of the people, who had amassed a huge fortune in his time, the blessed epoch of monopolies, by the sale of inferior liquor adulterated with stramonium; and brilliant General O. O., who has subdued something or other, is the pacificator of somebody or other, but, nevertheless, does not know what to do with himself, or how to make himself agreeable; and R. R., an amusing fat man, who regards himself as a very ailing and very clever fellow, but is as healthy as an ox and as stupid as a stump. This R. R. is almost the only person who in our day still preserves the tradition of the social lions of the '40's of the epoch of " The Hero of Our Times " [1] and of Countess Vorotýnsky. He has retained also the gait with its swing from the heels, and " *le culte de la pose* " (which cannot even be expressed in Russian), and the unnatural deliberation of movement, and the sleepy majesty of expression on the impassive, as it were offended, countenance, and the habit of interrupting other people's remarks with a yawn, carefully inspecting

[1] By M. Y. Lérmontoff.—TRANSLATOR.

his own fingers and nails the while, of laughing straight in people's faces, of suddenly tilting the hat from the nape of the neck over the brows, and so forth, and so forth. There were also even governmental officials, diplomats, big-wigs with European reputations, men of good counsel and sense, who imagine that the golden bull was issued by the Pope, and that the English " poor-tax " is an impost on the poor; there were, in conclusion, fiery but bashful admirers of the frail fair ones, young society dandies with their hair supremely well parted behind, with superb pendent side-whiskers, attired in real London costumes, young dandies whom, apparently, nothing could prevent from becoming the same sort of vulgar triflers as the renowned French chatterer; but no! nothing native-born is in vogue with us,—and Countess Sh., the well-known law-giver of fashion, and of the " grand genre," nicknamed by malicious tongues " The Tzarítza of the Wasps " and " The Medusa in a Mob-cap," preferred, in the absence of the prattler, to turn to the Italians, Moldavians, American " spiritists," dashing secretaries of foreign legations, petty Germans with effeminate but already cautious physiognomies, and so forth, who were hovering about there also. In imitation of the Countess's example, Princess Babette also, the one in whose arms Chopin died (there are about a thousand ladies in Europe in whose arms he yielded up his spirit), and Princess

Annette, who would have possessed every charm were it not that from time to time suddenly, like the odour of cabbage in the midst of the finest amber, the common country washerwoman had not cropped out; and Princess Pachette, to whom the following catastrophe happened: her husband lighted upon a conspicuous position and all of a sudden, *Dieu salt pourquoi,* he thrashed the mayor of the town and stole twenty thousand rubles of the government money; and that mirthful maiden —Princess Zizi, and tearful Princess Zozo; all of them deserted their fellow-country people and treated them ungraciously. . . But let us also desert them, these charming ladies, and quit the famous tree around which they are seated in such costly but rather tasteless toilettes, and may the Lord send them relief from the ennui which is tormenting them!

II

SEVERAL paces removed from the "Russian Tree," at a small table in front of Weber's café, sat a man about thirty years of age, of medium stature, lean and swarthy, with a manly and agreeable face. Bending forward and leaning on his cane with both hands, he sat quietly and simply, like a man to whom the idea would never occur that any one was noticing him or taking an interest in him. His large, expressive eyes, brown with a tawny tinge, gazed slowly about him, now blinking a little with the sunlight, again suddenly and intently following some eccentric figure that passed by, in which last case a swift, childlike smile barely moved his slight moustache, his lips and strong physiognomy. He was clad in a loose frock-coat of German cut, and his soft grey hat half concealed his lofty brow. At first sight he produced the impression of an honourable, active and rather self-confident young fellow, of which sort there are not a few in the world. He appeared to be resting from prolonged labours, and with all the more singleness of mind was diverting himself with the picture which unfolded itself before him, because his thoughts were far away, and because, moreover, those thoughts were revolving in a world which did not in the least resemble that which surrounded him at that moment. He was a Russian; his name was Grigóry Mikhaílovitch Litvínoff.

We must make his acquaintance, and therefore it becomes necessary to narrate, in a few words, his far from gay or complicated past.

The son of a retired plodding official from the merchant class, he had not been educated in town, as might have been expected, but in the country. His mother was a noble by birth, a girl from one of the Government Institutes, a very amiable and very enthusiastic being, yet not lacking in strength of character. Being twelve years younger than her husband, she remodelled his education as far as she was able, dragged him out of the official into the noble rut, tamed and softened his harsh, vigorous nature. Thanks to her, he had come to dress neatly and behave with propriety, and had left off swearing; he had come to respect learned men and learning,— although, of course, he never took a book in his hand,—and endeavoured in every way never to derogate from his dignity: he even began to walk more lightly, and he spoke in a subdued voice, chiefly on lofty subjects, which cost him no little trouble. " Ekh! I 'd like to take and spank you! " he sometimes said to himself, but aloud he remarked: " Yes, yes . . . of course; that is the question." Litvínoff's mother had put her house-

hold also on a European footing; she said " you "
to the servants, and permitted no one to overeat
at dinner to the point of snoring. So far as the
estate which belonged to her was concerned,
neither she nor her husband had been able to make
anything out of it: it had long been neglected,
but was extensive with various meadows, forests
and a lake, beside which, in times gone by, had
stood a large factory established by the zealous
but unsystematic owner, which had thriven in the
hands of a knavish merchant, and had finally
come to ruin under the direction of an honest
manager, a German. Madame Litvínoff was satisfied with not having impaired her property and
with having contracted no debts. Unfortunately,
she could not boast of good health, and died of
consumption during the very year that her son
entered the Moscow University. He did not finish his course, owing to circumstances (the reader
will learn later on what they were), and lounged
about in the country, where he enjoyed life for a
considerable time without occupation, or connections, almost without acquaintances. Thanks to
the nobles of his county, who were ill-disposed toward him, and imbued not so much with the
Western theory of the evils of " absenteeism " as
with the innate conviction that " charity begins at
home," he was got into the militia in 1855, and
came near dying of typhus in the Crimea, where,
without having beheld a single " ally," he was

quartered for six months in an earth-hut on the banks of the Putrid Sea; then he served in the elections, as a matter of course, not without unpleasantness, and finding himself at ease in the country he became passionately devoted to farming. He comprehended that his mother's property, badly and indolently managed by his now infirm father, did not yield a tenth part of the income which it was capable of yielding, and that in experienced and expert hands it might be converted into a regular gold mine; but he also comprehended that precisely what he lacked was this experience and skill—and he betook himself abroad to study agronomy and technology—to study them from the very foundation. He had spent more than four years in Mecklenburg, Silesia, Karlsruhe, he had travelled in Belgium and in England, he had laboured conscientiously, he had acquired information: it had not been easily acquired; but he had endured the ordeal to the end, and now, confident of himself, of his future, of the utility he could bring to his fellow-countrymen, even to the whole country, he was preparing to return to his native land, whither his father, utterly disconcerted by the emancipation, by the division of lands, by the redemption contracts,—by the new order of things, in short,— was summoning him with despairing adjurations and entreaties in every letter. . . But why was he in Baden?

He was in Baden because from day to day he was expecting the arrival there of his second cousin, his affianced bride,—Tatyána Petróvna Shestóff. He had known her almost from childhood, and had passed the spring and summer with her in Dresden, where she had settled with her aunt. He sincerely loved, he profoundly respected his young relative, and having completed his obscure preparatory work, and being on the point of entering upon a new career, of beginning active, not state service, he had proposed to her, as to a beloved woman, as to a comrade and friend, that she should unite her life to his life—for joy and for sorrow, for toil and for repose, " for better, for worse," as the English say. She had consented, and he had betaken himself to Karlsruhe, where he had left his books, his things and his papers. . . But why was he in Baden, you ask again?

He was in Baden because Tatyána's aunt, who had reared her, Kapitólina Márkovna Shestóff, an elderly spinster of fifty-five years, a most kind-hearted and honourable eccentric, a free soul, all burning with the fire of self-sacrifice and self-renunciation, an *esprit fort* (she read Strauss,— on the sly from her niece, it is true), and democrat, a sworn foe of grand society and the aristocracy, could not resist the temptation to take just one little peep at that same grand society in such a fashionable place as Baden. . . Kapitólina Márkovna dispensed with crinoline and clipped her white hair in a shock, but luxury and brilliancy secretly agitated her, and she found it joyful and sweet to rail against them and despise them. . . And how could one refuse to divert the kindly old lady?

But Litvínoff was so calm and simple, he gazed about him so confidently, because his life lay before him with precise clearness, because his fate had been settled, and because he was proud of that fate, and was rejoicing in it, as the work of his own hands.

III

"BA! ba! ba! here he is!" a squeaking voice suddenly rang out straight in his ear, and a flabby hand tapped him on the shoulder.

He raised his head,—and beheld one of his few Moscow acquaintances, a certain Bambáeff, a nice man, one of the triflers, no longer young, with cheeks and nose as soft as though they had been boiled, greasy, dishevelled hair, and a flabby, obese body. Eternally penniless and eternally in raptures over something or other, Rostisláff Bambáeff roamed to and fro, with a hurrah but without occupation, over the face of our long-suffering mother earth.

"The very person I wanted to see!"—he repeated, opening wide his fat-obscured little eyes, and thrusting out his thick little lips, above which a dyed moustache stuck out in a strange and inappropriate manner.—"Hurrah for Baden! Every one crawls hither like black beetles. How didst thou get here?"

Bambáeff addressed positively every one on earth as "thou."

"I arrived three days ago."

"Whence?"

" But why dost thou wish to know? "

" Why, indeed! But wait, wait, perhaps thou dost not know who else has arrived here? Gubaryóff! That's who is here! He came from Heidelberg yesterday. Of course thou knowest him? "

" I have heard of him."

" Only that? Good gracious! Instantly, this very minute, I shall drag thee to him. Not know such a man! And, by the way, here's Voroshíloff. . . . Stay, perhaps thou dost not know him either? I have the honour to present you to each other. Both of you are learned men. He's even a very phœnix. Kiss each other! "

And as he uttered these words, Bambáeff turned to a handsome young man with a rosy but already serious face, who was standing beside him. Litvínoff rose, and of course did not kiss him, but exchanged a brief salute with the " phœnix," who, judging by the stiffness of his demeanour, was not any too well pleased by this unexpected introduction.

" I said a phœnix, and I will not withdraw the word," continued Bambáeff:—" go to Petersburg, to the * * * Cadet Corps, and look at the golden board—roll of honour—whose name stands first there? Voroshíloff Semyón Yakóvlevitch! But Gubaryóff, Gubaryóff, my dear fellows! That's the man to whom we must run, run! I positively worship that man! And I'm not the only one; all, without distinction, adore him. What a work he is now writing, oh . . . oh . . . oh!"

"What is the work about?" inquired Litvínoff.

"About everything, my dear fellow, in the style of Buckle, you know . . only more profound—more profound. . . In it everything will be settled and made clear."

"And hast thou read that work thyself?"

"No, I have not; and it is even a secret which must not be divulged; but from Gubaryóff everything is to be expected, everything! Yes!"— Bambáeff sighed and folded his hands.—"What if two or three more such heads were bred among us in Russia, what would happen, O Lord my God! I'll tell thee one thing, Grigóry Mikhaílovitch: whatever thou mayest have been occupying thyself with of late,—and I do not know what thy interests in general are,—whatever may be thy convictions,—and I know nothing about them either,—thou wilt find something to learn from him, from Gubaryóff. Unfortunately, he will not be here long. We must take advantage of the opportunity, we must go. To him, to him!"

A passing dandy with small red curls and a sky-blue ribbon on his low-crowned hat turned round and stared at Bambáeff through his monocle with a sarcastic smile. Litvínoff was vexed.

"Why dost thou shout?" he ejaculated:—

" thou yellest as though after a hound! I have not yet dined."

" What of that! We can dine immediately at Weber's . . all three. . Capital! Hast thou the money to pay for me? " he added in an undertone.

" Yes, yes; only really I do not know . . ."

" Stop, please; thou wilt thank me, and he will be glad. Akh, my God! " Bambáeff broke off.— " They 're playing the finale from ' Ernani.' How charming! *A som . . . mo Carlo*. . . But what a fellow I am! I begin to cry at once. Well, Semyón Yakóvlevitch! Voroshíloff! Shall we go? "

Voroshíloff, who was still standing in a stiff and stately attitude, maintaining his original somewhat haughty dignity of mien, dropped his eyes significantly, frowned, and bellowed something through his teeth . . . but did not refuse; and Litvínoff said to himself: "Never mind! let 's do it, seeing there 's plenty of time." Bambaéff slipped his arm into his, but before setting out for the café he beckoned to Isabella, the famous flower-girl of the Jockey Club: it had occurred to him to buy a bouquet of her. But the aristocratic flower-girl did not stir; and why should she go to a gentleman without gloves, in a stained velveteen jacket, a variegated necktie, and patched boots, whom she had never beheld in Paris? Then Voroshíloff beckoned to her in his turn. She went to him, and he, selecting from her basket a

tiny bunch of violets, tossed her a gulden. He
had thought to astonish her with his lavishness;
but she never moved an eyelash, and when he
turned away from her she curled her closely-com-
pressed lips in scorn. Voroshíloff was very fop-
pishly, even elegantly, clad, but the experienced
eye of the Parisienne had instantly noted in his
toilette, in his very gait, which bore traces of early
military drilling, the absence of genuine, thor-
oughbred " chic."

When our acquaintances had seated themselves
in Weber's principal room and had ordered dinner, they entered into conversation. Bambáeff
talked loudly and fervently about the lofty significance of Gubaryóff, but soon fell silent, and
noisily sighing and chewing, clinked glass to
glass. Voroshíloff ate and drank little, and having questioned Litvínoff as to the nature of his
occupation, began to express his own opinions . . .
not so much with regard to that occupation as in
general about various " questions." . . He suddenly grew animated and started off at full gallop, like a good horse, adroitly and sharply em-
phasising every syllable, every letter, like a
fine dashing young cadet at his final ex-
amination, and waving his arms violently, but
not in accord. He became momentarily more vol-
uble, more energetic, as no one interrupted him:
it was exactly as though he were reading a disser-
tation or a lecture. The names of the newest

savants, with the year of each one's birth or death added, the title of pamphlets which had just been published, in general names, names, names,— fell thick and fast from his tongue, affording him the highest gratification, which was reflected in his flashing eyes. Voroshíloff evidently despised everything old, prized only the cream of culture, the latest, most advanced points of science; to mention, even inopportunely, the book of some Doctor Sauerbrengel about the prisons in Pennsylvania, or an article which had appeared the previous day in *The Asiatic Journal* about the Vedas and the Puranas (he said it in just that way: "Journal," although, of course, he did not know English)—was for him genuine delight, felicity. Litvínoff listened to him, listened and could not in the least understand what his own speciality was. Now he turned the conversation upon the rôle of the Celtic race in history; again it bore him off to the ancient world, and he argued about the marbles of Ægina, harped insistently on the sculptor Onatas, who lived before Phidias, but who, in his hands, was transformed into Jonathan, and thereby, in the twinkling of an eye, imparted to his whole argument a biblical or American colouring; then he suddenly jumped to political economy, and called Bastia a fool and a blockhead, " as much so as Adam Smith and all the physiocrats " . . . "Physiocrats! " Bambáeff whispered after him . . . " Aristocrats? . . ."

Among other things, Voroshíloff had evoked an expression of amazement on the countenance of that same Bambáeff by a remark carelessly and lightly dropped concerning Macaulay, as an obsolete author who had been left in the lurch by science; as for Gneist and Riehl, he declared that it was merely necessary to name them, and shrugged his shoulders. Bambáeff shrugged his shoulders also. "And all this at one burst, without any motive whatever, in the presence of strangers in a café," meditated Litvínoff, as he gazed at the blond hair, the light eyes, the white teeth of his new acquaintance (he was particularly disturbed by those huge, sugar-like teeth, and also by those arms, with their inappropriate flourishes) ; " and he does not smile even once; and yet he must be a kindly young fellow and extremely inexperienced. . ." Voroshíloff quieted down at last; his voice, youthfully resonant and hoarse as that of a young cock, broke a little . . . and Bambáeff in the nick of time began to declaim verses, and again almost fell to weeping, which produced the effect of a row at one neighbouring table, around which an English family was seated, and a tittering at another: two courtesans were dining at this second table with a very aged infant in a lilac wig. The waiter brought the bill; the friends paid it.

"Well," exclaimed Bambáeff, rising heavily from his chair:—" now for a cup of coffee, and march! But yonder it is, our Russia," he added, halting in the doorway, and almost with rapture pointing with his soft, red hand at Voroshíloff and Litvínoff. . . "What do you think of it?"

"Yes, Russia," thought Litvínoff; but Voroshíloff, who had already again succeeded in imparting to his face a concentrated expression, smiled condescendingly, and lightly clicked his heels together.

Five minutes later all three of them were mounting the stairs of the hotel where Stepán Nikoláevitch Gubaryóff was stopping. . . A tall, stately lady, in a bonnet with a short black veil, was descending the same staircase, and on catching sight of Litvínoff she suddenly turned to him and halted, as though struck with amazement. Her face flushed for a moment and then as swiftly paled beneath the close meshes of the lace; but Litvínoff did not notice her, and the lady ran more briskly than before down the broad steps.

IV

" GRIGÓRY LITVÍNOFF is a jolly good fellow, a
Russian soul; I recommend him,"exclaimed Bambáeff, conducting Litvínoff up to a man of short
stature and the appearance of the landed gentry
class, with an unbuttoned collar, in a short-tailed
coat, grey morning trousers, and slippers, who
was standing in the middle of a bright, capitally-
furnished room;—" and this," he added, turning
to Litvínoff,—" this is he, the very man; you understand? Well, in one word, Gubaryóff."

Litvínoff fixed his eyes with curiosity on " the
very man." At first he perceived nothing unusual
about him. He beheld before him a gentleman
of respectable and rather stupid appearance, with
a large forehead, large eyes, a large beard,
a thick neck, and an oblique glance, which was
directed downward. This gentleman simpered,
muttered: " Mmm . . . yes . . . that 's good . . .
I 'm delighted . . . ," raised his hand to his own
face, and immediately turning his back on Litvínoff, strode several paces across the carpet, wab-
bling slowly and strangely, as though he were
walking stealthily. Gubaryóff had a habit of
constantly walking to and fro, incessantly pluck-

23

ing at and combing his beard with the tips of his long, firm nails. In addition to Gubaryóff there was in the room a lady in a shabby silk gown, about fifty years of age, with a remarkably mobile face as yellow as a lemon, black down on her upper lip, and vivacious little eyes which seemed on the point of popping out; a thick-set man was also sitting there doubled up in a corner.

"Well, ma'am, respected Matróna Semyónovna," began Gubaryóff, addressing the lady, and evidently not considering it necessary to introduce her to Litvínoff;—"dear me, what was it that you had begun to tell us?"

The lady (her name was Matróna Semyónovna Sukhántchikoff; she was a widow, childless, not rich, and this was the second year that she had spent in wandering from land to land) immediately began to talk with a peculiar, embittered enthusiasm:

"Well, and so he presents himself to the Prince, and says to him: ' Your Illustrious Highness,' says he,—' with your dignity and your station, what does it cost you to alleviate my lot? You,' says he, ' cannot fail to respect the purity of my convictions! And is it possible,' says he, ' in our day to persecute a man because of his convictions?' And what do you think the Prince,— that cultured, highly-placed dignitary—did?"

"Well, what did he do?" ejaculated Gubaryóff, thoughtfully lighting a cigarette.

The lady drew herself up, and stretched out in front of her her bony right hand, with the index finger separated.

" He called his lackey, and said to him: ' Strip the coat off this man and take possession of it. I make you a present of his coat.' "

" And did the lackey strip it off? " inquired Bambáeff, clasping his hands.

" He stripped it off and took it. And that was done by Prince Barnaúloff, the famous rich man, the grandee, invested with special power, the representative of the government! What may we expect after that! "

Madame Sukhántchikoff's feeble body quivered all over with indignation, convulsive shivers flitted across her face, her emaciated bosom heaved violently beneath her flat bodice; it is unnecessary to mention her eyes: they fairly leaped. However, they were always leaping, whatever she was talking about.

" 'T is a crying, crying shame! " ejaculated Bambáeff.—" Hanging is too good for him! "

" Mmm . . . mmm . . . From top to bottom it 's all rotten," remarked Gubaryóff, but without raising his voice.—" It is n't a case for hanging; . . . 't is a case . . . for other measures."

" But stay; is it true? " said Litvínoff.

" Is it true? " retorted Madame Sukhántchikoff.—" Why, it 's impossible even to think of doubting, impossible to thi-i-i-ink of such a thing. ." She uttered the word with such force that she fairly writhed.—" It was told to me by a most reliable man. And you know him, Stepán Nikoláevitch—Kapitón Elistrátoff. He heard it himself from an eye-witness, from a witness of that outrageous scene."

" What Elistrátoff?" inquired Gubaryóff.— " The one who was in Kazán?"

" The very man. I know, Stepán Nikolá- itch, that a rumour was circulated about him that he had got money out of some contractor or distiller or other. But who says that? Peli- kánoff! And can one believe Pelikánoff, when everybody knows that he is simply—a spy?"

" No, permit me, Matróna Semyónovna," in- terposed Bambáeff:—" I am Pelikánoff's friend; I don't believe he is a spy."

" Yes, yes, exactly that, a spy!"

" But wait a bit, please. . ."

" A spy, a spy!" screamed Madame Sukhán- tchikoff.

" But he is n't, no, wait; I 'll tell you some- thing," shouted Bambáeff in his turn.

" A spy, a spy!" reiterated Madame Sukhán- tchikoff.

" No, no! There 's Tenteléeff—that 's quite another matter!" roared Bambáeff at the top of his voice.

Madame Sukhántchikoff became silent for a moment.

" I know it for a fact, with regard to that gentleman," continued Bambáeff in his ordinary voice, " that when the Third Section summoned him he crawled at the feet of Countess Blazenkampf and kept whining: ' Save me, intercede for me!' But Pelikánoff never descended to such baseness."

" Mm . . . Tenteléeff . . ." growled Gubaryóff:—" that . . that must be noted."

Madame Sukhántchikoff scornfully shrugged her shoulders.

" Both are good," she remarked:—"but I know a still better anecdote about Tenteléeff. As every one knows, he was the most dreadful tyrant with his people, although he gave himself out as an emancipator. Well, one day he was sitting with some acquaintances in Paris, when, all of a sudden, in comes Mrs. Beecher Stowe,—well, you know, ' Uncle Tom's Cabin.' Tenteléeff, a frightfully conceited man, began to urge the host to present him; but as soon as Mrs. Stowe heard his name: ' What?'—says she:—' how dares he make acquaintance with the author of ' Uncle Tom'? And, whack, she slapped his face!— ' Begone!' says she,—' this instant!'—And what do you think? Tenteléeff took his hat, and putting his tail between his legs, he slunk off."

" Well, that strikes me as exaggerated," remarked Bambáeff.—" That she did say ' Begone!' to him is a fact; but she did not slap his face."

"She did slap his face, she did slap his face," repeated Madame Sukhántchikoff, with convulsive intensity:—"I don't talk nonsense. And you are the friend of such people!"

"Excuse me, excuse me, Matróna Semyónovna, I never asserted that Tenteléeff was an intimate friend of mine; I was speaking of Pelikánoff."

"Well, if it was n't Tenteléeff, it was some one else: Mikhnyóff, for instance."

"What did he do?" asked Bambáeff, intimidated in advance.

"What? Don't you really know? On the Vosnesénsky Prospékt, in the presence of everybody, he shouted out that all liberals ought to be in prison; and then an old boarding-school comrade, a poor man, of course, comes up to him, and says: 'May I dine with you?' But he answered him: 'No, you cannot; two Counts are to dine with me to-day . . . . g' 'way!'"

"But good gracious, that is a calumny!" clamoured Bambáeff.

"A calumny? . . . a calumny? In the first place, Prince Vakhrúshkin, who also was dining with your Mikhnyóff . . ."

"Prince Vakhrúshkin," interposed Gubaryóff sternly,—"is my first cousin; but I will not receive him. . . Consequently, there is no use of mentioning him."

"In the second place," continued Madame Sukhántchikoff, submissively inclining her head in the direction of Gubaryóff:—"Praskóvya Yakóvlevna herself told me so."

"A fine person to allege as authority! She and Sarkísoff are first-class inventors of tales."

"Well, sir, you must excuse me; Sarkísoff is a liar, that's a fact, and that he pulled the brocade pall off his dead father I will never deny; but Praskóvya Yakóvlevna,—what a comparison! Recollect how nobly she separated from her husband! But you, I know, are always ready to . . . . ."

"Come, that will do, that will do, Matróna Semyónovna," Bambáeff interrupted her.—"Let us drop this tittle-tattle and soar aloft. I'm a poker of ancient make,[1] you see. Have you read 'M'lle de la Quintinie'? It's charming! And with exactly your principles!"

"I no longer read romances," replied Madame Sukhántchikoff, drily and curtly.

"Why?"

Because it is no time for such things; I have only one thing in my head now—sewing-machines."

"What sort of machines?" inquired Litvínoff.

"Sewing-, sewing-machines; all women, all,

1 An old-fashioned man.—TRANSLATOR.

29

must supply themselves with sewing-machines, and form a society; in that way they will all earn their living and will at once become independent. Otherwise, they cannot possibly free themselves. It is an important, an important social question. Boléslaff Stadnítzky and I had such a dispute about that. Boléslaff Stadnítzky has a wonderful nature, but he looks on these things in a frightfully frivolous way. He does nothing but laugh. . . . The fool!"

"All men will be summoned, in due season, to an accounting—all men will be held responsible," remarked Gubaryóff slowly, in a partly dogmatic, partly prophetic tone.

"Yes, yes," repeated Bambáeff:—"they will be held responsible—exactly so, held responsible. And how about your work, Stepán Nikoláitch," he added, lowering his voice:—"is it progressing?"

"I am collecting the materials," replied Gubaryóff, knitting his brows; and turning to Litvínoff, whose head was growing giddy with that mess of names which were unfamiliar to him, with that frenzy of gossip, asked him: with what did he occupy himself?

Litvínoff satisfied his curiosity.

"Ah! that is to say with the natural sciences. That is useful, as a school. As a school, not as a goal. The goal now should be . . . . mm . . . should be . . . something else. Permit me to inquire, with what opinions do you take sides?"

"What opinions?"

"Yes; that is to say, what are your political convictions?"

Litvínoff smiled.

"I really have no political opinions whatever."

At these words the thick-set man, who was sitting in the corner, suddenly raised his head, and gazed attentively at Litvínoff.

"How so?" said Gubaryóff, with strange gentleness.—"Have n't you gone into the subject yet, or have you already grown tired of it?"

"How shall I explain it to you? It seems to me that it is still too early for us Russians to have political opinions, or to imagine that we have them. Observe that I give to the word ' political ' the meaning which rightfully belongs to it, and that . . . ."

"Aha! you 're one of the unripe ones," Gubaryóff interrupted him with the same gentleness, and approaching Voroshíloff, he asked him:—had he read the pamphlet which he had given him?

Voroshíloff, who, to Litvínoff's surprise, had not uttered the smallest word since his arrival, but had merely scowled and rolled his eyes about (as a rule he either orated or maintained complete silence),—Voroshíloff thrust out his chest in military fashion, and clicking his heels together, nodded his head in the affirmative.

" Well, and what then? Were you pleased? "

" So far as the principal premises are concerned, but I do not agree with the deductions."

" Mmm . . . but Andréi Ivánitch praised that pamphlet to me very highly. You must state your doubts to me later on."

Gubaryóff was evidently surprised: he had not expected this; but after reflecting briefly, he articulated:

" Yes, in writing. By the way, I will ask you to state for me also your views . . . . as to . . . as to association."

" Would you like it after the method of Lassalle, or of Schulze-Delitzsch? "

" Mmm . . . after both methods. You understand that the financial side is especially important for us Russians. Well, and the workingmen's union [1] as the kernel. . . All that must be taken into consideration. It must be thoroughly investigated. And there is the question of the peasants' allotments. . ."

" And what is your opinion, Stepán Nikoláitch, as to the suitable amount of desyatínas? " inquired Voroshíloff, with respectful delicacy in his voice.

" Mmm . . . And the commune? " said Gubaryóff with profundity, and gnawing a tuft of

[1] The *artél*, which represents workingmen united in voluntary, elastic associations for the purpose of fulfilling contracts to advantage, insuring trustworthiness, and so forth.—TRANSLATOR.

his beard he riveted his eyes on the leg of the table.
—" The commune. . . Do you understand?
That is a grand word! And then, what is the
meaning of these conflagrations . . . . these governmental measures against Sunday-schools,[1]
reading-rooms, newspapers?—and, in conclusion,
that which is going on in Poland? Do you not see
to what all this is leading, that . . . mm . . .
that we . . . we must now fuse ourselves with the
people, must find out . . find out their opinion? "
—Gubaryóff was suddenly seized with a painful,
almost malignant, agitation; he even turned a
greyish-brown hue in the face and breathed more
vehemently, but still he did not raise his eyes, and
continued to chew his beard.—" Do you not
see . . . ."

" Evséeff is a scoundrel! " suddenly blurted out
Madame Sukhántchikoff, to whom Bambáeff was
narrating something in an undertone, out of respect for the host. Gubaryóff wheeled abruptly
round on his heels, and began again to hobble up
and down the room.

New guests began to make their appearance;
toward the end of the evening a considerable number of persons had assembled. Among them came
also Mr. Evséeff, who had been so harshly abused
by Madame Sukhántchikoff: she chatted with

[1] For the instruction in the common branches of workingmen who
are occupied on week-days. As religion forms a prominent subject
in all school-courses in Russia, Sunday-schools in the Western sense
of the word are unnecessary.—TRANSLATOR.

him in a very friendly manner, and asked him to
escort her home; there came also a certain Pishtchálkin, an ideal arbitrator of the peace,[1] precisely one of those men of whom, possibly, Russia
is in need, namely—narrow, badly educated and
untalented but conscientious, patient, and honourable; the peasants of his district almost worshipped him, and he treated himself with extreme
respect as an individual truly worthy of homage.
There came also several young officers who had
run off on a brief leave of absence to Europe,
and were delighted at the opportunity, cautiously,
of course, and without banishing from their minds
a mental reservation about the regimental commander, to indulge themselves with clever and
rather dangerous people; and two slender young
students had run over from Heidelberg: one kept
gazing scornfully about him, the other laughed
spasmodically . . and both were very ill at ease;
after them a Frenchman pushed his way in, a so-
called *p'tit jeune homme:* dirty, poor and stupid . . he was famous among his comrades, who
were travelling salesmen, because Russian Coun-
tesses fell in love with him; but he himself was
more intent on a gratuitous supper; last of all,
Tit Bindásoff presented himself, with the aspect
of a noisy student, but in reality he was a cur-
mudgeon and a crafty fellow, in speech a terror-

[1] An official appointed at the time of the emancipation of the serfs
to decide dissensions between them and the landed proprietors arising
out of the distribution of the land. — TRANSLATOR.

ist, by vocation a police-captain, the friend of Russian merchants' wives and of Parisian courtesans, bald, toothless, drunken; he presented himself in a very crimson and evil state, asserting that he had lost his last kopék to that " little rascal Benazet," when, in reality, he had won sixteen gulden. . . In a word, a great many persons assembled. The respect with which all the visitors treated Gubaryóff as a teacher or leader was remarkable—truly remarkable; they expounded to him their doubts, submitted them to his judgment; but he replied . . with a bellow, by tugging at his beard, by rolling his eyes, or by fragmentary, insignificant words, which were immediately caught up on the fly like utterances of the loftiest wisdom. Gubaryóff himself rarely joined in the discussion; on the other hand, the rest zealously strained their chests. It happened more than once that three or four were shouting simultaneously for the course of ten minutes, but every one was satisfied and understood. The conversation lasted until after midnight, and was distinguished, as usual, by the abundance and the variety of subjects. Madame Sukhántchikoff talked about Garibaldi, about some Karl Ivánovitch, who had been flogged by his own house-serfs, about Napoleon III., about female labour, about merchant Pleskatchyóff, who, according to common knowledge, had starved twelve working-girls to

death, and had, on that account, received a
medal with the inscription: " For a useful
deed "; about the proletariat, about the Georgian
Prince Tchuktcheulídzeff, who had fired his wife
from a cannon, and about the future of Russia;
Pishtchálkin also talked about the future of Russia, about government monopolies, about the significance of nationality, and about his detesting
commonplace things most of all; Voroshíloff suddenly broke out: in one breath, and almost choking himself in the process, he mentioned Draper,
Virchow, Mr. Shelgunóff, Bichat, Helmholtz,
Stahr, Stuhr, Raymond, Johannes Müller the
physiologist, Johannes Müller the historian,—evidently confounding them,—Taine, Renan, Mr.
Shtchápoff, and then Thomas Nash, Peel,
Greene. . . " What sort of birds are these? "
muttered Bambáeff in amazement. " The prede-
cessors of Shakespeare, who bear to him the same
relation that the ramifications of the Alps bear
to Mont Blanc! " replied Voroshíloff cuttingly,
and also touched upon the future of Russia.
Bambáeff, too, talked about the future of Russia, and even painted it in rainbow-tinted colours,
but was raised to special rapture by the thought
of Russian music, in which he beheld something
" Ukh! great," and in confirmation he struck up
a romance by Varlámoff, but was speedily interrupted by a unanimous shout to the effect: " He 's
singing the *Miserere* from ' Trovatore,' and singing it very badly at that." One young officer, un-

der cover of the uproar, reviled Russian literature, another quoted verses from the " Spark ";
but Tit Bindásoff behaved still more simply: he
announced that all those rascals ought to have
their teeth knocked out—and enough said! without, however, specifying who those rascals were.
The cigar-smoke became stifling; every one was
heated and languid, all had grown hoarse, every
one's eyes had grown dim, the perspiration was
coursing in streams from every face. Bottles of
cold beer made their appearance, and were instantly emptied. "What the deuce was it I
was saying?" insisted one; "and whom and
about what have I just been talking?" inquired
another. And in the midst of all this tumult
and smoke-laden atmosphere Gubaryóff strode
about untiringly, waddling and ruffling his
beard as before, now listening, with ear inclined,
to some one's argument, again putting in a word
of his own, and every one involuntarily felt that
he, Gubaryóff, was the matrix of the whole affair, that he was the master and chief personage
there. . . .

About ten o'clock Litvínoff's head began to
ache violently, and he quietly withdrew, availing
himself of a recrudescence of the general clam-
our: Madame Sukhántchikoff had recalled another piece of injustice on the part of Prince
Barnaúloff: he had practically ordered some
one's ear to be bitten off.

The fresh night air clung caressingly to Litvínoff's inflamed face, and flowed in a fragrant flood between his parched lips. "What is it?" he said to himself, as he strolled along the dark avenue: "what sort of a thing was it that I was present at? Why did they meet together? Why did they shout and quarrel, why did they get so excited? What's the use of it all?" Litvínoff shrugged his shoulders, and betook himself to Weber's, picked up a newspaper and ordered an ice. The newspaper discussed the Roman question, and the ice turned out to be bad. He was on the point of going home, when suddenly there stepped up to him a stranger in a broad-brimmed hat, who, remarking in Russian, "I hope I do not disturb you?" seated himself at his little table. Then only did Litvínoff, on gazing more attentively at the stranger, recognise in him the thick-set man who had hidden himself in the corner at Gubaryóff's and had scrutinised him with so much attention when the conversation turned on political convictions. During the whole course of the evening that gentleman had not opened his mouth, and now, having seated himself beside Litvínoff and removed his hat, he gazed at him with a friendly and somewhat embarrassed look.

V

"Mr. Gubaryóff, at whose house I had the pleasure of seeing you to-day," he began,—"did not introduce me to you; so, if you will permit me, I will introduce myself: Potúgin, retired court councillor, served in the Ministry of Finance, in St. Petersburg. I hope that you will not think it strange. . I am not generally in the habit of making acquaintance so quickly, . . but with you . . ."

Here Potúgin began to stammer, and asked a waiter to bring him a glass of cherry cordial. " To give me courage," he added, with a smile.

Litvínoff gazed with redoubled attention at this last one of all the new persons with whom it had been his lot to come in contact that day, and immediately said to himself: " This man is not like those others."

And, in fact, he was not. Before him, running his slender fingers along the edge of the table, sat a broad-shouldered man, with an ample body mounted on short legs, a drooping, curly head, very clever and very melancholy little eyes beneath thick eyebrows, a large, regular mouth, poor teeth, and that purely Russian nose to which the name of " potato " has been appropriated;

a man with an awkward and even a rather wild, but assuredly not a commonplace, aspect. He was negligently dressed: an old-fashioned coat sat on him like a bag, and his necktie had got twisted to one side. His sudden confidence not only did not impress Litvínoff as an intrusion, but, on the contrary, secretly flattered him: it was impossible not to perceive that this man was not in the habit of forcing himself upon strangers. He produced a strange impression upon Litvínoff: he evoked in him both respect and sympathy, and a certain involuntary pity.

"So I do not disturb you?" he repeated in a soft, rather hoarse and feeble voice, which suited his whole figure to perfection.

"Certainly not," replied Litvínoff;—"on the contrary, I am very glad."

"Really? Well, then, I am glad too. I have heard a great deal about you; I know what you are occupying yourself with and what your intentions are. 'T is a good occupation. That is the reason you were taciturn to-day, by the way."

"Yes, and it strikes me that you had very little to say also," remarked Litvínoff.

Potúgin sighed.

"The others argued a very great deal, sir. I listened. Well," he added, after a brief pause, and setting his brows in rather comical fashion, —"were you pleased with our babel of an uproar?"

" It was a regular babel. That was extremely well said on your part. I kept wanting to ask those gentlemen why they were making such a fuss."

Again Potúgin sighed.

" That's precisely the point, that they don't know themselves, sir. In former times people would have expressed themselves about them in this manner: ' They are the blind instruments of the highest aims '; well, but nowadays we employ harsher epithets. And observe that I myself have not the slightest intention of condemning them; I will say more, they are all . . that is, almost all, very fine people. I know a great deal that is good about Madame Sukhántchikoff, for example: she gave her last penny to two poor nieces. Let us assume that the motive there was a desire to show off, to brag, yet you must admit that it was a noteworthy bit of self-sacrifice on the part of a woman who is not wealthy herself! About Mr. Pishtchálkin it is unnecessary to speak: in due time the peasants of his district will infallibly present him with a silver cup in the shape of a watermelon, and possibly a holy image with the picture of his guardian angel, and although he will tell them in his speech of thanks that he does not deserve such an honour, he will be telling an untruth: he does deserve it. Your friend, Mr. Bambáeff, has a splendid heart; it is true that, with him, as with the poet Yazykóff, who, they say, extolled debauchery while he sat over a book and drank water, enthusiasm is really not directed at anything, but it is enthusiasm, nevertheless; and Mr. Voroshíloff is extremely kind also; he is like all the men of his school, the men of the gilded classes, who seem to be sent expressly as orderlies to science, to civilisation; and he even holds his tongue pompously: but he is so young still! Yes, yes, they are all excellent people, but the sum total is nothing; the provisions are first-class, but the dish is n't fit to put in your mouth!"

Litvínoff listened to Potúgin with increasing amazement: all his ways, all the turns of his deliberate, but self-confident speech, revealed both understanding and the desire to talk.

Potúgin, in fact, both liked and understood how to talk; but, as a man out of whom life had already succeeded in eliminating conceit, he awaited with philosophical composure his opportunity, an encounter after his own heart.

" Yes, yes," he began again, with a humour not sickly, but sad, which was peculiarly characteristic of him:—" all that is very strange, sir. And here is another thing which I will beg you to note. When ten Englishmen, for example, come together, they immediately begin to discuss the submarine telegraph, the tax on paper, the process of dressing rats' skins,—that is to say, something positive, something definite; let ten Germans

come together,—well, there, of course, Schleswig-
Holstein and the unity of Germany make their
appearance on the scene; if ten Frenchmen assemble the conversation will infallibly touch on
' piquant adventures,' let them evade it as they
will; but when ten Russians get together the question instantly arises,—you have had an opportunity to-day of convincing yourself on that point,
—the question as to the significance, the future
of Russia, and that in just such general terms,
beginning with Leda's eggs, insusceptible of
proof, without any issue. They chew and chew
on that question, as a small child does on a piece
of india rubber: there 's no juice or sense in it.
Well, and, by the way, of course the rotten West
catches it also. A pretty preachment, as you can
imagine! it beats us at every point, that West—
but it 's rotten! And even if we did really despise
it," continued Potúgin:—" nevertheless, all that
is mere phrase-making and lies. We certainly do
revile it, but its opinion is the only one we value
—that is to say, the opinion of Parisian cox-
combs. I have an acquaintance, and a very nice
sort of man he is, apparently, the father of a
family, and no longer young; and that man was
in a state of depression for several days because
he had ordered *une portion de biftek aux pommes
de terre,* while a real Frenchman immediately
shouted out: *'Garçon! biftek pommes!'* My friend
was consumed with shame! And afterward he

shouted everywhere: ' *Biftek pommes!* ' and taught others. The very courtesans are astounded at the devout tremor wherewith our young fellows from the steppes enter their ignominious drawing-rooms. . . ' Good heavens!' they say to themselves, ' am I really here? At Annah Deslions!' "

" Please tell me," inquired Litvínoff, " to what do you ascribe the indubitable influence of Gubaryóff on all the people around him? Not to his gifts or to his capacities? "

" No, sir; no, sir; he has nothing of that sort. . ."

" To his character, then? "

" He has not that either, but he has a great deal of will, sir. We Slavonians in general, as is well known, are not rich in that attribute, and we give up in presence of it. Mr. Gubaryóff desired to be a leader, and every one has recognised him as a leader. What would you have done about it? The government has released us from serfdom, and we thank it; but the habits of serfdom have taken too profound a root in us; we shall not soon rid ourselves of them. In everything and everywhere we want a master; this master, in the majority of cases, is a vivacious individual; sometimes some so-called tendency acquires a power over us . . . now, for example, we have all bound ourselves as slaves to the natural sciences. . . Why, by virtue of what reasons, we enroll ourselves as slaves, is an obscure matter; evidently

such is our nature. But the principal point is
that we should possess a master. Well, and there
we have him; that means he is ours, and we don't
care a copper about the rest! Purely bondmen!
Both the pride of the bondman and the humilia-
tion of the bondman. A new master has come
into existence—away with the old one! The other
was named Yákoff, this one is called Sídor; give
Yákoff a box on the ears, fall at the feet of Sídor!
Recollect how many tricks of that sort have taken
place among us! We prattle about renunciation
as our distinguishing characteristic; but we do not
exercise renunciation like a free man who smites
with his sword, but like a lackey, who administers
a thrashing with his fist, and, what is more, administers a thrashing at his master's behest. Well,
sir, and we are also a soft race; it is not difficult
to keep a tight hand over us. And that's the way
Mr. Gubaryóff has come to be a master; he hammered and hammered away at one point until he
attained his object. People perceive that a man
has a great opinion of himself, believes in himself,
issues orders—the principal thing is to issue orders; they conclude that he is right and that he
must be obeyed. All our sectarians, our sects
of Onúphry and of Akulína,[1] had their origin in

[1] Onúfry—the founder of the priestless sect of the Old Ritualists: born 1829.—Akulína Ivánovna was the name of three of the
so-called Birthgivers of God (Madonnas) in the Scourgers' and
Skóptzy sects. Hence, one heresy received from them the appella-
tion of "Akulínovshtchina."—TRANSLATOR.

precisely this manner. He who has seized the
staff is the commander."

Potúgin's cheeks had flushed crimson and his
eyes had grown dim; but, strange to say, his
speech, bitter and even malicious though it was,
did not smack of gall, but rather of sadness, and
upright, genuine sadness at that.

" How did you become acquainted with Gubaryóff? " inquired Litvínoff.

" I have known him for a long time, sir. And
observe another queer thing about us: a man—
for instance, an author possibly—has been revil-
ing drunkenness all his life, in verse and in prose,
and upbraiding . . . and, all of a sudden, he takes
and buys two distilleries himself and leases a hundred dram-shops—and it's nothing! People
would wipe another man off the face of the earth,
but they do not even reproach him. Now there's
Mr. Gubaryóff: he's a Slavophil, and a democrat, and a socialist, and anything else you like,
but his estate always has been managed and is still
managed by his brother, a master of the ancient
type, one of the sort who were called ' Danteists.'
And that same Madame Sukhántchikoff, who
represents Mrs. Beecher Stowe as slapping Tenteléeff's face, almost crawls before Gubaryóff.
But, you know, the only thing about him is that
he reads clever books and is forever trying to get
down into the depths. As to his gift of language,
you have been able to judge for yourself to-day;

and thank God, too, that he says but little, and only writhes all the time. Because, when he is in the mood and lets himself go freely, then it is more than even I, a long-suffering man, can tolerate. He begins to banter and to narrate filthy anecdotes,—yes, yes, our great Mr. Gubaryóff narrates filthy anecdotes and laughs so abominably the while . . . ."

" Are you really so long-suffering? " said Litvínoff.—" I should have supposed the contrary. . . . But permit me to inquire, what is your name and your patronymic? "

Potúgin sipped a little of the cherry cordial.

" My name is Sozónt . . Sozónt Ivánitch. They gave me that very beautiful name in honour of a relative, an Archimandrite, to whom I am indebted for this alone. I am of the ecclesiastical race, if I may be allowed to express myself thus. And you make a mistake in doubting that I am patient: I am patient. I served for two and twenty years under my uncle, actual state councillor Irinárkh Potúgin. You did not know him? "

" No."

" I congratulate you on that. No, I am patient. But ' let us return to the first point,' as my colleague, the burnt-alive Archpriest Avákkum [1] was accustomed to say. I am amazed, my

[1] Avákkum Petróvitch, an ardent preacher of the doctrines of the Old Ritualists, who refused to accept the corrections (typographical and other) made in the Scriptures and Church Service

dear sir, at my fellow-countrymen. They are all low-spirited, they all go about in a dejected way, and, at the same time, they are all filled with hope, and at the slightest excuse they fairly go mad. Now take the Slavophils, among whom Mr. Gubaryóff reckons himself: they are very fine people, but there's the same mixture of despair and irritation, and they also live in the future. It's all coming, it's coming, they say. There's nothing in hand at the present moment, and Russia, in the course of ten whole centuries, has never worked out a single thing of her own, neither in government, nor in courts of justice, nor in science, nor in art, nor even in the handicrafts. . . But wait; have patience: everything will come. And why will it come, allow me to inquire? Because, forsooth, we are cultured people,— —stuff and nonsense; but the people . . oh, it's a grand people! Do you see that peasant coat? that's what all will proceed from. All the other idols have been smashed; but let us have faith in the peasant coat. Well, and what if the peasant coat betrays you? No, it will not betray; read Madame Kokhanóvsky,[1] and roll your eyes up to the ceiling! Really, if I were an

books in the reign of Peter the Great's father. Avákkum was forced to become a monk, banished to Siberia, brought back to Moscow, imprisoned, and eventually banished again to Pustózersk, Arkhangel Government. For his persistent heretical propaganda he and his companions were burned alive in 1681.—TRANSLATOR.

[1] Nadézhda Stepánovna Sokhánsky (1825–1884), who wrote under the name of "Kokhanóvsky."—TRANSLATOR.

artist this is the sort of a picture I would paint:
a cultivated man is standing in front of a peasant
and bowing low to him: ' Heal me, my dear peasant, says he, ' I am perishing with disease '; but
the peasant, in his turn, bows low before the educated man. ' Please teach me, dear master,' says
he, ' I am perishing with ignorance.' Well, and
of course both of them stick right where they are.
But all that is needed is really to become humble,
—not in words alone,—and adopt from our elder
brothers that which they have invented—better
than we and earlier than we! Waiter, another
glass of cherry cordial! You must not think that
I am a drunkard, but alcohol loosens my tongue."

" After what you have just said," observed Litvínoff, with a smile,—" it is not worth while for
me to ask to what party you belong and what
opinion you hold concerning Europe. But permit me to make one remark. Here you say that
we ought to borrow, to adopt from our elder
brothers; but how can we adopt without taking
into consideration the conditions of climate and
soil, with local and national peculiarities? I remember that my father ordered from Butenop's
foundry a splendidly recommended winnowing-
machine; the winnowing-machine really was very
good. But what happened? For five whole years
it stood in the shed utterly useless, until it was replaced by a wooden American machine,—which
was much better suited to our manner of life and

to our habits, as American machines are, in general. It is impossible to adopt things at haphazard, Sozónt Ivánitch."

Potúgin raised his head a little.

" I did not expect that sort of retort from you, most respected Grigóry Mikhaílitch," he began, after a brief pause.—" And who forces you to adopt at haphazard? Surely you take a foreign thing not because it is foreign, but because you find it suitable: consequently, you do take the circumstances into consideration, you do make a selection. And so far as the results are concerned, pray do not disturb yourself: they will be original by virtue of precisely those local, climatic and other conditions to which you allude. All you have to do is to offer good food, and the natural stomach will digest it after its own fashion; and, in course of time, when the organism shall have gained strength, it will yield *its own* sap. Just take our language as an example. Peter the Great deluged it with thousands of foreign words —Dutch, French, and German: those words expressed conceptions with which it was necessary to make the Russian nation acquainted; without philosophising, and without standing on ceremony, Peter poured those words wholesale, by the bucketful, by the cask, into our bosom. At first, it is true, the result was something monstrous, but later on—precisely that digestive process set in which I have mentioned to you. The conceptions became grafted on and appropriated; the foreign forms gradually evaporated; the language found in its own bosom the wherewithal to replace them—and now, your humble servant, a very mediocre master of style, will undertake to translate any page you please from Hegel,—yes, sir; yes, sir; from Hegel,—without making use of a single non-Slavonic word. That which has taken place with the language will, it is to be hoped, take place in other spheres. The whole question lies here—is nature strong? But our nature is all right; it will stand the strain: that's not where the great difficulty lies. Only nervous invalids and weak nations can fear for their health, for their independence; and just so, only idle people are capable of going into raptures until they foam at the mouth, because, forsooth, we are Russians, say they. I am very solicitous about my health, but I don't go into raptures over it: I'm ashamed to, sir."

" All that is true, Sozónt Ivánitch," began Litvínoff in his turn:—" but why must we, inevitably, be subjected to such tests? You say yourself that the first result was something monstrous! Well—and what if that monstrous thing had remained monstrous? And it has remained so; you know it has."

" But not in the language—and that means a great deal! But I did not make our nation; I am not to blame if it is fated to pass through such a school. 'The Germans were developed regularly,' cry the Slavophils: 'give us regular development also!' But where is one to get it when the very first historical action of our tribe—summoning to themselves princes from over-sea—is an irregularity to start with, an anomaly which is repeated in every one of us, down to the present day; every one of us, at least once in his life, has infallibly said to something foreign, non-Russian: 'Come, exercise authority and reign over me!'— I am ready, if you like, to admit that, when we introduce a foreign substance into our own body, we cannot, by any means, know with certainty beforehand what it is we are introducing: a bit of bread or a bit of poison; for, assuredly, it is a familiar fact that you never pass from bad to good through better, but always through worse— and poison is useful in medicine. Only dolts or sharpers can decently point with triumph at the poverty of the peasants after the Emancipation, at their increased drunkenness after the abrogation of the liquor monopoly. . . . Through worse to good!"

Potúgin passed his hand over his face.

"You asked me my opinion concerning Europe," he began again:—"I am amazed at it and devoted to its principles to the last degree, and do not consider it necessary to conceal the fact. For a long time . . no, not for a long time . . for some time past I have ceased to be afraid to give utterance to my convictions . . . even you, you see, did not hesitate to announce to Guba-ryóff your mode of thought. I, thank God, have ceased to conform to the ideas, the views, the habits of the man with whom I am conversing. In reality, I know of nothing worse than that useless cowardice, that base-spirited willingness to please by virtue of which, as you see, one of our grave dignitaries humours some little student who is of no account in his eyes, almost sports with him, runs after him like a hare. Well, let us assume that the dignitary behaves in this manner out of a desire for popularity; but why should plebeians like me shift and shuffle? Yes, sir, yes, sir, I am an Occidentalist, I am devoted to Europe—that is, to speak more accurately, I am devoted to culture, to that same culture at which people so charmingly jeer nowadays in our country,—to civilisation—yes, yes, that word is even better, and I love it with all my heart, and I believe in it, and I have not and never shall have any other faith. That 's the word: ci-. . . . vi . . . li-. . . sa . . . tion " (Potúgin pronounced each syllable distinctly with emphasis) ; " it is intelligible, and pure, and holy, but all the others, whether it be nationality, or glory, smell of blood. . . I want nothing to do with them! "

" Well, but, Sozónt Ivánitch, you love Russia, your native land? "

Potúgin passed his hand over his face.

"I love it passionately, and I hate it passionately."

Litvínoff shrugged his shoulders.

"That's old, Sozónt Ivánitch, that's a commonplace."

"Well, what of that? What's the harm? A pretty thing to take fright at!—A commonplace! I know many fine commonplaces! Here now, for example: liberty and order—that's a familiar commonplace. Is it better, in your opinion, to have, as with us, servility and disorder? And, moreover, are all those phrases wherewith so many young heads become intoxicated: the despised bourgeoisie, *souveraineté du peuple,* the right to labor,—are not they also commonplaces? And how about love, inseparable from hatred? . ."

"Byronism," interrupted Litvínoff:—"romanticism of the '30's."

"You are mistaken, excuse me; Catullus, the Roman poet Catullus, was the first to point out that blending of sentiments, two thousand years ago.[1] I learned that by reading him, because I know something of Latin, in consequence of my ecclesiastical extraction, if I may venture so to express myself. Yes, sir, I both love and hate my Russia, my strange, dear, dreadful, beloved fatherland. Now I have abandoned it; I had to air myself a bit, after sitting for twelve years at

[1]Odi et amo. Quare id faciam, fortasse, requiris?
Nescio: sed fieri sentio et excrucior.
Catullus, LXXXVI.

a government desk, in a government building; I have abandoned Russia, and I find it agreeable and jolly here; but I shall soon return, I feel it. Garden soil is good—but cloudberries will not grow on it!"

"You find it pleasant and jolly, and I am at ease here," said Litvínoff.—"And I came hither to study; but that does not prevent my seeing such little pranks as that. . ." He pointed to two passing courtesans, around whom several members of the Jockey Club were grimacing and lisping, and at the gambling-hall, which was packed full, in spite of the late hour.

"But who told you that I was blind to that?" retorted Potúgin.—"Only, pardon me, but your remark reminds me of the triumphant way our unhappy journalists had of pointing, during the Crimean campaign, to the defects of the English military administration, revealed in the *Times*. I am not an optimist myself, and everything that pertains to man, all our life, that entire comedy with a tragic ending, does not present itself to me in a rosy light; but why tax the Occident, in particular, with that which, possibly, has its root in our human essence itself? That gambling-house is repulsive, it is true; well, but is our home-bred knavery, perchance, any the more beautiful? No, my dear Grigóry Mikhaílovitch, let us be more humble and more quiet; a good pupil perceives the errors of his teacher, but he respectfully holds his peace about them; for those very errors are of service to him, and direct him in the right way. But if you insist upon gossiping about the rotten West, here comes Prince Kokó at a jog-trot; he has, probably, dropped at the gaming-table in a quarter of an hour the toil-won, extorted quit-rents of a hundred and fifty families, his nerves are unstrung, and, moreover, I saw him to-day at Marks's, turning over the pages of Veuillot's pamphlet. . He 'll be a capital companion for you!"

"But pardon me, pardon me," said Litvínoff hastily, perceiving that Potúgin was rising from his seat.—"My acquaintance with Prince Kokó is very slight, and then, of course, I prefer conversation with you. . ."

"I am greatly indebted to you," said Potúgin, rising and bowing his farewell;—"but I have been conversing with you a pretty long time as it is—that is, strictly speaking, I have been doing all the talking myself, while you, probably, have observed from your own experience that a man always feels conscience-stricken somehow and uncomfortable when he has been talking a great deal —all alone. Especially so when it happens at a first meeting: as much as to say, 'Look at me, that 's the sort of man I am!' Farewell until our next pleasant meeting. . And I, I repeat it, am very glad at having made your acquaintance."

"But wait a bit, Sozónt Ivánitch; tell me, at

least, where you are living, and whether you intend to remain here long."

Potúgin seemed to wince a little.

" I shall remain about a week longer in Baden, but we can meet each other here, or at Weber's, or at Marks's. Or I will go to you."

" Nevertheless, I must know your address."

" Yes. But this is the point: I am not alone."

" You are married? " asked Litvínoff abruptly.

" Good gracious, no. . . Why talk so absurdly? . . But I have a young girl with me."

" Ah! " ejaculated Litvínoff, with a shrug, as though apologising, and dropped his eyes.

" She is only six years old," went on Potúgin. —" She is an orphan, . . the daughter of a lady . . of one of my good friends. Really, we had better meet here. Good-bye, sir."

He pulled his hat down over his curly head and walked rapidly away, appearing for an instant a couple of times under the gas-jets, which cast a rather scanty light upon the road which led to Lichtenthal Avenue.

VI

" A STRANGE man!" said Litvínoff to himself, as
he wended his way to the hotel where he was stopping: "a strange man! I must hunt him up."
He entered his room; a letter on the table caught
his eye. " Ah! from Tánya!" he thought, and
rejoiced in advance; but the letter was from his
father in the country. Litvínoff broke the large
heraldic seal and was about to begin reading. . A
powerful, very agreeable, and familiar odour attracted his attention. He glanced about him, and
perceived on the window-sill, in a glass of water,
a large bouquet of fresh heliotropes. Litvínoff
bent over them, not without surprise, touched
them, smelled them. . . Some memory seemed to
recur to him, something very remote, . . but precisely what he could not imagine. He rang for
a servant and asked him whence the flowers had
come. The servant replied that they had been
brought by a lady, who would not give her name,
but had said that he, " Herr Zluitenhoff," would
be sure to divine who she was from the flowers
themselves. . . Again Litvínoff caught a glimpse
of some memory. . . He asked the servant what
was the appearance of the lady? The servant ex-

plained that she was tall and very well dressed, but wore a veil over her face.

" Probably a Russian Countess," he added.

" Why do you assume that? " inquired Litvínoff.

" She gave me two gulden," replied the servant, with a grin.

Litvínoff sent him away, and for a long time thereafter stood before the window immersed in thought; but at last he waved his hand in despair, and again took up the letter from the country. In it his father poured forth his habitual complaints, asserted that no one would take the grain even as a gift, that the people had grown utterly unruly, and that, in all probability, the end of the world was at hand. " Just imagine," he wrote, by the way, " my last coachman, that little Kalmýk, you remember? has been bewitched, and the man would infallibly have perished and there would have been no one to drive me, but, luckily, some kind people gave me a hint and advised me to send the sick man off to Ryazán, to a priest who is a well-known expert in dealing with spells; and the treatment actually succeeded to perfection, in confirmation whereof I enclose the letter of the father himself, by way of document." Litvínoff ran his eye over this " document " with curiosity. It contained the statement that " the house-servant, Nikanór Dmítrieff, was afflicted with a malady which medical science could not reach;

and this malady was caused by malevolent persons; but the cause of it was Nikanór himself, for he had not fulfilled his promise to a certain maiden, hence she, through these persons, had rendered him unfit for anything, and if I had not been his helper, under these circumstances he must have perished utterly, like a cabbage-worm; but I, trusting in the All-seeing Eye, constituted myself his prop in life; and how I accomplished this is a secret; and I request Your Well-Born that henceforth that maiden may not occupy herself with those evil attributes, and it would even do no harm to threaten her, otherwise she may exercise a maleficent influence over him again." Litvínoff fell into thought over this document; it exhaled upon him a breath of the wilds of the steppe, the impassive gloom of stagnating life, and it seemed marvellous to him that he should have read that letter precisely in Baden. In the meantime, midnight had long since struck; Litvínoff went to bed and blew out his candle. But he could not get to sleep; the faces he had seen, the speeches he had heard, kept whirling and circling, strangely interweaving and mixing themselves in his burning head, which was aching with the tobacco-smoke. Now he seemed to hear Gubaryóff's bellow, and his downcast eyes, with their stupid, obstinate gaze, presented themselves; then, all of a sudden, those same eyes began to blaze and leap, and he recognised

Madame Sukhántchikoff, heard her sharp voice, and, involuntarily, in a whisper, repeated after her: " She did slap his face, she did! " then the shambling figure of Potúgin moved forward before him, and for the tenth, the twentieth time, he recalled his every word; then, like a puppet from a snuff-box, Voroshíloff sprang forward in his brand-new paletot, which fitted him like a new uniform, and Pishtchálkin wisely and gravely nodded his capitally-barbered and really well-intentioned head; and Bindásoff bawled and reviled, and Bambáeff went into tearful raptures. . . . But the chief thing was: that perfume, that importunate, insistent, sweet, heavy perfume, gave him no rest, and was exhaled with ever-increasing power in the darkness, and ever more persistently reminded him of something which he vainly endeavoured to grasp. . . It occurred to Litvínoff that the odour of flowers was injurious to the health at night in a bed-chamber, and he rose, felt his way to the bouquet, and carried it out into the adjoining room; but the insufferable fragrance penetrated to his pillow, under his coverlet, even from that point, and he tossed sadly from side to side. Fever was beginning to lay hold upon him; the priest, " the expert in dealing with spells," had already twice run across his path in the shape of a very nimble hare with a beard, and Voroshíloff, squatting in a General's plume, as in a bush, was beginning to trill like a nightingale before him . . . when, all of a sudden, he sat up in bed, and clasping his hands, exclaimed: " Is it possible that it is *she?* It cannot be! "

But in order to explain this exclamation of Litvínoff, we must ask the indulgent reader to go back several years with us.

VII

At the beginning of the '50's there resided in Moscow, in very straitened circumstances, almost in poverty, the numerous family of the Princes Osínin. They were genuine, not Tatár-Georgian, but pure-blooded princes, descendants of Rúrik; their name is frequently met with in our Chronicles under the first Grand Princes of Moscow, the collectors of the Russian land; they possessed extensive patrimonial estates and domains, had been repeatedly rewarded for " toils, and blood, and wounds," had sat in the Council of the boyárs; one of them even wrote his name with " vitch " ; [1] but had fallen into disgrace through the conspiracy of enemies for " witchcraft and knowledge of roots "; they were ruined " terribly and completely"; they were deprived of their honours, and banished to parts remote; the Osínins crumbled away, and never recovered themselves, never again attained to power; the decree of banishment was removed from them, in course of time, and their " Moscow homestead " and their " chattels " were even restored to them, but nothing was of any avail. Their race had become im-

[1] Formerly a sign of blood-royal.—Translator.

63

poverished, had " withered away "—it did not rise either under Peter or under Katherine, and becoming constantly more insignificant and reduced, it counted among its members private stewards, managers of liquor counting-houses, and police-captains. The family of the Osínins to which we have alluded consisted of husband, wife and five children. They lived near the Dogs' Square, in a tiny, one-story wooden house, with a striped principal porch opening on the street, green lions on the gates, and other devices appertaining to the nobility, and barely made the two ends meet, running into debt at the greengrocer's shop, and frequently going without fuel and lights in winter. The Prince himself was an indolent, rather stupid man, who had, once upon a time, been a handsome man and a dandy, but had utterly gone to pieces; not so much out of respect for his name, as out of courtesy to his wife, who had been a Maid of Honour at Court, he had been given one of the ancient Moscow posts with a small salary, a difficult title, and no work whatever; he never meddled with anything, and did nothing but smoke from morning till night, never abandoning his dressing-gown, and sighing heavily. His wife was a sickly and peevish woman, perpetually worried over domestic troubles, with getting her children placed in government institutions for education, and with keeping up her connections in St. Petersburg; she never could get reconciled to her position and expatriation from the Court.

Litvínoff's father, during his sojourn in Moscow, had made the acquaintance of the Osínins, had had an opportunity to render them several services, had once lent them three hundred rubles; and his son, in his student days, had frequently called to inquire after their health, as his lodgings chanced to be situated not very far from their house. But it was not the close vicinity which attracted him, neither did the wretched comforts of their mode of life allure him: he began to visit the Osínins frequently from the moment when he fell in love with their eldest daughter, Irína.

At that time she had just passed her seventeenth birthday; she had just left the Institute, from which her mother had taken her, on account of a quarrel with the directress. The quarrel had arisen from the circumstance that Irína was to have delivered the verses of greeting to the Curator at the commencement in the French language, and just before the ceremony another girl, the daughter of a very wealthy government monopolist, had been substituted for her. The Princessmother could not digest this affront; and Irína herself could not forgive the directress for her injustice; she had been dreaming in advance how, in the sight of every one, attracting universal attention, she would declaim her speech, and how Moscow would talk about her afterward. . . And,

in fact, Moscow probably would have talked about
Irína. She was a tall, slender girl, with a somewhat sunken chest and narrow, youthful shoulders, with a palely-opaque skin rare at her age, as
pure and smooth as porcelain, and thick, blond
hair, wherein dark locks were intermingled with
the blond ones in an original manner. Her features, elegantly, almost exquisitely regular, had
not yet lost that innocent expression which is peculiar to early youth; but in the slow inclinations
of her beautiful neck, in her smile, which, not exactly abstracted, nor yet exactly languid, denoted
the nervous young gentlewoman, and in the very
outline of those thin, barely smiling lips, of that
small, aquiline, somewhat compressed nose, there
was something wilful and passionate, something
dangerous both for others and for herself. Her
eyes were astounding, truly astounding, of a
blackish-grey, with green lights, languishing,
long as those of Egyptian divinities, with radiant
eyelashes, and a bold sweep of eyebrows. There
was a strange expression in those eyes: they
seemed to be gazing, gazing attentively and
thoughtfully, from out of some unknown depths
and distance. In the Institute Irína had borne the
reputation of being one of the best scholars as to
mind and capacities, but with an unstable, ambitious character, and a mischievous head; one of
the teachers had predicted to her that her passions
would ruin her—*"Vos passions vous perdront"*;

on the other hand, another teacher had persecuted her because of her coldness and lack of feeling, and called her *" une jeune fille sans cœur."* Irína's companions thought her proud and deceitful, her brothers and sisters were afraid of her, her mother did not trust her, and her father felt uneasy when she fixed her mysterious eyes upon him; but she inspired both father and mother with a sentiment of involuntary respect, not by virtue of her qualities, but by virtue of the peculiar, indistinct expectations which she aroused in them, God knows why.

" You will see, Praskóvya Danílovna," said the old Prince one day, taking his pipe-stem out of his mouth:—" Arínka will extricate us from our difficulties yet."

The Princess flew into a rage, and told her husband that he used *" expressions insupportables,"* but thought better of it afterward, and repeated, between her teeth: " Yes . . . and it would be a good thing if she did extricate us."

Irína enjoyed almost unbounded freedom in the parental abode; they did not pet her, they even held rather aloof from her, but they did not oppose her: that was all she wanted. . . . It sometimes happened when there was some quite too humiliating scene—when a shopkeeper would come and yell, so that the whole house could hear him, that he was tired of haunting them for his money, or when their servants, whom they owned,

took to abusing their masters to their face, saying, " A pretty sort of princes you are, with not
a copper in your purse to keep from starving "—
that I,ina would never move a muscle, but would
sit motionless, with a malign smile on her gloomy
face; and that smile alone was more bitter to her
parents than all reproaches, and they felt themselves guilty, innocently guilty, in the presence of
that being, who seemed, from her very birth, to
have been endowed with the right to wealth, to
luxury, to adoration.

Litvínoff fell in love with Irína as soon as he
saw her (he was only three years older than she),
but for a long time he could not win reciprocity
or even attention. Upon her treatment of him
there lay the imprint even of a certain hostility;
it was exactly as though he had offended her and
she were profoundly concealing the offence, but
were unable to forgive him. He was too young
and modest at that time to understand what might
be concealed beneath this hostile, almost scornful
harshness. There were times when, oblivious of
lectures and note-books, he would sit in the Osínins' cheerless drawing-room,—sit and stare cov-
ertly at Irína: his heart pined slowly and bitterly
away within him and oppressed his breast; but
she, as though she were angry or bored, would
rise, pace up and down the room, gaze coldly at
him, as at a table or a chair, shrug her shoulders,
and fold her arms; or, during the whole course of

the evening, she would deliberately refrain from
glancing at Litvínoff a single time, even when
talking with him, as though refusing him even
that alms; or, in conclusion, she would take up a
book and rivet her eyes upon it, without reading,
frown and bite her lips, or would suddenly inquire
of her father or brother: what was the German
word for patience?

He tried to tear himself away from the
enchanted circle, in which he incessantly suffered torment and struggled, like a bird which
has fallen into a trap; he absented himself from
Moscow for a week. After nearly losing his mind
with grief and irksomeness, he returned to the
Osínins, all haggard and ill. . . And, strange to
say, Irína also had grown emaciated during those
days, her face had turned yellow, her cheeks were
sunken; . . . but she greeted him with greater
coldness than ever, with almost malevolent scorn,
as though he had still further aggravated that
mysterious grievance which he had dealt her. . .

She tortured him in this manner for two
months; then one day everything underwent a
change. It was as though she had broken out in
conflagration, as though love had swooped down
upon her like a thunder-cloud. One day—he long
remembered that day—he was again sitting in the
Osínins' drawing-room, at the window, and irrele-
vantly staring into the street, and he was feeling
vexed and bored and despised himself, and yet he

could not stir from the spot. . . It seemed to him as though, if a river were flowing just there, beneath the window, he would hurl her into it with terror, but without compunction. Irína had placed herself not far from him, maintained a rather singular silence, and remained motionless. For several days past she had not spoken to him at all, and indeed she had not spoken to any one; she sat on and on, propped up on her arms, as though she found herself perplexed, and only from time to time did she cast a slow glance around her.

This cold torment became, at last, more than Litvínoff could endure; he rose, and, without taking leave, began to look for his hat. " Wait," a soft whisper suddenly made itself heard. Litvínoff's heart quivered; he did not at once recognise Irína's voice: something unprecedented resounded in that single word. He raised his head and stood petrified: Irína was gazing at him affectionately—yes, affectionately. Comprehending nothing, not fully conscious of what he was doing, he approached her and stretched out his hands. . . She immediately gave him both of hers, then smiled, flushed all over, turned away, and without ceasing to smile, she left the room. . . . A few minutes later she returned in company with her younger sister, again looked at him with the same gentle glance, and made him sit down beside her. . . At first she could say nothing: she merely sighed and blushed; then she began, as though overcome with timidity, to question him concerning his occupations, something which she had never done before. On the evening of that same day she several times endeavoured to excuse herself to him for not having known how to appreciate him up to that moment, assured him that she had now become an entirely different person, amazed him by an unexpected republican sally (at that time he worshipped Robespierre, and dared not condemn Marat aloud), but a week later he had already discovered that she had fallen in love with him. Yes; he long remembered that first day; . . . but he did not forget the following ones, either,—those days when, still striving to doubt, and afraid to believe, he clearly perceived, with tremors of rapture, almost of terror, how this unexpected happiness was engendered, grew and, irresistibly sweeping everything before it, at last fairly submerged him.

The luminous moments of first love ensued—moments which are not fated to be, and should not be, repeated in one and the same life. Irína suddenly became as tame as a lamb, as soft as silk, and infinitely kind; she undertook to give lessons to her younger sisters,—not on the piano,—she was not a musician,—but in the French and English languages; she read with them from their text-books, she took part in the housekeeping; everything amused her, everything interested her;

now she chattered incessantly, again she became
immersed in dumb emotion; she concocted various
plans, she entered into interminable speculations
as to what she would do when she married Litvínoff (they had not the slightest doubt that their
marriage would take place), what they would do
together. . . " Work? " suggested Litvínoff. .

" Yes, work," repeated Irína: " read . . . but,
principally, travel." She was particularly desirous of quitting Moscow as speedily as possible,
and when Litvínoff represented to her that he had
not yet completed his course in the university,
on each such occasion, after meditating a little,
she replied that he might finish his studies in Ber-
lin, or . . . somewhere there. Irína put little
constraint upon herself in the expression of her
feelings, and, therefore, her affection for Litvínoff did not long remain a secret to the Prince
and Princess. They were not precisely delighted,
but, taking all the circumstances into consideration, they did not consider it necessary to impose
their veto immediately. Litvínoff's property was
considerable. . . . . . " But family, family! . . ."
remarked the Princess. " Well, of course, family," replied the Prince; " but, at all events, he 's
not a plebeian, and that 's the chief thing; for
Irína will not listen to us. Was there ever a case
when she did not do as she pleased? *Vous con-
naissez sa violence!* Moreover, there 's nothing
definite as yet." Thus reasoned the Prince, and

yet, on the instant, added mentally: " Madame Litvínoff—nothing more? I expected something else."

Irína took complete possession of her future betrothed, and he himself willingly gave himself into her hands. He seemed to have fallen into a whirlpool, to have lost himself. . . And he found it painful and sweet, and he regretted nothing and kept back nothing. He could not make up his mind to reflect upon the significance, the duties of wedlock, or whether he, so irrevocably submissive, would make a good husband, and what sort of a wife Irína would turn out to be; his blood was on fire and he knew one thing only: to go after her, with her, onward and without end, and then let that happen which might! But, despite the absence of all opposition on the part of Litvínoff to the superabundance of impulsive tenderness on the part of Irína, matters did not progress without several misunderstandings and clashes. One day he ran in to see her straight from the university, in his old coat, with his hands stained with ink. She rushed to meet him with her customary affectionate greeting, and suddenly came to a halt:

" You have no gloves," she said slowly, with pauses, and instantly added:—" Fie! what a . . . student . . . you are! "

" You are too impressionable, Irína," remarked Litvínoff.

" You are . . a regular student," she repeated:
—"*Vous n' êtes pas distingué.*"

And turning her back on him, she left the room.
It is true that, an hour later, she entreated him to
forgive her. . . On the whole, she willingly pun-
ished herself and asked his pardon; only, strange
to say, she often, almost with tears, accused herself of bad motives which she did not have, and
obstinately denied her real defects. On another
occasion he found her in tears, with her head resting on her hands, and her hair falling unbound;
and when, thoroughly disquieted, he questioned
her as to the cause of her grief, she silently pointed
her finger at her breast. Litvínoff involuntarily
shuddered. " Consumption! " flashed through his
mind, and he seized her hand.

" Art thou ill? " he ejaculated with a quivering
voice (they had already begun, in important cases,
to call each other " thou ").—" If so, I will go at
once for the doctor . . ."

But Irína did not allow him to finish, and
stamped her little foot with impatience.

" I am perfectly well . . but it is this gown
. . . don't you understand? "

" What do you mean? . . this gown . . ." he
ejaculated in surprise.

" What do I mean? Why, that I have no
other, and that it is old, horrid, and that I
am compelled to put on this gown every day . .
even when thou . . even when you come. . It

will end in thy ceasing to love me, if thou seest me so slovenly."

"Good heavens, Irína, what art thou saying? Why, this gown is very pretty. . . And it is dear to me, moreover, because I saw thee in it for the first time."

Irína blushed.

"Please do not remind me, Grigóry Mikhaílovitch, that even then I had no other gown."

"But I assure you, Irína Pávlovna, it is charmingly becoming to you."

"No, it's horrid, horrid," she repeated, tugging nervously at her long, soft curls.—"Okh, this poverty, poverty, obscurity! How can I rid myself of this poverty? How get out, get out of the obscurity?"

Litvínoff did not know what to say, and slightly turned away.

Suddenly Irína sprang up from her chair and laid both her hands on his shoulders.

"But, surely, thou lovest me? Thou lovest me?" she cried, approaching her face to his, and her eyes, still filled with tears, beamed with the joy of happiness.—"Thou lovest me even in this horrid gown?"

Litvínoff flung himself on his knees before her.

"Akh, love me, love me, my dear one, my saviour," she whispered, bending down to him.

Thus the days rushed on, the weeks elapsed, and although no formal explanation had as yet taken place, although Litvínoff still delayed his demand, not, of course, by his own wish, but in expectation of a command from Irína (she had happened one day to remark, " We are both ridiculously young; we must add a few weeks more to our age "), yet everything was moving onward to a conclusion, and the immediate future was becoming more and more clearly defined, when suddenly an event occurred which scattered all these surmises and plans like the light dust of the highway.

VIII

THAT winter the Court visited Moscow. One festival followed another; then came the turn of the customary great ball in the Assembly of the Nobility. The news of this ball, it is true, penetrated even to the tiny house on the Dogs' Square, in the shape of an announcement in the *Police News*. The Prince was the first to take the initiative; he immediately decided that it was indispensable that they should go and take Irína, that it was unpardonable to miss the opportunity of seeing their sovereigns, that the ancient nobility were, in a manner, bound to do so. He insisted on his opinion with a peculiar warmth, which was not characteristic of him; the Princess agreed with him to a certain extent, and only sighed over the expense; but Irína displayed decided opposition. " It is unnecessary; I will not go," she replied to all the arguments of her parents. Her obstinacy assumed such proportions that the old Prince at last decided to ask Litvínoff to try to persuade her by representing to her, among the other " reasons," that it was improper for a young girl to avoid society, that it was proper for her " to test that," that, as it was, no one ever saw her any-

where. Litvínoff undertook to present these
" reasons " to her. Irína gazed at him so intently and attentively that he grew confused, and
toying with the ends of her sash, she calmly
said:

" You desire this?—you? "

" Yes . . . I think I do," replied Litvínoff
faltering.—" I agree with your father. . . And
why should not you go . . . to look at the people
and to show yourself? " he added, with a curt
laugh.

" To show myself," she slowly repeated.—
" Well, very good, I will go. . . Only, remember,
it is you yourself who have willed it. ."

" That is to say, I . . ." Litvínoff tried to
begin.

" It is you yourself who have willed it," she interrupted.—" And there is one more condition:
you must promise me that you will not be present
at that ball."

" But why? "

" I wish it."

Litvínoff flung his hands apart.

" I submit; . . but, I must confess, I should be
very happy to see you in all your majesty, to be
a witness of the impression which you will infallibly produce. . How proud I should be of you! "
he added, with a sigh.

Irína laughed.

" All that magnificence will consist of a white

frock; and as for the impression . . . well, in short, I will have it so."

" Irína, you seem to be angry? "

Irína laughed again.

" Oh, no! I am not angry. Only thou . . ." (She fixed her eyes upon him, and it struck him that never before had he beheld in them such an expression.) " Perhaps it is necessary," she added in a low voice.

" But, Irína, thou lovest me? "

" Yes, I love thee," she replied, with almost solemn impressiveness, and shook his hand in masculine fashion.

During all the succeeding days Irína sedulously occupied herself with her toilet, with her coiffure; on the eve of the ball she felt indisposed, could not sit still in one place, fell to weeping a couple of times when she was alone: in Litvínoff's presence she smiled in a monotonous sort of way . . . but treated him tenderly, as before, yet in an abstracted manner, and kept incessantly contemplating herself in the mirror. On the day of the ball she was extremely taciturn and pale, but composed. At nine o'clock in the evening Litvínoff came to take a look at her. When she came out to him in her white tarlatan frock, with a spray of small blue flowers in her hair, which was dressed rather high, he simply cried out in admiration: she seemed to him beautiful and majestic beyond her years. " Yes, she has grown taller since morning," he said to himself; " and what a carriage! What a thing good blood is!" Irína stood before him with pendent arms, without smile or affectation, and gazed with decision, almost with boldness, not at him, but at some point in the distance, straight in front of her.

" You are like a fairy princess," uttered Litvínoff at last;—" or, no: you are like the leader of an army before a victory. . . You have not permitted me to go to this ball,"—he continued, while she remained motionless, as before, and seemed not so much to be listening to him as to some other inward speech;—" but you will not refuse to accept from me these flowers, and to carry them?"

He gave her a bouquet of heliotropes.

She cast a quick glance at Litvínoff, stretched out her hand, and suddenly grasping the tips of the spray which adorned her head, she said:

" Do you wish it? Only say the word, and I will tear off all this and remain at home."

Litvínoff's heart fairly sang with joy. Irína's hand was already wrenching off the spray. . .

" No, no, why should you?" he said hastily, in a burst of grateful and noble sentiments;—" I am not an egoist; why should I restrict your liberty . . when I know that your heart . . ."

" Well, then, don't come near me; you will crush my gown," she said hastily.

Litvínoff was disconcerted.

" And you will take the bouquet?" he asked.

" Of course; it is very pretty, and I am very fond of that perfume. . *Merci.* . I will preserve it as a souvenir."

" Of your first appearance in society," remarked Litvínoff:—" of your first triumph. . ."

Irína contemplated herself in the mirror over her shoulder, bending her body a little.

" And am I really so pretty? Are not you a partial judge?"

Litvínoff grew diffuse in enthusiastic praises. But Irína was no longer listening to him, and lifting the bouquet to her face, she again began to gaze off into the distance with her strange eyes, which seemed to darken and widen, and the ends of the delicate ribbons, set in motion by a light current of air, elevated themselves on her shoulders like wings.

The Prince made his appearance with hair curled, in a white necktie, a shabby black dress suit, and with the Vladímir ribbon of the order of the nobility in his buttonhole; after him the Princess appeared in a chiné silk gown of antique cut, and with that grim anxiety beneath which mothers strive to conceal their agitation put her daughter to rights from behind—that is to say, she shook out the folds of her gown without any necessity whatever. An old-fashioned, four-seated hired carriage, drawn by two shaggy nags, crawled up to the entrance, its wheels creaking over the mounds of snow which had not been

swept away, and an infirm footman in a prepos-
terous livery ran in from the anteroom and rather
desperately announced that the carriage was
ready. . . After bestowing their blessing for the
night upon the remaining children, and donning
fur wraps, the Prince and Princess directed their
steps to the porch; Irína, in a thin, short-sleeved
cloak—how she did hate that cloak!—followed
them in silence. Litvínoff escorted them, in the
hope of receiving a parting glance from Irína,
but she took her seat in the carriage without turning her head.

About midnight he passed under the windows
of the Assembly. The innumerable lights in the
huge chandeliers pierced through the crimson curtains in luminous spots, and the sounds of a
Strauss waltz were being wafted, with a haughty,
festive challenge, all over the square encumbered
with equipages.

On the following day, at noon, Litvínoff betook
himself to the Osínins. He found no one at home
but the Prince, who immediately announced to
him that Irína had a headache, that she was in
bed, and would not rise until the evening, and
that, moreover, such an indisposition was not in
the least surprising after a first ball.

" *C'est très naturel, vous savez, dans les jeunes
filles,*" he added in French, which somewhat
amazed Litvínoff, who noticed, at the same moment, that the Prince was not wearing his dress-

ing-gown as usual, but a frock-coat.—" And, moreover," went on Osínin, " how could she help falling ill after the events of last night? "

" The events? " blurted out Litvínoff.

" Yes, yes, the events, the events, *vrais événements*. You cannot imagine, Grigóry Mikhaílovitch, *quel succès elle a eu!* The entire Court noticed her! Prince Alexander Feódorovitch said that her place was not here, that she reminded him of the Duchess of Devonshire . . well, you know . . the famous one. . . And old Blazenkampf declared, in the hearing of every one, that Irína was *la reine du bal,* and asked to be presented to her; and he introduced himself to me —that is to say, he told me that he remembered me as a hussar, and inquired where I was serving now. He 's very amusing, that Count, and such an *adorateur du beau sexe!* But what am I saying? . . . And my Princess also . . . . they gave her no peace either: Natálya Nikítishna herself conversed with her . . . what more would you have? Irína danced *avec tous les meilleurs cavaliers;* they kept introducing them and introducing them to me . . . . . until I lost count of them. Will you believe it, everybody thronged around us in crowds; in the mazurka they did nothing but choose her. One foreign diplomat, on learning that she was a native of Moscow, said to the Emperor: ' *Sire,*' said he,—' *décidément c'est Moscou qui est le centre de votre empire!* '

and another diplomat added:—' *C'est une vraie
révolution, Sire* '; revelation or revolution . . . .
something of that sort. Yes . . . yes . . . it
. . . it . . . I must tell you, it was something remarkable."

"Well, and Irína Pávlovna herself?" inquired
Litvínoff, whose feet and hands had turned cold
during the Prince's speech:—" did she enjoy herself, did she seem pleased?"

" Of course she enjoyed herself; as if she could
help being pleased! However, you know, one
cannot make her out immediately. Every one said
to me last night: ' How amazing! *jamais on ne
dirait que mademoiselle votre fille est à son premier bal.*' Count Reisenbach, among the rest;
. . . surely you must know him. . ."

" No, I do not know him at all, and never have
known him."

" He 's my wife's first cousin. . ."

" I do not know him."

" He 's a rich man, a Court Chamberlain; he
lives in Petersburg; he 's all the fashion; he twists
everybody in Livonia round his finger. Up to
now he has always despised us; . . . naturally, I
do not bear him any grudge for that. *J'ai
l'humeur facile, comme vous savez.* Well, now
there was he. He sat down beside Irína, conversed with her for a quarter of an hour, no more,
and then said to my Princess: ' *Ma cousine,*' says
he, ' *votre fille est une perle; c'est une perfection;*

every one is complimenting me on my niece. . . .'
And then I saw that he went up to . . an important personage, and kept staring at Irína all the
while . . . well, and the personage stared also. . . ."

" And so Irína Pávlovna will not be visible all
day?" inquired Litvínoff again.

" No; she has a very bad headache. She asked
to be remembered to you, and that we should
thank you for your bouquet, *qu'on a trouvé charmant*. She must rest. . . My Princess has gone
out to pay calls . . and I myself, you see . . . ."

The Prince coughed and began to shuffle his
feet about, as though at a loss what more to say.
Litvínoff took his hat, said that he had no intention of embarrassing him, and would call later to
inquire after his health, and took his departure.

A few paces from the Osínins' house he caught
sight of a dandified two-seated carriage, which
had halted in front of the police sentry-box. A
liveried footman, also dandified, was bending
carelessly down from the box and inquiring of the
sentry, who was a Finn, whereabouts in the vicinity dwelt Prince Pável Vasílievitch Osínin.
Litvínoff glanced into the carriage: in it sat a
middle-aged man, of sanguine complexion, with a
frowning and haughty face, a Grecian nose, and
evil lips, enveloped in a sable cloak,—a high dignitary, by all the signs.

IX

Litvínoff did not keep his promise to call later; he reflected that it would be better to defer his visit until the following day. When, about twelve o'clock, he entered the familiar drawing-room, he found there the two younger Princesses, Victorínka and Cleopátrinka. He greeted them, then inquired: was Irína Pávlovna feeling any better, and could he see her?

"Irínotchka has gone out wiv mamma," replied Victorínka; although she lisped, she was more vivacious than her sister.

"What . . . she has gone out?" repeated Litvínoff, and something shivered within him in the depths of his breast.—"Does n't . . . does n't . . . does n't she occupy herself with you at this hour—does n't she give you lessons?"

"Irínotchka ith n't going to give us lethonth any more," replied Victorínka.—"She is n't going to any more," Cleopátrinka repeated after her.

"And is your papa at home?" inquired Litvínoff.

"Papa ith n't at home, eiver," continued Victorínka;—"and Irínotchka is ill: she cwied, cwied all night long. . ."

86

" She cried? "

" Yeth, she cwied. . . Egórovna told me, and her eyes are so wed, as though they were swol—len. . ."

Litvínoff paced up and down the room a couple of times, shivering slightly, as though with cold, and returned to his lodgings. He experienced a sensation akin to that which takes possession of a man when he gazes down from the summit of a lofty tower: everything died away within him, and his head swam quietly and mawkishly. Dull surprise and a mouse-like scampering of thoughts, ill-defined alarm and dumb anticipation, and strange, almost malicious curiosity, in his compressed throat the bitterness of unshed tears, on his lips the effort at an empty smirk, and an entreaty addressed to no one . . oh, how cruel and humiliatingly repulsive it all was! " Irína does not wish to see me," kept whirling incessantly through his brain, " that is clear; but why? What can have taken place at that ill-starred ball? And how is such a change, all at once, possible? So suddenly. . ." (People are constantly observing that death comes unexpectedly, but they cannot possibly accustom themselves to its suddenness, and think it senseless.) —" She sends me no message, she does not wish to come to an explanation with me. . . ."

"Grigóry Mikhaílovitch," cried a strained voice in his very ear.

Litvínoff started, and beheld before him his man with a note in his hand. He recognised Irína's handwriting. . . Even before he had broken the seal of the note he had a foreboding of misfortune, and bowed his head upon his breast and hunched up his shoulders, as though warding off a blow.

At last he summoned his courage and tore off the envelope with one movement. On a small sheet of note-paper stood the following words:

"Forgive me, Grigóry Mikhaílitch. Everything is at an end between us. I am going to Petersburg. It distresses me dreadfully, but the deed is done. Evidently, it is my fate; . . but no, I will not try to justify myself. My forebodings have been realised. Forgive me, forget me; I am not worthy of you.

"Be magnanimous: do not try to see me.

"Irína."

Litvínoff read these five lines and sank back slowly on the couch, as though some one had dealt him a blow in the breast. He dropped the note, picked it up, read it again, whispered, " To Petersburg," dropped it again, and that was all. Tranquillity descended upon him; he even adjusted the cushion under his head with his hands, which were thrown behind him. " Those who are wounded unto death do not toss about," he said to himself; " as it has come, so it has gone. . . All this is natural; I have always expected this. . ."

(He lied to himself: he had never expected anything of the sort.) "Wept? She wept?.. What did she weep about? For she did not love me! However, it is all comprehensible and in consonance with her character. She, she is not worthy of me... The idea!" (He laughed bitterly.) "She herself did not know what force was concealed within her; well, but after convincing herself of its effects at the ball, how could she put up with an insignificant student? ... It is all intelligible enough."

But here he recalled her tender words, her smiles, and those eyes—those unforgettable eyes, which he would never see again, which both beamed and melted at the mere encounter with his eyes; he recalled also one swift, timid, burning kiss—and all of a sudden he burst out sobbing, and sobbed convulsively, wildly, venomously, turned over on his face, and choked, and sighed with fierce enjoyment, as though thirsting to rend himself and everything about him, thrust his inflamed face into the cushion of the divan and bit it...

Alas! The gentleman whom Litvínoff had seen on the previous day in the carriage was precisely that first cousin of the Princess Osínin, the wealthy man and Chamberlain of the Court, Count Reisenbach. On perceiving the impression which Irína had made on persons of the highest position, and instantaneously calculating what advantages, *"mit etwas Accuratesse,"* might be derived from that fact, the Count, being an energetic man and one who understood how to render obsequious service, immediately drew up his plan. He decided to act promptly, in Napoleonic fashion. "I will take that original young girl into my own house," he reflected; "in Petersburg I will make her my heiress, devil take it, well, of almost all my estate; I happen to have no children; she is my niece, and my Countess finds life tiresome alone. . . At any rate, it will be more agreeable when there is a pretty little face in the drawing-room. . . Yes, yes; that's so: *es ist eine Idee, es ist eine Idee!"* He must dazzle, confuse, startle her parents.—"They have nothing to eat," the Count pursued his meditations, as he sat in his carriage and was being driven to the Dogs' Square, "therefore, in all probability, they will not prove obstinate. They're not so very sensitive. I might give them a sum of money. But she? And she will consent also. Honey is sweet . . . she got a taste of it last night. It is a caprice of mine, let us assume; then let them profit by it . . . the fools. I shall say to them: thus and so; come to a decision. Otherwise, I shall take some other girl; an orphan—which is more convenient. Yes or no, I give you twenty-four hours to make up your minds, *und damit Punctum."*

With these same words upon his lips, the Count presented himself before the Prince, whom he had

already, on the previous evening at the ball, fore-
warned of his visit. It seems not worth while to
enter at length into the results of this visit. The
Count had made no mistake in his calculations:
the Prince and Princess really did not prove re-
fractory, and accepted the sum of money, and
Irína really did consent, without waiting for the
expiration of the appointed term. It was not easy
for her to break her bond with Litvínoff; she loved
him, and, when she had sent him the note, she
almost took to her bed, wept incessantly, grew
thin and sallow. . . But, nevertheless, a month
later the Princess took her away to Petersburg,
and settled her at the Count's, confiding her to
the guardianship of the Countess, a very kind
woman, but with the mind of a chicken and the
exterior of a chicken.

But Litvínoff then abandoned the university,
and went off to his father in the country. Little
by little his wound healed. At first he heard nothing about Irína, and he avoided talking about
Petersburg and Petersburg society. Then gradually reports began to circulate about her, not evil,
but strange reports; rumour began to busy itself
with her. The name of the young Princess Osínin, surrounded with splendour, stamped with a
special seal, came to be more and more frequently
mentioned in provincial circles. It was uttered
with curiosity, with respect, with envy, as the
name of Countess Vorotýnsky had formerly been

uttered. At last the news of her marriage was spread abroad. But Litvínoff paid hardly any attention to this last bit of news: he was already betrothed to Tatyána.

And now it has probably become intelligible to the reader precisely what it was that recurred to Litvínoff, when he exclaimed: " Is it possible! " and therefore we will now return to Baden and resume the thread of our interrupted story.

X

IT was very late when Litvínoff got to sleep, and he did not sleep long: the sun had only just risen when he rose from his bed. The summits of the dark hills which were visible from his windows were glowing with a moist crimson hue against the clear sky. "How fresh it must be yonder, under the trees!" he said to himself, and he hastily dressed himself, cast an abstracted glance at the bouquet, which had blossomed out even more luxuriantly during the night, took his cane, and betook himself to the well-known " Cliffs," behind the "Old Castle." The morning enveloped him in its strong and tranquil caress. He breathed vigorously, he moved vigorously; the health of youth played in his every sinew; the earth itself seemed to rise up to meet his light tread. With every step he felt more amiably disposed, more cheerful: he walked along in the dewy shade, over the coarse sand of the paths, past the pines, the tips of all whose twigs were rimmed with the vivid green of the spring shoots. "How glorious this is!" he kept saying to himself. All at once he heard voices that were familiar to him: he glanced ahead and descried Voroshíloff and Bambáeff, who were walking toward him. He fairly writhed: he darted aside, like a school-boy evading his teacher, and hid behind a bush. . . "Oh, my Creator!" he prayed, " carry my fellow-countrymen past!" It seemed to him at that moment that he would have begrudged no amount of money, if only they might not catch sight of him. . . And, in fact, they did not catch sight of him: the Creator bore his fellow-countrymen past. Voroshíloff, with his cadet-like self-complacent voice, was explaining to Bambáeff about the various " phases " of Gothic architecture, while Bambáeff merely grunted approvingly; it was evident that Voroshíloff had already been overwhelming him for a long time with his " phases," and the good-natured enthusiast was beginning to be bored. Long did Litvínoff, biting his lip, and craning his neck, listen to the retreating footsteps; long did cadences, now guttural, now nasal, of that instructive harangue resound; at last all became silent. Litvínoff heaved a sigh of relief, emerged from his ambush, and pursued his way.

For three hours he roamed about the mountains. Now he deserted the path, and leaped from rock to rock, occasionally slipping on the smooth moss; again he seated himself on a fragment of the cliff, beneath an oak or a beech, and indulged in pleasant thoughts, to the ceaseless murmur of the brooks, overgrown with ferns, the soothing rustle of the leaves, and the ringing song of a solitary blackbird; a slight drowsiness, also agreeable, stole upon him, seemed to embrace him from behind, and he fell asleep . . . but suddenly he smiled and cast a glance about him: the green and gold of the forest, of the forest air, beat gently on his sight—and again he smiled, and again he closed his eyes. He felt like breakfasting, and betook himself in the direction of the " Old Castle," where, for a few kreutzers, he would be able to obtain a glass of good milk and coffee. But he had not succeeded in taking his place at one of the small white-painted tables, which stood on the platform in front of the castle, when he heard the laboured snorting of horses, and three calashes made their appearance, from which poured forth a rather numerous party of ladies and cavaliers . . . . Litvínoff immediately recognised them for Russians, although they were all talking in French . . because they were talking in French. The toilets of the ladies were distinguished by exquisite smartness; the cavaliers wore brand-new coats, but tight-fitting and with a well-defined waist, which is not altogether usual in our day, trousers of grey figured material, and very shiny city hats. A low, black neckcloth closely encircled the neck of each cavalier, and something military made itself felt in their whole bearing. As a matter of fact, they were military men; Litvínoff had happened upon a picnic of young generals, persons of the highest society, and of con-

siderable importance. Their importance was announced in every point: in their discreet ease of
manner, in their gracefully majestic smiles, in the
strained abstraction of their glance, in the effeminate twitching of their shoulders, in the swaying
motion of their figures, and in the bend of their
knees; it was betrayed by the very sound of their
voices, which seemed to be amiably and fastidi-
ously returning thanks to a subservient throng.
All these warriors were splendidly washed,
shaved, perfumed through and through with some
scent or other which is a genuine appurtenance of
the nobility and the Guards, a mixture of the most
capital cigar smoke and the most astonishing
patchouli. And all their hands were those of
nobles—white, large, with nails as strong as ivory;
the moustaches of all fairly shone, their teeth
gleamed, and their very delicate skin was red on
the cheeks, blue on the chin. Some of the young
generals were playful, others were thoughtful;
but the stamp of superior propriety lay upon them
all. Each one, apparently, was profoundly conscious of his own worth, and of the dignity of his
future part in the empire, and bore himself se-
verely and boldly, with a faint tinge of that frisk-
iness, that " devil-take-me " air, which so naturally makes its appearance during travels abroad.
Having noisily and pompously seated themselves, the company summoned the bustling waiters. Litvínoff made haste to finish his glass of

milk, paid what he owed, and pulling his hat well down over his eyes, he was on the point of slipping past the picnic of generals. . .

" Grigóry Mikhaílitch," said a woman's voice. —" Don't you know me? "

He involuntarily halted. That voice. . That voice had but too often caused his heart to beat in days gone by. . . He turned round and beheld Irína.

She was sitting at a table, and with her arms crossed on the back of a chair which had been pushed aside, she was gazing at him courteously, almost joyously, with her head bent on one side, and smiling.

Litvínoff instantly recognised her, although she had changed since he had seen her for the last time, ten years previously, although from a young girl she had become a woman. Her slender figure had developed and blossomed out, the lines of her formerly compressed shoulders now suggested those of the goddesses who start forth from the ceilings of ancient Italian palaces. But her eyes remained the same, and it seemed to Litvínoff that they were gazing at him in the same manner as then, in that tiny house in Moscow.

" Irína Pávlovna . . . ." he began irresolutely.

" You recognise me? How glad I am! . . . how I . . ." (She paused, blushed slightly, and drew herself up.) " This is a very pleasant meeting," she went on in French.—" Allow me to in-

troduce you to my husband. *Valérien,* Monsieur
Litvínoff, *un ami d'enfance;* Valerián Vladímirovitch Ratmíroff, my husband."

One of the young generals, almost the most elegant of them all, rose from his chair, and bowed
to Litvínoff with extreme courtesy, while his remaining comrades knit their brows slightly, or,
not so much knit their brows, as became immersed,
for the moment, each one in himself, as though
protesting in advance at any connection with a
strange civilian, while the other ladies who were
taking part in the picnic considered it necessary
to screw their eyes up a trifle and to grin, and
even to express dissatisfaction on their faces.

" You. . . . Have you been long in Baden? " inquired General Ratmíroff, assuming an affected
air, in a certain non-Russian fashion, and evidently not knowing what to talk about with the
friend of his wife's youth.

" Not long," replied Litvínoff.

" And do you intend to remain long? " went
on the polite general.

" I have not yet made up my mind."

" Ah! That is very pleasant . . . very."

The general became dumb. Litvínoff also
maintained silence.

Both held their hats in their hands, and with
bodies inclined forward and teeth displayed, they
stared at each other's brows.

" *Deux gendarmes un beau dimanche,*" struck

up, out of tune, as a matter of course,—we have
yet to meet the Russian noble who does not sing
out of tune,—a mole-eyed, sallow general with an
expression of perpetual irritation on his face, as
though he could not pardon himself for his own
appearance. He was the only one among all those
comrades who did not resemble a rose.

"But why do not you sit down, Grigóry Mikhaílitch?" remarked Irína at last.

Litvínoff obeyed and sat down.

"I say, Valerian, give me a light," said (in
English) another general, also young but already
obese, with immovable eyes, which seemed to be
riveted on the air, and with thick, silky side-
whiskers, in which he slowly plunged his snow-
white fingers. Ratmíroff gave him a silver box
filled with matches.

"*Avec vous des papiros?*" inquired one of the
ladies, with a lisp.

"*De vrais papelitos, comtesse.*"

"*Deux gendarmes un beau dimanche,*" struck
up the mole-eyed general again, almost gnashing
his teeth.

"You certainly must call upon us," Irína was
saying, meanwhile, to Litvínoff.—"We are living in the Hotel de l'Europe. I am always at
home from four until six. You and I have not
seen each other for a long time."

Litvínoff cast a glance at Irína; she did not
lower her eyes.

"Yes, Irína Pávlovna, it is a long time. Not since Moscow days."

"Since Moscow days—since Moscow days," she repeated haltingly.—"Do come; we will have a chat and recall old times. But, do you know, Grigóry Mikhaílitch, you have not altered much."

"Really? But you have changed, Irína Pávlovna."

"I have grown old."

"No, that was not what I meant to say. . ."

"Irène?" in an inquiring tone of voice, said one of the ladies, with a yellow bonnet on yellow hair, after a preliminary whisper and giggle with the cavalier who sat beside her.—"Irína?"

"I have grown old," repeated Irína, making no reply to the lady; "but I have not changed. No, no, I have not changed in any way."

"*Deux gendarmes un beau dimanche!*" rang out again. The irritable general could recall only the first line of the familiar song.

"It still pricks, Your Illustriousness," said the fat general with the side-whiskers in a loud voice, pronouncing his *os* broadly, probably in allusion to some amusing story familiar to the whole *beau monde,* and uttering a curt, wooden laugh, he again fixed his eyes on the air. All the rest of the party broke out laughing also.

"What a sad dog you are, Bóris!" remarked (in English) Ratmíroff in a low tone. He even

pronounced the name " Borís " in English
fashion.

" Irène? " inquired for the third time, the lady
in the yellow bonnet. Irína turned quickly toward her.

" *Eh, bien! quoi? Que me voulez-vous?* "

" *Je vous le dirai plus tard,*" replied the lady
affectedly. Although possessed of an extremely
unattractive exterior, she was constantly indulg-
ing in affectations and grimaces; a certain wit
had once said of her that she *"minaudait dans le
vide "*—made grimaces at empty space.

Irína frowned and impatiently shrugged her
shoulders.

" *Mais que fait donc Monsieur Verdier? Pourquoi ne vient-il pas?* " exclaimed one lady, with
those drawling accents which are insufferable to
French ears, and which constitute the specialty of
the Great Russian pronunciation.

" Akh, you, akh, you, Monsieur Verdier, Monsieur Verdier," groaned a lady, who had certainly
been born in Arzamás.

" *Tranquillisez-vous, mesdames,*" interposed
Ratmíroff:—" *Monsieur Verdier m'a promis de
venir se mettre à vos pieds.*"

" Ha, ha, ha! "—the ladies began to flutter
their fans.

The waiter brought several glasses of beer.

" *Bairisch-bier?* " inquired the general with the
side-whiskers, intentionally speaking in a bass

voice, and pretending to be surprised.—"*Guten Morgen.*"

"Well? Is Count Pável still there?" one young general coldly and languidly asked another.

"Yes,"—replied the other, with equal coldness. —"*Mais c'est provisoire.* Serge, they say, is in his place."

"Oho!" hissed the other through his teeth.

"Ye-es," hissed the first.

"I cannot understand," began the general who had been humming the song:—"I cannot understand what possessed Pólya to defend himself, to allege various excuses. . . Well, he molested the merchant, *il lui a fait rendre gorge* . . . well, but what of that? He may have had his reasons."

"He was afraid . . of being shown up in the newspapers," muttered some one.

The irritable general flared up.

"Well, that is the very worst of all! The newspapers! Shown up! If it had depended on me, all I would permit your newspapers to print would be the fixed prices of meat and of bread, and the advertisements of the sale of fur cloaks and boots."

"And of noblemen's estates at auction," put in Ratmíroff.

"If you like, under present conditions. But what a conversation in Baden, at the Vieux Château!"

"*Mais pas du tout! pas du tout!*" lisped the lady in the yellow bonnet.—"*J'adore les questions politiques.*"

"*Madame a raison*," interposed another general, with an extremely agreeable and rather effeminate face.—"Why should we avoid those questions . . . even in Baden?" At these words he glanced politely at Litvínoff, and smiled condescendingly.—"An upright man ought nowhere, under any circumstances, to renounce his convictions. Is not that true?"

"Of course," replied the irritable general, also casting his eyes on Litvínoff, and, as it were, indirectly reproving him:—"but I do not perceive the necessity . . ."

"No, no," interrupted the condescending general, with his former mildness.

"Here our friend, Valerián Vladímirovitch, alluded to the sale of noblemen's estates. What of that? Is it not a fact?"

"But it is impossible to sell them now; nobody wants them!" exclaimed the irritable general.

"Possibly . . . possibly. Therefore, it is necessary to declare that fact . . . that sad fact, at every step. We are ruined—very good. We are humiliated,—it is impossible to dispute that; but we large proprietors, we represent a principle . . *un principe* . . . nevertheless. It is our duty to uphold that principle. Pardon, madame, I think you have dropped your handkerchief. When a

certain blindness, so to speak, takes possession of
even the loftiest minds, we ought to point out—
humbly point out " (the general stretched out
his finger),—" point out with the finger to the
citizen the abyss whither everything is hastening.
We ought to utter a warning: we ought to say
with respectful firmness: ' turn back, turn back. .'
That is what we ought to say."

" But it is impossible to turn back completely,"
remarked Ratmíroff thoughtfully.

The condescending general merely grinned.

" Completely; completely back, *mon très cher*.
The further back the better."

Again the general cast a polite glance at Litvínoff. The latter could restrain himself no longer.

" You would not have us return to the time of
the Seven Boyárs, Your Excellency? "

" Even that! I expressed my meaning without
any ambiguity; we must do over . . . yes . . .
do over everything that has been done."

" And the nineteenth of February also? "

"Yes,the nineteenth of February[1] also,—so far
as that is possible. *On est patriote ou on ne l'est
pas*. ' But freedom?' I shall be asked. Do you
think this freedom is sweet to the people? Just
ask them. . . ."

" Try," retorted Litvínoff:—" try to deprive
them of that freedom. . ."

[1] The date of the Emancipation Proclamation, March 3,
1861.—Translator.

"*Comment nommez-vous ce monsieur?*" whispered the general to Ratmíroff.

"But what are you talking about there?" suddenly began the fat general, who, evidently, played the part of a spoiled child in this company. "Still about the newspapers? About quill-drivers? Let me tell you what an experience I had with a quill-driver—it was splendid! I was told: '*un folliculaire* has written a libel on you.' Well, of course, I immediately called him to account. They brought the dear man. . . 'How come you,' says I, 'my friend, *folliculaire,* to be writing libels? Have you conquered your patriotism?' 'I have,' says he. 'Well, and do you love money, *folliculaire?*' says I. 'I do,' says he. So then, my dear sirs, I let him smell of the knob of my cane.—'And do you love this also, my angel?'—'No,' says he, 'I don't love that.'—'Well,' says I, 'you smell of that in proper fashion—my hands are clean.'—'I don't like it,' says he, 'and that's enough.'—'But I, my dear fellow,' says I, 'love it very much, only not for myself. Do you understand this allegory, my treasure?'—'I understand,' says he.—'Then look to it, be a good boy hereafter, and now here's a ruble for you; take yourself off, and bless me day and night.' And the *folliculaire* departed."

The general broke into a laugh, and all the others again followed his example and laughed—all, with the exception of Irína, who did not even smile, and stared in a somewhat gloomy manner at the story-teller.

The condescending general tapped Borís on the shoulder.

"You invented the whole of that, my beloved friend. . As if you would menace any one with a cane. . . You have n't even any cane. *C'est pour faire rire ces dames.* It was just for the sake of a joke. But that's not the point. I said a while ago that we must return completely. Understand me, I am not an enemy to so-called progress; but all those universities and seminaries there, and schools for the common people, those students, priests' sons, plebeians, and that small fry, *tout ce fond du sac, la petite propriété, pire que le proletariat*"— (the general spoke in a subdued, almost prostrated voice) —"*voilà ce qui m'effraie* . . . that is what must be stopped . . . and it will stop." (Again he cast a caressing glance at Litvínoff.) "Yes, sir, we must call a halt. Do not forget that with us no one demands anything, asks anything. Does any one ask for self-government, for example? Do *you* ask for it? Or dost thou? or thou? or do you, mesdames? For you not only govern yourselves but also all the rest of us." (The general's extremely handsome countenance lighted up with an amused smile.) "My dear friends, why flee like a hare? Democracy delights in you, it burns incense before you, it is ready to subserve your ends . . for you know this sword is two-edged. The old ways of times gone by are the best, after all . . They are much safer. Do not permit the common people to reason, and put your trust in the aristocracy, in which alone there is power. . . Really, it will be better so. But as for progress . . . personally, I have no objection to progress. Only, do not give us any lawyers, and jurors, and some county officials or other—but discipline, most of all, do not meddle with discipline; but you can build bridges, and quays, and hospitals, and why should not the streets be illuminated with gas? "

" Petersburg has been fired on all four sides, and there's progress for you! " hissed the irritable general.

" Well, I perceive that you are rancorous," remarked the fat general languidly, as he swayed to and fro.—" It would be a good thing to appoint you Chief Procurator of the Holy Synod; but, in my opinion, *avec Orphée aux enfers le progrès a dit son dernier mot.*"

"Vous dites toujours des bêtises," giggled the lady from Arzamás.

The general assumed an air of dignity.

" *Je ne suis jamais plus sérieux, madame, que quand je dis des bêtises.*"

" Monsieur Verdier used that phrase several times," remarked Irína, in a low tone.

" *De la poigne et des formes!* " exclaimed the fat general:—"*de la poigne surtout.* And that may be translated into Russian thus: be courteous, but give it to them straight in the teeth!"

"Akh, you scamp, you incorrigible scamp!" interposed the condescending general.—"Please do not listen to him, mesdames. He would not hurt a gnat. He contents himself with devouring his own heart."

"Well, but no, Borís," began Ratmíroff, exchanging a glance with his wife:—"a jest is a jest, but this is carrying the thing too far. Progress is a manifestation of social life, and that must be borne in mind; it is a symptom. One must keep an eye on it."

"Well, yes," returned the fat general, and wrinkled up his nose.—"'T is a well-known fact that your aim is to be a statesman!"

"My aim is not in the least, to become a statesman. . . What has statesmanship to do with that? But one must not refuse to admit the truth."

"Bóris" again plunged his fingers into his whiskers, and riveted his eyes on the air.

"Social life is very important, because in the development of a nation, in the fate, so to speak, of the fatherland . . ."

"Valérien," interrupted "Bóris" impressively:—"*il y a des dames ici.* I did not expect this from you. Or do you wish to get on a committee?"

"But they are all discontinued now, thank God," interposed the irritable general, and again began to hum: "*Deux gendarmes un beau dimanche. . . . .*"

Ratmíroff raised his batiste handkerchief to his nose, and gracefully subsided into silence; the irritable general repeated: " The scamp! the scamp!" But " Bóris " turned to the lady who was making grimaces into empty space, and, without lowering his voice, without even altering the expression of his face, he began to ask her when she "would crown his flame," as he was amazingly in love with her, and was suffering to an unusual degree.

With every moment that passed during the course of this conversation Litvínoff felt more and more uncomfortable. His pride, his honourable, plebeian pride, fairly rose up in revolt. What was there in common between him, the son of a petty official, and those military aristocrats from Petersburg? He loved everything which they hated, he hated everything which they loved; he recognised that fact too plainly: he felt it with his whole being. He considered their jests insipid, their tone intolerable, their every movement artificial; in the very softness of their speech his ear detected scorn which revolted him—and yet he seemed to have grown timid in their presence —in the presence of those people, those enemies. . .
" Faugh, how disgusting! I embarrass them, I seem ridiculous to them," kept whirling through his brain:—" and why do I remain here? Let me

go, let me go at once!" Irína's presence could
not detain him: she also aroused melancholy emotions in him. He rose from his chair and began
to take leave.

"Are you going already?" said Irína, but
after a little reflection she ceased to insist, and
merely made him promise that he would not fail
to call on her. General Ratmíroff, with the same
refined courtesy as before, took leave of him, shook
hands with him, and escorted him to the edge of
the platform. . . But Litvínoff had barely passed
round the first turn in the road, when a hearty
burst of laughter rang out behind him. This
laughter did not refer to him, but to the long-
expected Monsieur Verdier, who suddenly made
his appearance on the platform, in a Tyrolean
hat, a blue blouse, and mounted astride of an ass;
but the blood fairly rushed to Litvínoff's cheeks,
and he felt bitter, as though wormwood had glued
his tightly-compressed lips together. "The de-
spicable, vulgar creatures!" he muttered, without
taking into consideration that the few moments
spent in company of those people had not furnished him any cause to express himself so
harshly. And Irína, the Irína who had once been
his, had got into that set! She moved in it, lived
in it, reigned in it, for it she had sacrificed her
own dignity, the best sentiments of her heart. . .
Evidently, all was as it should be; evidently, she
deserved no better fate! How glad he was that

it had not occurred to her to question him as to his intentions! He would have been obliged to state them before " them," in " their " presence. . . " Not for any consideration! Never!" whispered Litvínoff, inhaling a deep breath of the fresh air, and descending the path to Baden almost at a run. He thought of his affianced bride, of his dear, good, holy Tánya, and how pure, how noble, how upright, she appeared to him! With what genuine emotion he recalled her features, her words, even her habits . . . with what impatience did he await her return!

His rapid pace calmed his nerves. On reaching home he seated himself at the table, took a book in his hand, and suddenly threw it down, and even shuddered. . What had happened to him? Nothing had happened to him, but Irína . . . Irína . . . his encounter with her suddenly struck him as surprising, strange, unusual. Was it possible he had met, had talked with that same Irína? . . . And why did not that repulsive, worldly stamp, wherewith all the others were so plainly marked, lie upon her also? Why did it seem to him that she was bored, or grieved, or oppressed by her position? She was in their camp, but she was not an enemy. And what could have made her treat him with such cordiality, ask him to come to her?

Litvínoff gave a start.—" Oh Tánya, Tánya! " he exclaimed impulsively:—" thou art my angel, my good genius—I love thee alone and will always love thee. And I will not go to that woman. I will have nothing whatever to do with her! Let her amuse herself with her generals!"

Litvínoff again took up a book.

XI

Litvínoff took up a book, but he could not read. He left the house, strolled about a little, listened to the music, stared a while at the gaming, and again returned to his room—again made an attempt to read—still without success. Time, for some reason, dragged on with particular slowness. Pishtchálkin, the well-meaning arbitrator of the peace, came in, and sat there for about three hours. He conversed, explained, put questions, argued in the intervals—now on lofty themes, now on useful ones, and at last diffused such tedium that poor Litvínoff almost set up a howl. In the art of inspiring tedium, melancholy, cold, helpless, hopeless tedium, Pishtchálkin had no rival, even among the people of the loftiest morality, who are well-known masters in that line. The mere sight of his closely-clipped, smoothly-brushed head, of his light, lifeless eyes, his well-formed nose, inspired involuntary despondency, and his slow, baritone, apparently slumbering voice, seemed to have been created for the purpose of uttering, with conviction and perspicuity, apophthegms to the effect that two and two make four, and not five, and not three; that water is wet, and that virtue is laudable; that a private person, equally with an empire, and an empire, equally with a private person, must have credit for financial operations. And withal, he was a most excellent man! But such is the fate decreed to Russia: our most excellent people are tiresome. Pishtchálkin withdrew; Bindásoff took his place, and slowly, with immense impudence, demanded that Litvínoff should lend him one hundred guldens, which the latter gave him, in spite of the fact that he not only took no interest in Bindásoff, but even loathed him, and knew for a certainty that he would never get his money back again; moreover, he needed it himself. Then why did he give it to him? the reader asks. The devil knows why! The Russians are great fellows at that. Let the reader lay his hand on his heart and recall how many acts in his own life have had, positively, no other cause. But Bindásoff did not even thank Litvínoff: he demanded a glass of Affenthaler (the red wine of Baden) and went away, without wiping his lips, and with a rude clumping of his boots. And how angry Litvínoff was with himself, as he gazed at the red neck of the departing monopolist! Just before evening he received a letter from Tánya, in which she informed him that in consequence of her aunt's illness she could not reach Baden in less than five or six days. This news produced an unpleasant effect on Litvínoff: it aggravated his vexation, and he went to bed early in an evil

frame of mind. The following day turned out
no better than the preceding, worse, if anything.
From early morning Litvínoff's room was filled
with his fellow-countrymen: Bambáeff, Voroshíloff, Pishtchálkin, the two officers, the two Heidelberg students, all thronged in at once, and
never took their departure until almost dinner-
time, although they speedily talked themselves
out, and were evidently bored. They simply
did not know what to do with themselves, and
having once got into Litvínoff's quarters, they
" stuck " there, as the expression is. At first they
discussed the fact that Gubaryóff had gone back
to Heidelberg, and that they must betake themselves to him; then they philosophised a little,
touched on the Polish question; then they proceeded to argue about gambling, courtesans, began to narrate scandalous anecdotes; at last a
conversation arose about strong men, fat men,
and gluttons. Ancient anecdotes were dragged
out into the light of day, about Lúkin, about the
deacon who devoured, on a wager, thirty-three
herrings, about the colonel of Uhlans, Izyédinoff,
well known for his obesity, about the soldier who
broke a beef-bone over his own forehead; and then
came downright lies. Pishtchálkin himself narrated, with a yawn, that he knew a peasant woman
in Little Russia, who, at her death, weighed
twenty-seven puds [1] and several pounds, and a

[1] A *pud* is thirty-six pounds.—TRANSLATOR.

landed proprietor, who had devoured three geese and a sturgeon for breakfast. Bambáeff suddenly went into raptures, and declared that he himself was in a condition to eat a whole sheep, " of course, with condiments," while Voroshíloff rashly made such an absurd remark about his comrade, the muscular cadet, that all became silent, remained silent, stared at one another, took their hats, and dispersed. When he was left alone, Litvínoff tried to occupy himself with some work, but it seemed exactly as though soot had got into his head; he could do nothing of value, and the evening also was wasted. On the following morning, as he was preparing to breakfast, some one knocked at his door. " O Lord!"—said Litvínoff to himself,—" there's some one of those friends of yesterday again," and not without considerable shuddering, he called out:

" Herein!"

The door opened very softly, and Potúgin entered the room.

Litvínoff was extremely glad to see him.

" This is delightful!" he exclaimed, warmly pressing the hand of his unexpected guest:— " thank you! I should certainly have called on you, but you would not tell me where you live. Sit down, please, lay aside your hat. Sit down, I say!"

Potúgin made no reply to Litvínoff's friendly

speeches, but stood shifting from foot to foot in the middle of the room, and merely laughed and rocked his head. Litvínoff's joyous reception evidently touched him, but there was something constrained in the expression of his face.

" There . . is a little misunderstanding here . . ." he began, not without hesitation.—" Of course I am always pleased . . . but, to tell the truth . . I have been sent to you."

" That is, you mean to say," remarked Litvínoff in a mournful tone,—" that you would not have come to me of your own accord?"

" O, no, good gracious! . . . But I . . I—perhaps I should not have made up my mind to intrude upon you to-day, if I had not been requested to call on you. In short, I have a message for you."

" From whom, permit me to inquire?"

" From a person of your acquaintance: from Irína Pávlovna Ratmíroff. Two days ago you promised to call upon her, and you have not done so."

Litvínoff fixed his eyes in amazement upon Potúgin.

" Are you acquainted with Madame Ratmíroff?"

" As you see."

" And do you know her intimately?"

" I am her friend, to a certain degree."

Litvínoff said nothing.

"Allow me to ask you," he began at last:—
"do you know why Irína Pávlovna wishes to
see me?"

Potúgin walked to the window.

"Yes, to a certain extent I do know. So far
as I am able to judge, she was greatly delighted
at her meeting with you,—well, and so she wishes
to renew your former relations."

"Renew!" repeated Litvínoff.—"Excuse my
indiscretion, but permit me to ask you still another question. Do you know the nature of those
relations?"

"To tell the truth,—no, I do not. But I assume," added Potúgin, suddenly turning to Litvínoff, and gazing at him in a friendly way:—"I
assume that they were of a good sort. Irína Pávlovna praised you highly, and I had to give
her my word that I would bring you. You will
go?"

"When?"

"Now . . . immediately."

Litvínoff merely flung out his hands with a
gesture of surprise.

"Irína Pávlovna," went on Potúgin,—"takes
it for granted that that . . . how shall I express
it . . . that set of people, let us say, in which you
found her two days before yesterday, could not
have aroused any special sympathy in you; but
she has commanded me to say that the devil is not
as black as he is painted."

" H'm. . . . . Is that expression applied precisely to that . . . . set? "

" Yes . . and in general."

" H'm . . . Well, and what is your own opinion about the devil, Sozónt Ivánitch? "

" I think, Grigóry Mikhaílitch, that, in any case, he is not what he is represented to be."

" Is he better? "

" Whether he is better or worse it is difficult to decide, but he is not as represented. Well, how is it to be? Shall we go? "

" You sit here a while first. I must confess, that it strikes me as rather strange. ."

" What does, if I may presume to inquire? "

" How have you—you in particular—been able to become the friend of Irína Pávlovna? "

Potúgin surveyed himself with a glance.

" With my figure and my position in society, it really does seem incredible; but you know— Shakespeare said: ' There are many things, friend Horatio,' and so forth. Life also does not like to jest. Here 's a comparison for you: a tree stands before you, and there is no wind; how can a leaf on the lowest bough touch a leaf on the highest bough? In no way whatever. But let a storm arise, and everything gets mixed up—and those two leaves come into contact."

" Aha! That means that there has been a storm? "

" I should think so! Can one get along in life

without storms? But away with philosophy. It
is time to go."

But Litvínoff still hesitated.

"O Lord!" exclaimed Potúgin, with a comical grimace:—"how queer the young men have
become nowadays! The most charming of
women invites them to her, sends a messenger
after them, a special messenger, and they stand
on ceremony! Shame on you, my dear sir, shame
on you! Here 's your hat. Take it, and '*vor-
wärts!*' as our friends the ardent Germans say."

Litvínoff still stood for a space in thought, but
ended by taking his hat, and sallying forth from
his chamber with Potúgin.

XII

THEY came to one of the best hotels in Baden, and asked for Madame Ratmíroff. The hall-porter first inquired their names, then immediately replied, *" die Frau Fürstin ist zu Hause,"* and himself conducted them up the stairs, knocked on the door of the room with his own hand, and announced them. *" Die Frau Fürstin "* received them at once; she was alone: her husband had gone off to Karlsruhe to meet an official big-wig, one of "the influential personages,"who was passing through. Irína was seated beside a small table and embroidering on canvas when Potúgin and Litvínoff crossed the threshold. She hastily threw aside her sewing, pushed the table away, and rose; an expression of unfeigned satisfaction spread over her face. She wore a morning gown, closed to the throat; the beautiful outlines of her shoulders and arms were visible through the thin material; her carelessly twisted hair had become loosened, and fell low on her slender neck. Irína cast a swift glance at Potúgin, whispered *"merci,"* and offered her hand to Litvínoff, amiably reproaching him for his forgetfulness. " And an old friend at that," she added.

Litvínoff began to make excuses. *"C'est bien, c'est bien,"* she said hastily, and taking his hat from him with gracious force, she made him sit down. Potúgin also seated himself, but immediately rose, and saying that he had business which could not be deferred, and that he would drop in after dinner, he took his leave. Irína again threw him a swift glance and gave him a friendly nod, and as soon as he had disappeared behind the portière, she turned to Litvínoff with impatient vivacity.

"Grigóry Mikhaílovitch," she began in Russian, in her soft and resonant voice:—"here we are alone at last, and I can say to you that I am very glad of our meeting, because it . . . it affords me the opportunity . . ." (Irína looked him straight in the face), "to ask your forgiveness."

Litvínoff involuntarily shuddered. He had not anticipated such a rapid attack. He had not anticipated that she herself would turn the conversation on bygone days.

"For what . . forgiveness . . ." he stammered out.

Irína blushed.

"For what? . . you know for what," she said, and turned aside a little.—"I was to blame toward you, Grigóry Mikhaílitch . . although, of course, such was my fate" (Litvínoff recalled her letter), "and I do not regret it . . in any case, it would be too late; but when I met you so un-

expectedly, I said to myself that we must become
friends without fail—without fail . . . and I
should have felt deeply pained if it had not succeeded . . . and it seems to me, that to that end,
you and I must have an explanation without
delay, and once for all, in order that thereafter
there might be no . . . *gêne,* no awkwardness,
—once for all,—Grigóry Mikhaílovitch; and that
you ought to tell me that you forgive me,
otherwise I shall suspect in you . . . *de la ran-
cune. Voilà!* It may be a great piece of assump-
tion on my part, because you, in all probability,
have long ago forgotten everything, but, nevertheless, do tell me that you have forgiven me."

Irína uttered this entire speech without taking
breath, and Litvínoff could see that tears glis-
tened in her eyes . . yes, actually tears.

"Pray, Irína Pávlovna," he hastily began:—
"are n't you ashamed to excuse yourself, to ask
forgiveness . . it is an affair of the past, it has
utterly lapsed out of existence, and I can but feel
surprised that you, in the midst of the splendour
which surrounds you, can still have preserved a
memory of the gloomy companion of your early
youth. . ."

"Does that surprise you?" said Irína softly.

"It touches me," replied Litvínoff:—"because I could not possibly imagine . . ."

"But you have not yet told me that you have
forgiven me," interrupted Irína.

" I rejoice sincerely in your happiness, Irína Pávlovna; with all my soul I wish you the very best on earth. . . ."

" And you bear no ill-will? "

" I remember only those fair moments, for which I was, in times past, indebted to you."

Irína extended both her hands to him. Litvínoff pressed them warmly, and did not immediately release them. . . . A mysterious something which had long ceased to exist began to stir in his heart at that soft contact. Again Irína looked him straight in the face; but this time he smiled. . . And for the first time he gazed directly and intently at her. . . Again he recognised the features, once so dear, and those deep eyes with their unusual lashes, and the little mole on the cheek, and the peculiar sweep of the hair above the brow, and her habit of curling her lips in a certain gracious and amusing way, and of imparting to her eyebrows the suspicion of a quiver, he recognised all, all. . . But how much more beautiful she had grown! What charm and power in the young feminine body! And there was neither red paint, nor white, nor blackening for the eyebrows, nor powder, nor any sort of artificiality on the fresh, pure face. . . Yes, she was a real beauty!

A meditative mood took possession of Litvínoff. . . . He continued to gaze at her, but his thoughts were already far away. . . Irína observed this.

" Well, that's capital," she said aloud:—
" Well, now my conscience is at ease, and I can
satisfy my curiosity. . . ."

" Curiosity," repeated Litvínoff, as though in
perplexity.

" Yes, yes. . . I insist upon knowing what you
have been doing all this time, what your plans
are; I want to know everything just the same as
when . . . everything, everything . . . and you
must tell me the truth, because, I warn you, that
I have not lost sight of you . . . so far as that
has been possible. . ."

" You have not lost sight of me, you . . . there
. . in Petersburg?"

" In the midst of the splendour which surrounds me, as you just expressed it. Yes, exactly that; I have not lost sight of you. You and
I will discuss the splendour later on; but now you
must narrate to me a great deal, narrate at
length; no one will disturb us. Akh, how splendid that will be!" added Irína, merrily, seating
herself in an arm-chair and putting on a pretty
air.—" Come, now, begin."

" Before I tell my story, I must thank you,"
began Litvínoff.

" What for?"

" For the bouquet of flowers which made its
appearance in my chamber."

" What bouquet? I know nothing about it."

" What?"

" I tell you, I know nothing about it. . . But

I am waiting . . . waiting for your story.—Akh, what a clever fellow that Potúgin is to have brought you!"

Litvínoff pricked up his ears.

"Have you been acquainted long with that Mr. Potúgin?" he inquired.

"Yes, for a long time . . . but tell your story."

"And do you know him intimately?"

"Oh, yes!"—Irína sighed.—"There are peculiar reasons for it. . . You have heard of Eliza Byélsky, of course. . . The one who died such a frightful death last year?—Akh, yes, I had forgotten that our stories are not known to you. Happily, happily, you do not know them. Oh, *quelle chance!* at last, at last, there is one man, a live man, who knows none of our affairs! And one can talk Russian with him, bad Russian, but Russian all the same, and not that eternal, affected, repulsive Petersburg French!"

"And you say that Potúgin had some connection with . . ."

"It is very painful to me to recall that," interposed Irína.—"Eliza was my best friend at the Institute, and afterward, in Petersburg, we saw each other constantly. She confided to me all her secrets: she was very unhappy, she suffered much. Potúgin behaved splendidly in that affair, like a genuine knight! He sacrificed himself. It was only then that I prized him at his true value! But we have digressed again. I am waiting for your story, Grigóry Mikhaílovitch."

" But my story cannot in the least interest you, Irína Pávlovna."

" That is no concern of yours."

" Remember, Irína Pávlovna, we have not met for ten years. How much has happened,—how much water has flowed past since then!"

" Not water only! not water only!" she repeated, with a peculiar, bitter expression:—" and that is why I wish to hear you. . ."

" And, moreover, I really cannot think where to begin."

" At the beginning. From the very time when you . . . when I went away to Petersburg. You then remained in Moscow. . . Do you know, I have never been back to Moscow since that day!"

" Really? "

" At first it was not possible, and afterward, when I married . . ."

" And have you been married long? "

" Three years."

" You have no children? "

" No," she replied drily.

Litvínoff fell silent.

" And until your marriage you lived altogether with that—what 's his name—Count Reisenbach? "

Irína contemplated him fixedly, as though desirous of comprehending why he asked that question.

" No . . ." she said at last.

" Consequently, your parents. . . By the way, I have not asked you about them. How are they? . . ."

" They are both well."

" And they live in Moscow as formerly? "

" Yes."

" And your brothers and sisters? "

" All is well with them; I have provided for them all."

" Ah! "—Litvínoff cast a sidelong glance at Irína.—" As a matter of fact, Irína Pávlovna, it is not I who ought to relate the story, but you, if only . . ."

He suddenly caught himself up, and stopped speaking.

Irína raised her hands to her face, and began to twist her wedding ring round on her finger.

" Do you think so? I do not refuse," she said at last.—" Some time, if you like. . . But it is your turn first . . because, you see, I have kept watch over you, yet I know almost nothing about you; but about me . . . well, about me, you surely must have heard a good deal. Is n't that true? Tell me, you have heard things? "

" You have occupied too prominent a place in the world, Irína Pávlovna, not to start rumours

. . . especially in the country districts where I was, and where every rumour is believed."

" And you believed those rumours? And of what sort were they? "

" I must confess, Irína Pávlovna, that those rumours very rarely reached my ears. I led an extremely isolated life."

" How so? Were not you in the Crimea, in the militia? "

" And is that known to you? "

" As you see. I tell you that you were watched."

Again Litvínoff was forced to wonder.

" Why should I tell you what is already known to you without that? " said Litvínoff, in a low voice.

" Because . . because . . in order to comply with my request. I entreat you, Grigóry Mikhaílovitch."

Litvínoff inclined his head, and began . . . began rather confusedly, in general outlines, to communicate to Irína his far from complicated adventures. He paused frequently, and cast an inquiring glance at Irína, as much as to say: " Isn't this enough? " But she insistently demanded that he should continue his narration, and pushing her hair back behind her ears, and resting her elbows on the arms of the easy-chair, seemed to be seizing every word with strained attention. Any one looking at her from a distance, and watching the

expression of her face, might have thought that
she was not listening to what Litvínoff was telling her, but was merely immersed in meditation.
. . But she was not meditating upon Litvínoff,
although he became embarrassed, and flushed
crimson beneath her persistent gaze. Before her
had started forth a whole life, another life, not
his—her own life.

Litvínoff did not finish, but fell silent, under
the influence of a disagreeable sensation of constantly augmenting, inward discomfort. This
time Irína said nothing to him, did not ask him
to continue, and pressing her palm to her eyes,
as though weary, she slowly leaned against the
back of her chair and remained motionless. Litvínoff waited a while, and reflecting that his visit
had already lasted more than two hours, was on
the point of extending his hand to take his hat,
when suddenly, in the adjoining room, the swift
squeak of thin, lacquered boots resounded, and,
preceded by that same odour of nobility and the
Guards, Valerián Vladímirovitch Ratmíroff entered the room.

Litvínoff rose from his chair, and exchanged
a bow with the good-looking general. But Irína,
without any haste, removed her hand from her
face, and bestowing a cold glance upon her husband, remarked, in French:—" Ah! So you have
returned! But what time is it?"

" It is almost four o'clock, *ma chère amie,* and

you are not yet dressed—the Princess will be waiting for us," replied the general, and with an elegant inclination of his body in the direction of Litvínoff, with the almost effeminate playfulness in his voice which was peculiar to him, he added: —" Evidently, your amiable guest has made you forget the time."

The reader will permit us to impart to him, at this point, a few facts concerning General Ratmíroff. His father was the natural . . . what do you think? You are not mistaken, but we did not wish to say it . . . the natural son of a prominent grandee of the times of Alexander I., and of a pretty little French actress. The grandee had opened a career for his son, but had left him no property,—and that son (the father of our hero) had not succeeded in becoming rich either: he had died with the rank of colonel, in the vocation of chief of police. A year before his death he had married a pretty young widow, who had been obliged to have recourse to his protection. His son and the widow's, Valerián Vladímirovitch, having got into the Pages Corps through influence, had attracted the attention of the authorities—not so much by proficiency in his studies as by his military bearing, his good manners, and his good morals (although he had been subjected to everything, which all former pupils of the government military institutions must undergo),—and had graduated into the Guards. He

had made a brilliant career, thanks to the modest
gaiety of his disposition, his skill in dancing, his
masterly riding as orderly officer at parades—
mostly on other people's horses—and, in conclusion, to a special art of familiarly-respectful be-
haviour toward the loftiest personages, a mourn-
fully-caressing, almost forlorn, obsequiousness,
not devoid of a dash of liberalism, light as down.
. . This liberalism did not prevent him, nevertheless, from soundly flogging fifty peasants in a
revolted White Russian village, which he had been
sent to pacify. He was the possessor of an at-
tractive and extremely youthful exterior; smooth,
ruddy, supple and adhesive: he enjoyed remarkable success with the women: distinguished old
ladies fairly went wild over him. Cautious by
habit, taciturn through calculation, General Ratmíroff, like the industrious bee, which extracts
juice even from wretched flowers, was constantly
circulating in the highest society—and, devoid of
morality, devoid of every sort of knowledge, but
with the reputation of a capable man, with a good
scent for people, and comprehension of circumstances, and chief of all—with an inflexibly firm
desire of good things for himself—he at last saw
all roads open before him. . .

Litvínoff smiled in a constrained way and Irína
merely shrugged her shoulders.

" Well," she said, in the same cold tone,—" did
you see the Count? "

" Of course I saw him. He asked to be remembered to you."

" Ah! Is he still as stupid as ever, that protector of yours? "

General Ratmíroff made no reply, and only laughed a little through his nose, as though making allowance for the precipitancy of woman's judgment. Benevolent adults reply to the absurd sallies of children with precisely that sort of a laugh.

" Yes," added Irína:—" the stupidity of your Count is too astounding, and it strikes me that I have had plenty of opportunity to observe it."

" It was you yourself who sent me to him," remarked the general, through his teeth, and turning to Litvínoff, he asked him, in Russian:— " Was he undergoing a cure of the Baden waters? "

" I am well, thank God," replied Litvínoff.

" That's the best thing of all," went on the general, with an amiable grin:—" yes, and in general, people do not come to Baden for the sake of taking the cure; but the waters here are very efficacious, *je veux dire, efficaces;* and for any one who, like myself, for instance, is suffering from a nervous cough. . . ."

Irína rose in haste.—" We shall meet again, Grigóry Mikhaílovitch, and that soon, I hope,"— she said in French, scornfully interrupting her husband's speech:—" but now I must go and dress. That old Princess is insufferable with her eternal *parties de plaisir,* where there is nothing but tedium."

" You are very severe on everything to-day," muttered her husband, and slipped into the other room.

Litvínoff went toward the door.

" You have told me everything," she said, " but you have concealed the principal thing."

" What is that? "

" It is said that you are going to marry? "

Litvínoff crimsoned to his very ears. . . In fact, he had deliberately refrained from mentioning Tánya; but he felt frightfully vexed, in the first place, because Irína knew about his marriage, and in the second, because she had caught him, as it were, in a desire to hide the marriage from her. Decidedly, he did not know what to say, but Irína never took her eyes from him.

" Yes, I am about to marry," he said at last, and immediately took his departure.

Ratmíroff returned to the room.

" Well, why don't you get dressed? " he inquired.

" Go alone; my head aches."

" But the Princess . . ."

Irína measured her husband with a glance from head to foot, turned her back on him, and went off to her dressing-room.

XIII

Litvínoff was extremely dissatisfied with himself, as though he had lost money at roulette, or had broken his pledged word. . An inward voice told him, that as an affianced bridegroom, as a staid grown man, and no longer a boy, it was not proper for him to listen to the instigations of curiosity, nor to the seductions of memory. " Much need there was for me to go! " he argued. " On her side it was nothing but coquetry, a whim, caprice. . She is bored, she has grown tired of every thing, she caught at me . . . a dainty person sometimes suddenly longs for black bread . . . well, and that 's all right. But why did I run to her? Could I . . help despising her? " This last word he did not utter, even mentally, without an effort.—" Of course, there is no danger whatever, and there can be none ": he resumed his argument. " For I know with whom I have to deal. But, nevertheless, one should not play with fire. . . I won't set foot in her house again." Litvínoff did not dare, or could not yet, admit to himself, to what a degree Irína had seemed beautiful to him, and how powerfully she had aroused his emotion.

Again the day passed in a dull and languid manner. At dinner he chanced to sit beside a *" bel homme,"* of fine bearing, with dyed moustache, who uttered not a word, but merely puffed and opened his eyes very wide . . . but, being suddenly seized with hiccough, proved to be a fellow-countryman, for he instantly said in Russian: " Did n 't I say that I ought not to eat melons! " In the evening also nothing cheering happened: Bindásoff, before Litvínoff's very eyes, won a sum four times as large as the one he had borrowed from him, but not only did not repay the debt, but even looked him in the face with a menacing glance, as though preparing to castigate him even more painfully for having been a witness of his winnings. On the following morning the horde of fellow-countrymen descended upon him again; it was with difficulty that Litvínoff got rid of them, and betaking himself to the mountains, hit upon Irína the very first thing— he pretended that he did not recognise her, and passed swiftly by;—then on Potúgin. He was on the point of entering into conversation with Potúgin, but the latter answered him unwillingly. He was leading by the hand a smartly attired little girl, with fluffy, almost white locks, great dark eyes in a pale, sickly little face, and that peculiar imperious, impatient expression, which is characteristic of spoiled children. Litvínoff spent a couple of hours on the mountains, and then re-

turned home, along Lichtenthaler Avenue. . . .
A lady with a blue veil over her face, who was
sitting on a bench, hastily rose and approached
him. . . He recognised Irína.

"Why do you avoid me, Grigóry Mikhaílovitch," she said in an unsteady voice, such as a
person uses whose heart is seething.

Litvínoff was embarrassed.—"Do I avoid you,
Irína Pávlovna?"

"Yes, you . . . you . . . ."

Irína seemed agitated, almost incensed.

"You are mistaken, I assure you."

"No, I am not mistaken. Did not I see this
morning—when we met,—did not I see that you
knew me? Tell me, did n't you recognise me?
Tell me?"

"I really . . Irína Pávlovna . . ."

"Grigóry Mikhaílovitch, you are a straight-
forward man, you have always spoken the truth:
tell me—tell me, surely you recognised me? you
turned aside deliberately."

Litvínoff glanced at Irína. Her eyes shone
with a strange brilliancy, but her lips and cheeks
gleamed with a death-like pallor through the close
meshes of her veil. In the expression of her face,
in the very sound of her impetuous whisper, there
was something so irresistibly mournful, beseeching. . . . Litvínoff could dissimulate no longer.

"Yes. . . I recognised you," he said, not without an effort.

Irína shuddered softly, and softly dropped her hands.

"Why did not you come to me?" she whispered.

"Because . . . because!"—Litvínoff stepped aside from the path. Irína silently followed him. —"Why?" he repeated, and his face suddenly lighted up, and a feeling akin to malice oppressed his chest and his throat.—"You . . . you ask that, after all that has taken place between us? Not now, of course, not now, but there . . . there . . . in Moscow."

"But surely, you and I decided, surely you promised . . ." Irína began.

"I promised nothing. Pardon the harshness of my expressions, but you demand the truth—therefore judge for yourself: to what, if not to coquetry,—which is, I confess, incomprehensible to me,—to what, if not to a desire to try how much power you still possess over me, can I attribute your . . I do not know what to call it . . . your persistence? Our paths have become so widely separated! I have forgotten everything, I have long ago lived down the pain of it all, I have become an entirely different man; you are married, happy, in appearance at least; you enjoy an enviable position in society; why then, to what end, a renewal of acquaintance? What am I to you, what are you to me? We cannot understand each other now, we have absolutely nothing in common now, either in the past or in the present! Especially . . . especially in the past!"

Litvínoff pronounced the whole of this speech hurriedly, abruptly, without turning his head. Irína did not stir, and only from time to time, almost imperceptibly, extended her hands toward him. She seemed to be entreating him to stop and listen to her, and at his last words slightly bit her under lip, as though crushing down a sentiment of keen, swift injury.

" Grigóry Mikhaílovitch," she began at last, in a more composed voice, and retreated still further from the path, along which, now and then, people passed. . .

Litvínoff, in turn, followed her.

" Grigóry Mikhaílovitch, believe me: if I could have imagined that I still retained an atom of power over you, I would have been the first to avoid you. If I did not do so, if I made up my mind, in spite of . . . of my past fault, to renew acquaintance with you, it was because . . . because . . ."

" Because?" inquired Litvínoff, almost roughly.

" Because," replied Irína, with sudden force: —" because that society, that enviable position of which you speak, have become unbearable, insufferable to me; because, on meeting you, a live man, after all those dead dolls—you were able to view specimens of them three days ago at the

Vieux Château,—I rejoiced as at a well in the desert, but you call me a coquette, and suspect me, and repulse me under the pretext that I really was to blame toward you, and still more toward myself!"

"You chose your own destiny, Irína Pávlovna," said Litvínoff surlily, and still without turning his head.

"I did, I did . . . and I do not complain; I have no right to complain," hastily said Irína, to whom Litvínoff's very sternness afforded secret delight;—"I know that you must condemn me, and I do not defend myself; I only wish to explain to you my sentiment, I wish to convince you that I am not disposed to coquet now. . I coquet with you! Why, there is no sense in that! . . . When I saw you, all that was good, all that was young in me, awoke . . . the time when I had not yet chosen my destiny, everything which lies there in that bright zone, beyond those ten years. . . ."

"But permit me, at last, Irína Pávlovna! So far as I am aware, the bright zone in your life began precisely with the moment of our parting. . ."

Irína raised her handkerchief to her lips.

"What you say is very cruel, Grigóry Mikhaílovitch; but I cannot be angry with you. Oh, no, that was not a brilliant time; it was not for my happiness that I quitted Moscow. Not one in-

stant, not one minute of happiness have I known
. . . believe me, whatever you may have been told.
If I had been happy, could I talk with you as I
am doing now? . . I repeat it, you do not know
what those people are like. . Why, they understand nothing, sympathise with nothing, they
have not even any minds, *ni esprit, ni intelligence,*
but only cunning and tact; why, in reality, music,
poetry, and art are alike unknown to them. . .
You will say that I myself was fairly indifferent
to all this; but not to that degree, Grigóry Mikhaílovitch . . . not to that degree! It is not a
fashionable woman whom you now see before
you. You have only to look at me, not a lioness
. . . it seems that is what we are called . . . but
a poor, poor creature, who is really deserving of
compassion. Be not astonished at my words. . .
I am not disposed to be proud now! I reach out
my hand to you as a beggar, understand it, at
last, as a beggar. . . I entreat alms," she added
suddenly, in an involuntary, irrepressible impulse:—" I ask for alms, and you . . . ."

Her voice failed her. Litvínoff raised his head
and looked at Irína; she was breathing rapidly,
her lips were quivering. His heart suddenly began to beat hard, and his feeling of wrath vanished.

"You say that our paths have parted," resumed Irína:—" I know you are marrying for
love; you have the plan for your whole life al-

ready drawn up; yes, it is so; but we have not become strangers to each other, Grigóry Mikhaílovitch, we can still understand each other. Or do you suppose that I have become utterly stupid—that I have become utterly mired in this swamp? Akh, no, do not think that, please! Let me ease my soul, I beg of you, if only in the name of those by-gone days, if you are not bent on forgetting them. Let not our meeting have been in vain; that would be too bitter, and it will not last long, in any case. . . I do not know how to express myself as I should; but do understand me, for I ask little, very little . . . only a trifle of happiness, only that you will not repulse me, that you will give me a chance to ease my soul. . ."

Irína paused, tears resounded in her voice. She sighed and gazed at Litvínoff with a timid, rather sidelong, searching glance, and offered him her hand. . .

Litvínoff slowly took that hand, and faintly pressed it.

" Let us be friends," whispered Irína.

" Friends," repeated Litvínoff thoughtfully.

" Yes, friends . . . but if that is too great a demand, then let us be, at least, good acquaintances. . . Let us not stand on ceremony—just as though nothing had ever happened. . . ."

" As though nothing had ever happened . ." repeated Litvínoff again.—" You just told me, Irína Pávlovna, that I am not willing to forget by-gone days. . Well, and what if I cannot forget them? "

A blissful smile flashed across Irína's face, and instantly vanished, making way for an anxious, almost terrified expression.

" Do as I do, Grigóry Mikhaílovitch: remember only what is pleasant; but, above all, give me your word now, your word of honour. . ."

" What about? "

" Not to avoid me . . . not to grieve me needlessly. . . Do you promise? tell me! "

" Yes."

" And you will banish all evil thoughts from your mind? "

" Yes . . . but I still renounce the effort to understand you."

" That is not necessary . . wait, however, and you will understand me. But you promise? "

" I have already said: Yes."

" Thanks. Observe that I have become accustomed to believe you. I shall expect you to-day or to-morrow; I shall not leave the house. But now I must leave you. The Duchess is walking in the avenue. . . She has seen me, and I cannot avoid going to her. . . Until we meet again. . . Give me your hand, *vite, vite*. . Farewell for the present."

And with a vigorous clasp of Litvínoff's hand, Irína directed her steps toward a middle-aged person who was walking heavily along the sanded path, accompanied by two other ladies and a very good-looking lackey.

" *Eh, bonjour, chère madame,*" said this person, while Irína respectfully courtesied before her.—" *Comment allez-vous aujourd'hui? Venez un peu avec moi.*"—" *Votre Altesse a trop de bonté,*" Irína's insinuating voice could be heard in reply.

XIV

Litvínoff allowed the Duchess and all her suite to depart, and then emerged upon the avenue himself. He could not give himself a clear account of his sensations; he felt both ashamed and alarmed, and his self-love was flattered. . . The unexpected explanation with Irína had taken him unawares; her burning, hurried words had swept over him like a downpour of rain. " Queer people those society women," he thought;—" there 's no coherence about them . . . and how the circle in which they live perverts them, and the anomalousness of it they feel themselves!" . . . As a matter of fact, he did not think that at all, but was merely repeating mechanically those hackneyed phrases, as though desirous thereby of ridding himself of other and more painful thoughts. He comprehended that it ill-befitted him to meditate seriously at present, that, in all probability, he would be obliged to censure himself: and he strolled slowly along, almost compelling himself to turn his attention to everything which he encountered. . . All at once he found himself in front of a bench, perceived beside it some one's legs, ran his eyes up them. . . The legs belonged to a man who was sitting on the bench and reading a newspaper; the man proved to be Potúgin. Litvínoff gave vent to a slight exclamation. Potúgin laid his paper on his knees and stared attentively, unsmilingly, at Litvínoff, and Litvínoff also stared attentively and unsmilingly at Potúgin.

" May I sit down beside you? " he asked at last.

" Pray, do. Only I give you warning; if you wish to enter into conversation with me you must not be offended—I 'm in the most misanthropic frame of mind just now, and all objects present themselves to me in an exaggeratedly-evil light."

" That 's nothing, Sozónt Ivánitch," said Litvínoff, dropping down on the bench:—" it is even extremely opportune. . . But why has this mood come upon you? "

" As a matter of fact, I ought not to be in a rage," began Potúgin.—" Here I have just been reading about the project for judicial reforms in Russia, and with genuine satisfaction I perceive that we have at last got some common sense, and no longer intend under the pretext of independence there, of nationality or of originality, to tack a home-made tail on to pure, clear European logic; but, on the contrary, . . they are going to take the foreign thing which is good complete. That one concession in the affair of the peasants was sufficient. . . Just try to get rid of com-

munal tenure! . . Quite true, quite true, I ought
not to be in a rage; but, to my misfortune, I have
happened upon a self-made Russian—I have been
talking with him, and those rough nuggets—born
geniuses, and self-taught folks will worry me
into my grave!"

"What sort of a born genius?" inquired Litvínoff.

"Why, that sort of a gentleman is running
about, who fancies himself a gifted musician.—
'I,' says he, 'of course am nothing; I'm a cipher
because I never had any education, but I possess
incomparably more melodies and more ideas than
Meyerbeer.' In the first place, I will remark:
why were not you educated? and, in the second,
not only Meyerbeer, but the meanest German
flute-player, who modestly whistles his part in
the meanest German orchestra, has twenty times
more ideas than all our born geniuses; only the
flute-player keeps his ideas to himself, and does
not thrust himself forward with them into the
company of Mozarts and Haydns; but our Russian genius gets out a little waltz or a little romance, slap dash, and behold—there he is, hands
thrust into his pockets, and a scornful curl on his
mouth: 'I'm a genius,' says he. And it's just
the same with painting and everywhere. How I
detest those born geniuses! Who does not know
that people pride themselves upon them only in
places where there is no real science which has

been assimilated into blood and flesh, nor real art.
Is n't it time to file away in the archives this
boastfulness, this vulgar rubbish, along with the
familiar phrases, to the effect that among us, in
Russia, no one dies of hunger, and that travelling
by road is of the swiftest sort, and that we can
kill everybody with a slap of our caps? They be-
siege me with the giftedness of the Russian nature, with the instinct of genius, with Kulíbins.[1]
But what sort of giftedness is it, gentlemen, for
heaven's sake? It is the babbling of a man half
asleep, or a half-savage sagacity. Instinct! A
pretty thing to brag about, truly! Take an ant
in the forest, carry him off a verst away from his
hill: he will find the way back home; a man can
do nothing of the sort; what of that? is he lower
than the ant? Instinct, be it ever so talented, is
unworthy of man: reason—simple, sound, commonplace reason—that's our real fortune, our
pride; reason never plays any such pranks; and
that's why everything is founded on it. But as
for Kulíbin, who, without knowing anything
about mechanics, has constructed some extremely
absurd clocks or other,—I would order those
same clocks to be placed on a pillar of scorn;
' come, see, good people,' I would say, ' what you
must not do.' Kulíbin is not to blame in the matter, but his work is worthless. To praise Telúsh-

[1] A character in Ostróvsky's famous drama, "The Thunderstorm;"
a self-taught genius of a clockmaker.—TRANSLATOR.

kin, because he climbed the spire of the Admiralty, for his daring and skill—that is permissible; why should not he be praised? But it is not proper to shout out something to the effect, ' Has n't he made a laughing-stock of the foreign architects? and what 's the good of them? they only take your money.' . . He did not make a laughing-stock of them at all: afterward they were obliged to erect a scaffolding around the spire, and repair it in the ordinary way. For God's sake, do not encourage such ideas among us in Russia, as that anything can be attained without teaching! No; though you be as wise as Solomon, yet learn, learn from the alphabet up! Otherwise, sit down, and hang your tail between your legs! Faugh! I 've even got heated! "

Potúgin took off his hat, and fanned himself with his handkerchief.

" Russian art," he began again:—" Russian art! . . I know all about Russian limitations, and I know Russian impotency also, but as for Russian art, excuse me, but I have never met with it. For twenty years in succession we bowed down before that bloated cipher, Briullóff, and imagined, if you please, that a school had been founded among us, and that it was even destined to be better than all the others. . . Russian art, ha-ha-ha! ho-ho! "

" But permit me, Sozónt Ivánitch," remarked

Litvínoff.—" That means that you do not recognise Glínka either? "

Potúgin scratched behind his ear.

" Exceptions, you know, only prove the rule, but even in this case we could not get along without bragging! If you were to say, for example, that Glínka really was a remarkable musician, who was prevented by circumstances, external and internal, from becoming the founder of the Russian opera, no one would dispute you; but no; how is that possible! It immediately becomes necessary to promote him to be commander-in-chief, chief marshal of the Court in the department of music, and rob other nations by the way: ' they have nothing of the sort, if you please,' and then you have pointed out to you some ' mighty ' home-bred genius, whose compositions are nothing more than a sorry imitation of second-class foreign workers—second-class, precisely that: they are more easily imitated. Nothing of the sort. Oh, wretched fools and savages, for whom there exists no heritage of art, and artists—something in the style of Rappeau: as much as to say, a foreigner can lift six *puds* with one hand, but our man can lift twelve! Nothing of the sort! Let me inform you that I cannot get the following memory out of my head. This spring I visited the Crystal Palace, in the suburbs of London; in that palace, as you are aware, there is something in the nature of an exhibition of everything to which man's inventiveness has attained,—the encyclopædia of humanity, it must be called. Well, sir, I walked and walked past all those machines and implements, and statues of great men; and all the while I was thinking: if a decree were issued to the effect that, together with the disappearance from the face of the earth of any nation, everything which that nation had invented should immediately vanish from the Crystal Palace,—our dear mother, Orthodox Russia, might sink down to the nethermost hell, and not a single tack, not a single pin, would be disturbed, the dear creature: everything would remain quite calmly in its place, because even the samovár, and linden-bast slippers, and the shaft-arch, and the knout—those renowned products of ours— were not invented by us. It would not be possible to try a similar experiment with the Sandwich Islands even; their inhabitants have invented some sort of boats and spears: visitors would notice their absence. That is calumny! that is too harsh—you may say. . . But I say: in the first place, I do not know how to censure with a grumble; in the second, it is evident that no one can make up his mind to look not merely the devil, but himself, straight in the eye, and it is not the children only, with us, who like to be lulled to sleep. Our ancient inventions were brought to us from the East, our new ones we have dragged over, after a fashion, from the

West, and yet we continue to chatter about independent Russian art! Some daring persons have even discovered a Russian science: ' with us, if you please, twice two make four, but somehow it comes out in a more dashing way.' ''

" But stay, Sozónt Ivánitch," exclaimed Litvínoff.—" Stay! Surely, we send something to the International Expositions, and Europe procures some supplies from us."

" Yes, raw material, raw products. And observe, my dear sir: our raw material is chiefly good, only because it depends upon other, and very evil circumstances: our bristles, for example, are large and stiff merely because the pigs are poor; our hides are firm and thick, because the cows are thin; our tallow is fat, because it is boiled half and half with the beef. . . However, why am I dilating to you about this? Surely you, who occupy yourself with technology, must know all these things better than I do. People say to me: ' inventiveness! Russian inventiveness! ' There are our landed proprietors complaining bitterly, and suffering loss, because no satisfactory grain-dryer exists, which would relieve them of the necessity of placing their sheaves of grain in the kiln, as in the days of Rúrik: those kilns are frightfully detrimental, no better than linden-bast slippers, or bast mats, and they are constantly burning down. The landed proprietors complain, and still the grain-dryer does not make its appearance. And why not? Because the foreigner does not need it; he grinds his grain raw, consequently does not bother about inventing one, and we . . . are not capable of doing it! Not capable of doing it—and that's the end of the matter! You might try it! I vow, that from this day forth, as soon as a born genius or a self-taught man drops down on me, I shall say to him—' halt, my respected sir! and where's that grain-dryer? Hand it over!' But how can they? We are capable of picking up an old patched shoe, which long ago fell from the foot of Saint-Simon or Fourier, and placing it respectfully on our head, treating it like a holy thing; or of scribbling an article about the historical and contemporary significance of the proletariat in the principal cities of France—that also we can do; but I once tried to suggest to a writer and political economist, after the fashion of your Mr. Voroshíloff, to name to me twenty towns in that same France, and do you know the result? The result was, that the political economist, in despair, finally mentioned, among the towns of France, Mont Fermeil, probably recalling Paul de Kock's romance. And the following experience occurred to me. One day I was making my way, with gun and dog, through the forest. . ."

" And are you a sportsman?" inquired Litvínoff.

" I shoot a little. I was making my way to

a marsh in search of quail; other sportsmen had told me about that marsh. I looked, and in the midst of a field, in front of a cottage, sat a merchant's clerk, fresh and lusty as a husked nut,— sat there grinning, I did not know at what. And I asked him: ' Where is the marsh,' said I, ' and are there quail in it?'—' Certainly, certainly,' he drawled slowly, and with an expression as though I had presented him with a ruble; ' with great pleasure, sir: it 's a first-class marsh; but as for all sorts of wild birds—my God!—there 's a capital abundance of them also.' I went off, but I not only did not find a single wild bird,—the marsh itself had dried up long before. Now tell me, if you please, why does the Russian man lie? Why does the political economist lie, and about wild-fowl, to boot?"

Litvínoff made no reply, and only sighed sympathetically.

" And start a conversation with that political economist," resumed Potúgin:—" about the most difficult problems of social science, only, in general terms, without facts . . phrrrr! and the bird will soar off like an eagle! But I once succeeded in catching a bird of that sort: I employed a good visible bait, as you will see. We were talking with one of our present-day ' new youngsters,' about divers questions, as they express it. Well, sir, he flew into a great rage, as is usual; among other things, he rejected marriage, with truly childish obstinacy. I suggested to him arguments of one sort and another . . . it was like knocking my head against a wall! I saw that it was impossible to approach him from that quarter. And suddenly a happy thought flashed across me! 'Permit me to inform you,' I began, —one must always address the 'minnows' with respect—' that I am amazed at you, my dear sir; you are interested in the natural sciences—and hitherto you have not noted the fact that all carnivorous and rapacious animals, birds and beasts, all those who are obliged to sally forth in search of prey, and toil over procuring live food for themselves and their offspring . . . and, of course, you reckon man in the list of such animals?'—'Of course I do,' replied the 'minnow': 'man, after all, is nothing but a carnivorous animal.'—' And a rapacious one,' I added.—' And a rapacious one,' he assented.—' That is very well said,' I assented. ' So, then, I am amazed that you have not observed that all such animals stick to monogamy?' The new youngster shuddered.— ' How so?'—' Why, just so. Recall the lion, the wolf, the fox, the vulture, the hawk; and be so good as to consider how could they act otherwise? The two of you can hardly feed the children, as it is.'—My 'minnow' fell to thinking.—'Well,' says he, ' in that case, the beast is no model for man.' —' Then I called him an idealist, and how angry he became! He almost wept. I was obliged to

soothe him, and to promise him that I would not
betray him to his comrades. Is it a small thing
to deserve the name of idealist? And therein lies
the joke, that the present young generation has
made a mistake in its calculations. It has imagined that the day of old-fashioned, dark, under-
ground toil is past, that it was all well enough for
their aged fathers to dig like tortoises; but for us
such a rôle is humiliating, if you please, we will
act in the open air, we will act. . . The dear in-
nocents! and even your children will not act; and
would n't you like to go back to the cave, to the
cave again, in the footprints of the old men?"

A brief silence ensued.

" I, my dear sir, am of this opinion," Potúgin
began again:—" that we are indebted to civilisation not alone for knowledge, art, and law, but for
the fact that even the very sentiment of beauty
and poetry is developed and enters into force under the influence of that same civilisation; and
that so-called national, ingenuous, unconscious,
creative genius is stuff and nonsense. Even in
Homer traces are already discernible of a refined
and wealthy civilisation; even love is ennobled
thereby. The Slavyanophils would gladly hang
me for such a heresy if they were not such ten-
der-hearted creatures; but, nevertheless, I insist
upon my view—and however much they may re-
gale me with Madame Kokhanóvsky and ' The
Hive at Rest,' I will not inhale that *triple extrait*

de mougik russe; for I do not belong to the highest society, which finds it indispensably necessary, from time to time, to assure itself that it has not become completely Frenchified, and for whose special use that literature *en cuir de Russie* is composed. Try the experiment of reading to the common people—the genuine populace—the most incisive, the most ' national ' passages from the ' Hive '; they will think you are communicating some new plot about usury or hard drinking. I repeat it, without civilisation there is no poetry. Would you like to obtain an illustration of the unpoetic ideal of the uncivilised Russian man? Open our epic songs, our legends. I am not talking now about the fact that love always is represented in them as the result of witchcraft, of sorcery—is produced by drinking ' a love-philtre,' and is even called soldering, chilblain; neither am I referring to the fact that our so-called epic literature alone, among all the others, European and Asiatic,—alone, observe,—has not presented—unless you count Vánka-Tánka as such —a single typical pair of loving human beings; that the paladin of Holy Russia always begins his acquaintancewith his fated affinity by beating her ' mercilessly ' on her white body—whence ' also the feminine sex lives swollen up '; of all that I will not speak; but permit me to direct your attention to that elegant specimen of youth, the *jeune premier,* as he was depicted by the imagi-

nation of the primitive, uncivilised Slavonian.
Here, be pleased to note, comes the leading lover;
he has made himself a nice little cloak of marten-
fur, stitched along all the seams: a belt of the
seven silks is girt about him just under the arm-
pits, and the collar of the cloak is made higher
than his head; from the front his ruddy face,
from the back his white neck is not visible, his cap
rests on one ear, and on his feet are morocco
boots, with awl-like toes, his heels are pointed,—
around the little tips an egg might roll; under
the high heels a sparrow might fly and flutter.—
And the dashing young fellow walks with a short,
mincing step, that famous ' flaunting ' gait,
wherewith our Alcibiades, Tchurílo Plenkóvitch,
produced such a wonderful, almost medicinal effect on the old women and the young maidens,
that same gait wherewith, down to the present
day, our waiters, limbered in every joint, that
cream, that flower of Russian foppishness, that
nec plus ultra of Russian taste, trip about in so in-
imitable a manner. I am not saying this in jest:
dawdling dash is our artistic ideal. Well, is the
picture true? Does it contain many materials for
painting, for sculpture? And the beauty who
fascinates the young men, and whose ' blood in
her face is as though in that of a hare? ' . . . . . .
But, apparently, you are not listening to me? "

Litvínoff started. He really had not heard
what Potúgin had been saying to him: he had

been thinking, importunately thinking about Irína, about his last meeting with her. . .

" Excuse me, Sozónt Ivánitch," he began:— " but I want to put my former question to you once more, about . . . about Madame Ratmí-roff."

Potúgin folded his newspaper, and thrust it into his pocket.

" Again you wish to know how I became acquainted with her? "

" No, not that; I should like to hear your opinion . . . about the part which she has played in Petersburg. As a matter of fact, what was that part? "

" But I really do not know what to say to you, Grigóry Mikhaílovitch. I became pretty intimately acquainted with Madame Ratmíroff . . . . . but quite accidentally, and not for long. I have never taken a peep into her society, and what took place there has remained unknown to me. People have chattered somewhat in my presence, but you know scandal reigns among us not in democratic circles only. Moreover, I never had the curiosity to inquire. But I perceive," he added, after a brief pause:—" that she interests you."

" Yes; we have had a couple of pretty frank conversations. Still, I ask myself: Is she sincere? "

Potúgin dropped his eyes.—" When she gets

carried away—she is sincere, like all passionate women. Pride also sometimes keeps her from lying."

" But is she proud? I should suppose, rather —that she is capricious."

" As proud as the devil; but that's nothing."

" It seems to me that she sometimes exaggerates. . ."

" That's nothing, either; she is sincere, all the same. Well, and speaking in general, from whom would you care to have the truth? The very best of those young noble ladies are corrupt to the very marrow of their bones."

" But, Sozónt Ivánitch, call to mind, did not you call yourself her friend? Was it not you who, almost by force, took me to her? "

" What of that? She asked me to get you: why not? But I really am her friend. She is not devoid of good qualities: she is very kind— that is to say, generous,—that is to say, she gives to others that which she does not need herself. However, you certainly must know her quite as well as I do."

" I used to know Irína Pávlovna ten years ago; but since then . . ."

" Ekh, Grigóry Mikhaílovitch, what are you saying? Do people's characters change? As they are in the cradle, so they are in the grave. Or, perhaps . . . ."—Here Potúgin bent still lower;

—" perhaps you are afraid of falling into her hands? That really . . . well, you cannot avoid falling into some one's hands."

Litvínoff laughed in a constrained way.— " You think so? "

" You cannot avoid it. Man is weak, woman is strong, chance is all-powerful; it is difficult to reconcile one's self to a colourless existence, it is impossible wholly to forget one's self . . . but yonder is beauty and sympathy—yonder is warmth and light,—why resist? And you run to it like a child to its nurse. Well, and afterward, of course, there is cold, and darkness, and emptiness . . as is proper. And the end of it is, that you will grow unused to everything, you will cease to understand anything. At first you will not understand how it is possible to love; and afterward you will not understand how it is possible to live."

Litvínoff looked at Potúgin, and it seemed to him that never before had he met a more solitary, a more deserted . . . . a more unhappy man. On this occasion he was not timid, he did not stand on ceremony; all despondent and pale, with his head on his breast, and his hands on his knees, he sat motionless, and merely smiled a melancholy smile. Litvínoff felt sorry for this poor, queer, splenetic fellow.

" Irína Pávlovna mentioned to me, among

other things," he began in a low tone,—"one of her intimate friends, whom she called, I think, Madame Byélsky or Dólsky. . ."

Potúgin cast his sorrowful eyes on Litvínoff.

"Ah!" he exclaimed in a dull tone. . . "She mentioned her . . . well, and what of it? However," he added, with an unnatural sort of yawn: "I must go home—to dinner. I ask your pardon."

He sprang up from the bench and moved rapidly away before Litvínoff could manage to utter a word. . . His pity gave way to vexation—vexation at himself, of course. Every sort of indiscretion was unnatural to him; he had wished to express his sympathy for Potúgin and the result had been something in the nature of an awkward hint. With secret dissatisfaction at heart, he returned to his hotel.

"Corrupt to the very marrow of their bones," he thought some time later . . . "but proud as the devil! She, that woman, who is almost on her knees before me, proud? proud, not capricious?"

Litvínoff tried to expel Irína's image from his head, but did not succeed. For that very reason, also, he did not recall his affianced bride; he felt to-day that image would not surrender its place. He resolved to await the solution of all this "strange affair," without troubling himself further; the solution could not be long delayed, and Litvínoff had not the slightest doubt that it would be of the most abundant and natural sort. So he thought, but, in the meantime, it was not Irína's image alone which would not leave him—all her words recurred in turn to his memory.

A waiter brought him a note: it was from Irína.

"If you have nothing to do this evening, come: I shall not be alone; I have guests—and you will have a closer view of us, of our society. I am very anxious that you should see them: I have a premonition that they will display themselves in all their glory. And you ought to know what sort of air I breathe. Come; I shall be glad to see you, and you are not bored [Irína meant to say: you will not be bored]. Prove to me that our explanation of to-day has rendered impossible any misunderstanding between us. Faithfully yours, I."

Litvínoff put on his dress suit and a white tie, and went to Irína's. "All this is of no importance," he kept repeating to himself, in thought, on the way,—" but take a look at *them* . . . why should not I take a look? It is curious." A few days previously these same people had aroused in him a different feeling: they had aroused his indignation.

He walked with hurried steps, with his hat pulled far down over his eyes, with a constrained smile on his lips, and Bambáeff, who was sitting in front of Weber's Café, and pointed him out from a distance to Voroshíloff and Pishtchálkin, exclaimed enthusiastically: "Do you see that man? He's stone! He's a rock!! He's granite! ! !"

XV

Litvínoff found quite a number of guests at
Irína's. In a corner, at the card-table, sat three
of the generals of the picnic: the fat, the irritable, and the condescending ones. They were
playing whist with a dummy, and there are no
words in human language wherewith to express
the pompousness with which they dealt, took
tricks, played clubs, played diamonds . . . . .
just like statesmen! Leaving to plebeians, *aux
bourgeois,* the comments and adages customary
during a game, the generals uttered only the most
indispensable words; but the fat general permitted himself between two deals to say, with
energetic distinctness: *" Ce satané as de pique! "*
Among the visitors Litvínoff recognised the
ladies who had taken part in the picnic; but there
were others also whom he had not hitherto seen.
One was so old that it seemed as though she must
collapse immediately: she was wriggling her
dreadful bare, dark-grey shoulders about,—and
covering her mouth with her fan; she was casting sidelong glances at Ratmíroff, with her already quite dead eyes; he was paying court to
her; she was greatly respected in high society

as the last Maid of Honour of the Empress
Katherine II. By the window, dressed as a shep-
herdess, sat Countess Sh., " the Tzarítza of the
Wasps," surrounded by young men; among
them, distinguished by his arrogant bearing, his
perfectly flat skull, and his soullessly-brutal expression of countenance, worthy of a Khan of
Bokhará or of a Roman Heliogabalus, was Fínikoff, famous for his wealth and his good looks;
another lady, also a Countess, and known by the
diminutive name of *Lise,* was chatting with a
long-haired blond, pale " spirit-medium "; beside
them stood a gentleman, also pale and long-
haired, sneering significantly: this gentleman was
also a believer in spiritualism, but busied himself,
in addition, with prophecy, and, on the foundation of the Apocalypse and the Talmud, foretold
all sorts of remarkable events; not one of these
events took place,—but he was not discomfited,
and went on prophesying. That same heaven-
born genius who had aroused such ire in Potúgin
had placed himself at the piano; he was striking
chords in an absent-minded way, *d'une main dis-
traite,* and carelessly gazing about him. Irína
was sitting on the divan between Prince Kokó
and Madame X., formerly renowned as the
beauty and wit of All-Russia, and who had long
ago turned into a worthless wrinkled mushroom,
whence exhaled an odour of fast-tide oil and
putrid poison. On catching sight of Litvínoff,

Irína blushed, rose, and when he approached her, pressed his hand warmly. She wore a black crape gown, with barely visible gold embellishments; her shoulders gleamed with a dull whiteness, and her face, which was also pale beneath the momentary wave of crimson which had swept over it, breathed forth the triumph of beauty, and not of beauty only: a secret, almost mocking joy, sparkled in her half-closed eyes, quivered around her lips and nostrils. . .

Ratmíroff approached Litvínoff, and after exchanging with him the customary greetings, which were not, however, accompanied by his habitual playfulness, presented him to two or three ladies: to the aged ruin, to the Empress of the Wasps, to Countess Liza. . . They received him with a tolerable amount of graciousness. Litvínoff did not belong to their set . . . but he was not ill-looking, even very far from it, and the expressive features of his youthful face aroused their attention. Only he did not understand how to rivet this attention on himself; he had grown disused to society, and felt somewhat embarrassed, and then, too, the fat general had fixed his eyes on him. "Aha! the civilian! the freethinker!" that immovable, heavy glance seemed to say: " so he has crawled into our society; please let me kiss your hand," says he. Irína came to Litvínoff's rescue. She managed matters so cleverly that he found himself in a corner, near the door, a little behind her. When she addressed him she was obliged every time to turn toward him, and every time he admired the beautiful curve of her gleaming neck he inhaled the delicate perfume of her hair. The expression of profound and silent gratitude never left her face: he could not but admit that it was precisely gratitude which was expressed by those smiles, those glances, and he also began to seethe all over with the same sentiment, and he felt ashamed, yet found it sweet and painful . . . and at the same time she seemed constantly desirous of saying: "Well? What do you think of this?" This wordless question became audible to Litvínoff with especial clearness every time any of those present uttered or perpetrated a stupidity, and this happened more than once in the course of the evening. Once, even, she could not contain herself, and laughed aloud.

Countess Liza, a very superstitious lady and inclined to everything extraordinary, after having talked her fill to the light-haired medium about Hume, table-tipping, self-playing accordeons, and the like, wound up by asking him whether any animals existed upon whom magnetism produced an effect.

"One such animal exists, at any rate," remarked Prince Kokó from a distance.—"You know Milanóvsky, I believe? They put him to sleep in my presence, and he even snored, aï, aï!"

"You are very malicious, *mon prince;* I am talking about real animals, *je parle des bêtes.*"

"*Mais moi aussi, madame, je parle d'une bête. . .*"

"There are real animals also," interposed the spiritualist;—"for example—crabs; they are very nervous, and easily fall into a cataleptic state."

The Countess was amazed.—"What? Crabs! Is it possible? Akh, that is extremely curious! How I should like to see it! Monsieur Lúzhin," she added, addressing a young man with a stony face, such as new dolls have, and stony collar (he was famed for having wet that same face and collar with dashes of Niagara and the Nubian Nile, but he remembered nothing about all his travels, and loved only Russian puns . . . .), "Monsieur Lúzhin, be so good as to get us a crab."

Monsieur Lúzhin grinned.—"A live one or only a lively one?" he inquired.

The Countess did not understand him.—"*Mais oui,* a crab," she repeated, "*une écrevisse.*"

"What—what's the meaning of this?—a crab? a crab?" interposed Countess Sh. sternly. The absence of Monsieur Verdier irritated her: she could not understand why Irína had not invited that most charming of Frenchmen. The ruin, who had long ago ceased to understand anything,—in addition to which, deafness had seized upon her,—only waggled her head.

"*Oui, oui, vous allez voir.* Monsieur Lúzhin, please . . . ."

The young traveller bowed, left the room, and speedily returned. A waiter followed him, and grinning to the full extent of his mouth, bore a platter whereon was visible a large black crab.

"*Voici, madame,*" exclaimed Lúzhin;—"now you can set about the operation on the crab.[1] Ha, ha, ha!" (Russians are always the first to laugh at their own witticisms.)—"He, he, he!" echoed Prince Kokó, in the quality of a patriot and patron of all national products.

(We beg the reader not to feel astonished and not to get angry: who can answer for himself, that, when seated in the parterre of the Alexandrínsky Theatre, and invaded by its atmosphere, he will not perpetrate even a worse pun?)

"*Merci, merci,*" said the Countess.—"*Allons, allons, Monsieur Fox, montrez-nous ça.*"

The waiter placed the platter on a small round table. A slight movement ensued among the guests; several necks were outstretched; only the generals at the card-table preserved the serene solemnity of their pose. The medium rumpled up his hair, frowned, and approaching the table, began to make passes with his hands in the air: the crab bristled up, drew back, and elevated its

---

[1] The word also means *cancer* in Russian.—TRANSLATOR.

claws. The medium repeated and quickened his motions: the crab bristled as before.

"*Mais que doit-elle donc faire?*" inquired the Countess.

"*Elle doâ rester immobile et se dresser sur sa quiou,*" replied Mr. Fox, with a strong American accent, convulsively agitating his fingers over the platter; but the magnetism did not act, the crab continued to move about. The medium announced that he was not at his best, and retreated from the table with a dissatisfied aspect. The Countess undertook to console him, asserting that similar failures sometimes happened, even with Monsieur Hume. . . Prince Kokó confirmed her words. The expert in the Apocalypse and the Talmud stole up to the table on the sly, and poking his fingers swiftly, but violently, in the direction of the crab, also tried his luck, but without success: no symptoms of catalepsy manifested themselves. Then the waiter was summoned, and ordered to remove the crab, which command he obeyed, grinning to the full capacity of his mouth, as before; he could be heard to snort outside the door. . . . In the kitchen, later on, there was a great deal of laughter *über diese Russen.* The born genius had continued to strike chords during the whole time of the experiment with the crab, keeping to minor tones, because, you know, no one could tell what would prove effectual in that case,—then the born genius played his inevitable waltz, and, of course, received the most flattering approval. Carried away by the spirit of emulation, Count X., our incomparable dilettante (see Chapter I), "recited" a chansonette of his own invention, stolen entire from Offenbach. Its playful refrain on the words "*Quel œuf? quel bœuf?*" made the heads of almost all the ladies roll to right and to left; one even moaned gently, and the irresistible, inevitable "*Charmant! charmant!*" flitted across every one's mouth. Irína exchanged a glance with Litvínoff, and again that mysterious, mocking expression hovered about her lips. . . . But it came more powerfully into action a little later, —it even assumed a malevolent cast,—when Prince Kokó, that representative and defender of the interests of the nobility, took it into his head to set forth his views to that same medium, and, as a matter of course, immediately made use of his famous phrase about the shock to property in Russia, in which connection, incidentally, democracy caught it. The American blood in the medium made itself felt; he began to argue. The Prince, as was fitting, immediately began to shout, at the top of his voice, in place of proofs incessantly repeating: "*C'est absurde! cela n'a pas le sens commun!*" The wealthy Fínikoff began to utter impertinences, without stopping to think to whom they applied; the Talmudist set up a squeak; even Countess Sh. took to rattling.

. . . In short, there arose almost identically the same detestable uproar as at Gubaryóff's; only, in this case, there were no beer and tobacco-smoke, and all present were better dressed. Ratmíroff. endeavoured to restore silence (the generals had expressed dissatisfaction, an exclamation from Borís had made itself audible: "*Encore cette satanée politique!*"), but the effort proved fruitless; and a dignitary who was present, one of the softly-penetrating sort, on undertaking to present *le resumé de la question en peu de mots,* suffered defeat; it is true that he so mumbled and repeated himself, so evidently did not know how either to hear or answer objections, and so indubitably did not himself know precisely in what *la question* consisted, that no other issue could have been expected; and Irína, too, urged on the wranglers on the sly, and hounded them one upon the other, constantly glancing at Litvínoff, and nodding her head slightly at him. . . And he sat there as though bewitched, heard nothing, and only waited for those magnificent eyes to flash upon him once again, for that pale, tender, mischievous, charming face to flit once more across his vision. . . The end of it was that the ladies rebelled, and demanded that the dispute should cease. . Ratmíroff invited the dilettante to repeat his chansonette, and the born genius played his waltz again. . .

Litvínoff remained until after midnight, and

took his departure later than all the others. The conversation had touched upon many topics during the course of the evening, sedulously avoiding everything which was in the slightest degree interesting; the generals, after they had finished their majestic game, had majestically joined in it: the influence of these statesmen immediately made itself felt. A conversation was in progress about the notorieties of the Parisian *demi-monde,* with whose names and talents every one appeared to be intimately acquainted, about Sardou's last play, about About's romance, about Patti in " Traviata." Some one suggested that they play at " secretary," *au secretaire:* but this was not a success. The replies were insipid, and not devoid of grammatical errors; the fat general told how he, on one occasion, in answer to the question, *Qu'est ce que l'amour?* had replied: *Une colique remontée au cœur,* and immediately began to laugh with his wooden laugh; the ruin, with a sweeping gesture, tapped him with her fan on the arm; a bit of whitewash fell off of her forehead at this vigorous gesture. The dried mushroom undertook to recall the Slavonic principalities and the indispensability of an Orthodox propaganda beyond the Danube, but finding no echo, began to hiss, and withdrew into the background. In fact, they talked more about Hume than about anything else; even the " Empress of the Wasps " narrated how hands had crept over her, and how she had seen them, and had put her own ring on one of them. In truth, Irína triumphed: even if Litvínoff had paid more attention to what was being said around him, still he would not have carried away a single sincere word, a single intelligent thought, or a single new fact out of all that incoherent and lifeless chatter. No enthusiasm was audible even in the cries and exclamations; even in the reproaches no passion was to be felt: only from time to time, from beneath the mask of pseudo-civic indignation, pseudo-scornful indifference, did the fear of possible losses give forth a shriek, and a few names, which posterity will not forget, were uttered with gnashings of teeth. . . . And not one drop of living current beneath all this rubbish and litter! What ancient stuff, what useless nonsense, what insipid trifles absorbed all those brains, those souls, and absorbed them not on that one evening only, not only in society, but at home, at all hours, every day, in all the breadth and depth of their beings! And what ignorance, in conclusion! What lack of comprehension of everything upon which human life is founded, by which it is adorned!

As she took leave of Litvínoff, Irína slightly pressed his hand, and significantly whispered: " Well, what do you think of it? Are you satisfied? Have you sufficiently admired? Is it nice?" He made her no reply, but merely bowed silently and low.

When she was left alone with her husband Irína was on the point of retiring to her bedroom. . . He stopped her.

"*Je vous ai beaucoup admirée ce soir, madame,*"—he said, as he lighted a cigarette, and leaned his elbows on the mantelpiece:—"*vous vous êtes parfaitement moquée de nous tous.*"

"*Pas plus cette fois-ci que les autres,*"—she replied indifferently.

"How do you wish me to understand that?" —inquired Ratmíroff.

"As you please."

"H'm. *C'est clair.*"—Ratmíroff cautiously, in a feline way, knocked the ashes from his cigarette with the long nail of his little finger.— "Yes, by the way! That new acquaintance of yours—what's his name? . . . Mr. Litvínoff— must enjoy the reputation of being a very clever man."

At Litvínoff's name Irína turned swiftly round.

"What do you mean?"

The general grinned.

"He never utters a word; . . . evidently, he's afraid of compromising himself."

Irína laughed also, only not at all in the same way as her husband.

"It is better to hold one's tongue than to talk . . . . as some people do."

"Attrapé!"—said Ratmíroff, with feigned humility.—" Jesting aside, he has a very interesting face. Such a . . . concentrated expression . . and, altogether, a bearing. . . . Yes."—The general adjusted his necktie, and throwing back his head, scrutinised his own moustache.—" I assume that he is a republican, after the fashion of that other friend of yours, Mr. Potúgin; he's another of the clever men who are taciturn."

Irína's brows slowly elevated themselves above the widely-opened, brilliant eyes, and her lips became compressed, almost contorted.

" What is your object in saying this, Valerián Vladímiritch? "—she remarked, as though sympathetically.—" You are only wasting your powder on the empty air. . . We are not in Russia, and no one is listening to us."

Ratmíroff writhed.

" That is not my opinion only, Irína Pávlovna,"—he began, with a voice that, somehow, seemed suddenly to have become guttural:— " others also think that that gentleman looks like a carbonaro. . ."

" Really? And who are those others? "

" Why, Borís, for example. . ."

" What? And that fellow must needs express his opinion? "

Irína shrugged her shoulders, as though shuddering from cold, and softly passed the tips of her fingers over them.

" That fellow . . . yes, that fellow . . that

fellow. Permit me to inform you, Irína Pávlovna, you appear to be losing your temper; and you know yourself that the person who loses his temper . . . ."

" I am losing my temper? For what reason? "

" I don't know; perhaps the remark displeases you which I permitted myself to make concerning . . . ."

Ratmíroff began to stammer.

" Concerning? "—repeated Irína inquiringly. —" Akh, pray omit irony and speak more quickly. I am tired, I am sleepy."—She took a candle from the table.—" Concerning? . . ."

" Well, concerning that same Mr. Litvínoff. As there is no longer any doubt that you take a very great interest in him . . ."

Irína raised the hand in which she held the candlestick; the flame came on a level with her husband's face, and, after looking him straight in the eye, with attention and almost with curiosity, she suddenly burst out laughing.

" What 's the matter with you? "—asked Ratmíroff, with a scowl.

Irína continued to laugh.

" Come, what is it? " he repeated, and stamped his foot.

He felt insulted, exasperated, yet, at the same time, the beauty of this woman, who stood there before him so lightly and so boldly, involuntarily surprised him . . . it tormented him. He saw everything—all her charms, even the rosy gleam of the elegant nails on the delicate fingers, which firmly clasped the dark bronze of the heavy candlestick—even that gleam did not escape him . . . and the insult ate still more deeply into his heart. But Irína went on laughing.

"What? You? You are jealous?"—she said, at last, and turning her back on her husband, she left the room.—"He is jealous!"—was audible outside the door, and again her laughter rang out.

Ratmíroff gazed gloomily after his wife,— even then he could not fail to observe the enchanting grace of her figure, of her movements, —and crushing his cigarette with a heavy blow against the marble slab of the chimney-piece, he flung it far from him. His cheeks suddenly paled, a convulsive quiver flitted across his chin, and his eyes wandered dully and fiercely over the floor, as though in search of something. . . . Every trace of elegance had vanished from his face. That must have been the sort of expression it had assumed when he flogged the white Russian peasants.

But Litvínoff came to himself in his own room, and seating himself on a chair by the table, he clutched his head in both hands, and, for a long time, remained motionless. He rose, at last, opened a drawer, and taking out a portfolio, drew from an inner pocket of it Tatyána's photo-

graph. Her face, distorted and, as usual, made
to look older by the photograph, gazed sadly at
him. Litvínoff's betrothed was a young girl of
Great Russian descent, golden-haired, rather
plump, and with somewhat heavy features, but
with a wonderful expression of goodness and
gentleness in the light-brown eyes, and a tender
white brow, upon which the sunshine seemed always to linger. For a long time Litvínoff did
not take his eyes from the picture: then he softly
pushed it from him, and again clasped his head
with both hands. " All is over! "—he whispered
at last.—" Irína! Irína! "

It was only now, only at this moment, that he
comprehended that he was irrevocably, madly in
love with her, had fallen in love with her on the
very day of his first meeting with her at the Old
Château, that he never had ceased to love her.
And yet how astonished he would have been, how
incredulous; how he would have laughed if any
one had told him that a few hours earlier.

"But Tánya, Tánya, my God! Tánya!
Tánya! "—he kept repeating, with compunction;
but Irína's image kept rising up before him in her
black gown that looked like mourning, with the
radiant tranquillity of conquest on her marble-
white face.

XVI

LITVÍNOFF did not sleep all night long, and did not undress. He felt very heavy at heart. As an honourable and upright man, he understood the importance of obligations, the sacredness of duty, and would have regarded it as a disgrace to deal disingenuously with himself, with his weakness, with his conduct. At first a torpor descended upon him: for a long time he could not free himself from the weight of a persistent, semi-conscious, obscure sensation; then terror took possession of him at the thought that the future, his future so nearly won, was again enveloped in gloom, that his house—his house which had but just been erected—was reeling to its fall. . . He began pitilessly to upbraid himself, but immediately put a stop to his own outbursts. " What dastardliness is this? "—he thought.—" This is no time for reproaches; I must act; Tánya is my affianced bride, she has trusted my love, my honour, we are united forever, and we cannot, we must not part." He set before himself, in vivid colours, all Tatyána's qualities, he mentally sorted them over and enumerated them; he tried to arouse in himself emotion and tenderness.

" There is but one thing left to do,"—he thought
again:—" to flee, flee instantly, without waiting
for her arrival, to flee to meet her, even if I shall
suffer, even if I shall torture myself with Tánya,
—which is improbable,—but, in any case, it is useless to argue about that, to take that into consideration; I must do my duty, even if I die afterward!—" But thou hast no right to deceive her,"
another voice whispered to him, " thou hast not
the right to conceal from her the change which
has taken place in thy feelings; perchance, on
learning that thou hast fallen in love with another, she will not wish to become thy wife?"
" Nonsense! Nonsense! " he retorted:—" All that
is sophistry, shameful guile, false conscientious-
ness; I have no right not to keep my plighted
word, that's how the case stands. Well, very
good. . . Then I must go away from here without seeing her. . ."

But at this point Litvínoff's heart contracted,
a chill overcame him, a physical chill: a momentary shiver ran through his body, his teeth chattered. He stretched and yawned as though in a
fever. Without insisting further on his last
thought, stifling that thought, turning away from
it, he began to feel perplexed and astonished that
he could again have . . . again have fallen in
love with that depraved, worldly creature,
with all her repulsive, hostile surroundings. He
tried to ask himself: " But hast thou fallen thor-

oughly, actually in love?" and could only wave
his hand in despair. He still continued to feel
surprised and perplexed, and lo! there before
him, as though from a soft, fragrant mist, started
forth the bewitching countenance, the starry eyelashes were raised—and silently, irresistibly, the
enchanting eyes penetrated his heart, and the
voice rang out sweetly, and the gleaming shoulders—the shoulders of a young empress—exhaled the freshness and the fervour of tenderness. . . .

Toward morning a decision matured, at last, in
Litvínoff's soul. He decided to set out, on that
very day, to meet Tatyána, and in a final interview with Irína to tell her, if it could not be
avoided, the whole truth—and part from her
forever.

He arranged and packed his things, waited until twelve o'clock, and went to her. But at the
sight of her half-veiled windows, Litvínoff's
heart seemed to sink within him . . . he lacked
the courage to cross the threshold of the hotel.
He walked several times up and down Lichtenthaler Avenue. "My respects to you, Mr. Litvínoff!"—suddenly rang out a mocking voice from
the heights of a swiftly-rolling dog-cart. Litvínoff raised his eyes, and beheld General Ratmíroff seated beside Prince M., a well-known sportsman and lover of English equipages and horses.

The Prince was driving, but the general bent to one side and displayed his teeth, lifting his hat high above his head. Litvínoff bowed to him, and instantly, as though in obedience to a secret command, set out at a run for Irína.

She was at home. He ordered the servants to announce him: he was immediately received. When he entered she was standing in the middle of the room. She wore a loose morning gown, with wide, flowing sleeves; her face, pale as on the preceding day, but not fresh as it had then been, expressed weariness; the languid smile with which she greeted her guest still more clearly defined that expression. She offered him her hand, and gazed at him affectionately but abstractedly.

"Thank you for coming,"—she began, in a mournful voice, and sank into an arm-chair.—" I do not feel quite well to-day; I passed a bad night. Well, what have you to say about last evening? Was not I right?"

Litvínoff seated himself.

"I have come to you, Irína Pávlovna,"—he began . . .

She instantly straightened herself up and turned round; her eyes fairly bored into Litvínoff.

"What is the matter with you?"—she exclaimed.—"You are as pale as a corpse—you are ill. What is the matter with you?"

Litvínoff became confused.

"With me, Irína Pávlovna?"

"You have received bad news? A catastrophe has happened, tell me, tell me. . ."

Litvínoff, in his turn, stared at Irína.

"I have received no bad news,"—he said, not without an effort:—"but a catastrophe has really happened, a great catastrophe . . . and it has brought me to you."

"A catastrophe? What is it?"

"Such a one . . . . . that . . . ."

Litvínoff tried to go on . . . and could not. But he clasped his hands so hard that the fingers cracked. Irína bent forward, and seemed turned to stone.

"Akh! I love you!"—burst at last in a dull groan from Litvínoff's breast, and he turned away, as though desirous of hiding his face.

"What, Grigóry Mikhaílovitch, you . . . ." Irína also was unable to finish her phrase, and leaning back in her chair, she raised both hands to her face.—"You . . . love me?"

"Yes . . . yes . . . yes,"—he repeated with exasperation, turning his face more and more aside.

All became silent in the room: a butterfly which had flown in, agitated its wings and struggled between the curtain and the window.

Litvínoff was the first to speak.

"This, Irína Pávlovna,"—he began:—"this is the catastrophe which has . . . stunned me,

which I ought to have foreseen and avoided, if I
had not as in former days, in the Moscow time,
fallen immediately into the whirlpool. Evidently,
it has pleased fate to take me again unawares,
and experience again, through you, those tor-
ments which, it would have seemed, ought never
more to have been repeated. . . But I have resisted . . have tried to resist . . in vain; yes,
plainly, what is fated to be cannot be avoided.
But I am telling you all this for the purpose of
putting an end, as soon as possible to this . . .
this tragi-comedy,"—he added with a fresh access
of exasperation and shame.

Again Litvínoff fell silent; the butterfly continued to struggle and flutter. Irína did not remove her hands from her face.

" And you are not deceiving yourself?"—her
whisper became audible from beneath those white,
seemingly bloodless hands.

" I am not deceiving myself,"—replied Litvínoff in a hollow voice.—" I love you as I have
never loved, or loved any one but you. I am not
going to reproach you: that would be too foolish;
I will not repeat to you that perhaps nothing of
this sort would have happened had you behaved
differently toward me. . . . Of course, I alone
am to blame, my self-confidence has been my un-
doing; but I am rightly chastised, and you could
not possibly have expected this. Of course, you
did not take into consideration that it would have

been far less dangerous for me if you had not felt your fault so vividly . . . your imaginary fault toward me, and had not wished to atone for it . . . but what is done cannot be undone, of course. . . I only wanted to explain to you my position: it is sufficiently painful as it is. . . At all events, there will be no misunderstanding, as you say, but the frankness of my confession will, I hope, mitigate that feeling of insult which you cannot fail to feel."

Litvínoff spoke without raising his eyes; and if he had glanced at Irína, still he could not have seen what was going on in her face, because, as before, she did not remove her hands. Nevertheless, what was taking place on her face would, in all probability, have amazed him: it expressed both fear and joy, and a certain blissful exhaustion and agitation; the eyes barely glimmered beneath the drooping lids, and the long-drawn, broken breathing chilled the lips which were parted as though in thirst. . . .

Litvínoff maintained silence, waited for a reply, a sound. . . Nothing!

" But one thing is left for me to do,"—he began again:—" to go away; I am come to bid you farewell."

Irína slowly dropped her hands upon her knees.

" But I remember, Grigóry Mikhaílovitch,"— she began:—" that . . that person, of whom you spoke to me, was to come hither. You are expecting her?"

"Yes; but I shall write to her . . . she will stop somewhere on the way . . in Heidelberg, for instance."

"Ah! In Heidelberg. . . Yes. . It is pleasant there. . . But all this must disturb your plans. Are you sure, Grigóry Mikhaílovitch, that you are not exaggerating, *et que ce n'est pas une fausse alarme?*"

Irína spoke quietly, almost coldly, and with little pauses, and glances aside, in the direction of the window. Litvínoff did not answer her last question.

"But why have you alluded to the insult?"—she went on.—"I am not insulted . . . oh, no! And if either of us is to blame, then, in any case, it is not you; not you alone. . . Remember our last conversations, and you will be convinced that it is not you."

"I have never had any doubt of your magnanimity,"—ejaculated Litvínoff through his teeth: —"but I should like to know: do you approve of my intention?"

"To go away?"

"Yes."

Irína continued to gaze to one side.

"At the first moment your intention seemed to me to be premature . . . but now I have thought over what you said . . . and if you really are not making a mistake, then I suppose that you ought to go. It will be better so . . . better for both of us."

Irína's voice had grown more and more quiet, and her very speech became slower and slower.

" General Ratmíroff, really, might notice it," —Litvínoff began. . . .

Irína's eyes dropped again, and something strange flickered around her lips . . flickered and vanished.

" No, you do not understand me,"—she interrupted him.—" I was not thinking of my husband. Why should I? There would be nothing for him to notice. But, I repeat it: separation is indispensable for both of us."

Litvínoff took up his hat, which had fallen to the floor.

" Everything is over,"—he thought:—" I must go."—" And so it only remains for me to take leave of you, Irína Pávlovna,"—he said aloud, and suddenly dread fell upon him, exactly as though he were on the point of pronouncing his own sentence.—" I can only hope that you will not bear me any ill-will . . . . and that if, sometimes, we . . . ."

Again Irína interrupted him:

" Wait, Grigóry Mikhaílovitch, do not bid me farewell yet. That would be over-hasty."

Something quivered within Litvínoff, but a

burning bitterness surged up on the instant, and with redoubled force, in his heart.

"But I cannot remain!"—he exclaimed.— "To what end? Why prolong this anguish?"

"Do not bid me farewell yet,"—repeated Irína. . "I must see you once more. . . Again the same sort of dumb parting as in Moscow,— no, I will not have that. You may go now, but you must promise me, give me your word of honour, that you will not take your departure without having seen me once more."

"You wish that?"

"I demand it. If you go away without having taken leave of me, I will never, never forgive you. Do you hear: never!"—"It is strange!" —she added, as though speaking to herself:—"I cannot possibly realise that I am in Baden. . . I keep feeling that I am in Moscow. . . Go. ."

Litvínoff rose.

"Irína Pávlovna," he said,—"give me your hand."

Irína shook her head.

"I have told you that I will not bid you farewell. . ."

"I am not asking it for a farewell. . ."

Irína was on the point of giving him her hand, but glanced at Litvínoff for the first time since his confession,—and drew it back.

"No, no,"—she whispered,—"I will not give you my hand. No . . . no. Go."

Litvínoff bowed and left the room. He could not know why Irína had refused him a last friendly pressure. . . . . He could not know that she was afraid.

He left the room, and Irína again sank down in the arm-chair, and again covered her face.

XVII

LITVÍNOFF did not return home: he went off to
the mountains, and making his way into the den-
sity of the forest, threw himself on the earth, face
downward, and lay there for about an hour. He
did not suffer, he did not weep; he lay in a sort
of painful, agonising swoon. Never before had
he experienced anything of the sort: there was an
intolerably aching, gnawing sensation of emptiness, of emptiness in himself, around him everywhere. . . He did not think either of Irína or of
Tatyána. He felt one thing: the blow had fallen,
and life had been cut in twain like a rope, and he
was entirely drawn forward and seized upon by
something unknown, yet cold. Sometimes it
seemed to him that a whirlwind had descended
upon him, and he felt its swift gyrations and the
confused beatings of its dark pinions. . . But his
decision did not waver. . Remain in Baden . . .
such a thing was not even to be mentioned. Mentally, he had already taken his departure: he was
already seated in the rattling and smoking rail-
way-carriage, and fleeing, fleeing into the dumb,
dead distance. He rose up, at last, and leaning
his head against a tree, remained motionless; only

with one hand, without himself being conscious of it, he had grasped the highest frond of a fern, and was swaying it to and fro with a regular beat. The sound of approaching footsteps aroused him from his torpor; two charcoal-burners, with large sacks on their shoulders, were making their way along the steep path. " It is time! " whispered Litvínoff, and followed the charcoal-burners down the path to the town, turned into the railway building, and despatched a telegram to Tatyána's aunt, Kapitólina Márkovna. In this telegram he informed her of his immediate departure, and appointed a meeting with her in Schrader's hotel, in Heidelberg. " If an end is to be made, it had better be made at once,"—he thought;— " there is no use in deferring it until to-morrow." Then he entered the gaming-room, with dull curiosity stared two or three players in the face, descried from afar Bindásoff's hideous nape, Pishtchálkin's irreproachable face, and, after standing for a little while under the colonnade, he betook himself, without haste, to Irína. It was not at the instigation of a sudden, involuntary impulse that he went to her; when he had made up his mind to depart, he had also made it up to keep the word he had pledged, and to see her once again. He entered the hotel without being perceived by the door-porter, ascended the staircase without meeting any one, and, without knocking at the door, mechanically pushed it open, and entered the room. In the room, in the same arm-chair, in the same gown, in the same attitude as three hours before, sat Irína. . . It was evident that she had not stirred from the spot, had not moved during all that time. She slowly raised her head, and on perceiving Litvínoff, shuddered all over, and grasped the arms of the chair.— "You have frightened me,"—she whispered.

Litvínoff regarded her with speechless amazement. The expression of her face, of her sunken eyes, impressed him.

Irína smiled in a forced way and adjusted her hair, which had fallen out of curl.

"It does not matter. . . I, really, I do not know. . I think I have been asleep here."

"Excuse me, Irína Pávlovna,"—began Litvínoff,—"I entered without being announced. . I wished to comply with what you were pleased to demand of me. And, as I am going away to-day . . ."

"To-day? But I thought you told me that you wished first to write a letter. . ."

"I have sent a telegram."

"Ah! You found it necessary to make haste. And when do you leave? At what o'clock, I mean?"

"At seven o'clock in the evening."

"Ah! At seven o'clock! And you have come to say farewell?"

"Yes, Irína Pávlovna, to say farewell."

Irína remained silent for a while.

" I must thank you, Grigóry Mikhaílitch; you probably did not find it easy to come hither."

" No, Irína Pávlovna, it was very far from easy."

" Life is not easy, altogether, Grigóry Mikhaílitch; what do you think? "

" That depends on the person, Irína Pávlovna."

Again Irína remained silent for a space, as though in meditation.

" You have shown your friendship for me by coming,"—she said, at last.—" I thank you. And, altogether, I entirely approve of your decision to make an end of it all as speedily as possible, . . . because every delay . . . because . . . because I, that very same I whom you accused of coquetry, whom you called a comedian,—I believe that was what you called me? . ."

Irína rose hastily, and seating herself in another arm-chair, bent over and pressed her face and hands against the edge of the table. . .

" Because I love you . . ." she whispered, through her tightly-clasped fingers.

Litvínoff staggered back, as though some one had struck him in the breast. Irína sadly turned her head away from him, as though desirous, in her turn, of hiding her face from him, and laid it on the table.

" Yes, I love you. . . . I love you . . . and you know it."

" I? I know it? "—Litvínoff uttered, at last. —" I? "

" Well, and now you see,"—pursued Irína,— " that you really must go, that there must be no delay,—that we, that I can suffer no delay. It is dangerous, it is terrible. . . Good-bye! " she added, rising impetuously from her chair.

She took several steps in the direction of the door to her boudoir, and thrusting her hand behind her back, she hastily moved it through the air, as though desirous of encountering and pressing Litvínoff's hand; but he stood, as though rooted to the spot, at a distance. . . . Once more she said, " Farewell, forget," and without glancing behind her, fled from the room.

Litvínoff was left alone, and still could not recover himself. He came to his senses at last, swiftly approached the door of the boudoir, uttering Irína's name once, twice, thrice. . . He had already laid his hand on the handle of the door. . . The ringing voice of Ratmíroff made itself audible from the porch of the hotel.

Litvínoff pulled his hat down over his eyes and went out to the staircase. The elegant general was standing in front of the porter's lodge, and explaining to him, in imperfect German, that he wished to hire a carriage for the whole of the following day. On catching sight of Litvínoff, he again raised his hat abnormally high, and again expressed his " respect ": he was evidently scoffing at him, but Litvínoff cared nothing for that. He barely returned Ratmíroff's salutation, and on reaching his own quarters, he paused in front of his trunk, already packed and closed. His head was in a whirl, and his heart was quivering like a chord. What was to be done now? And could he have foreseen this?

Yes, he had foreseen it, incredible as it might seem. It had stunned him like a clap of thunder, but he had foreseen it, although he had not dared to admit it. But he had known nothing with certainty. Everything had got jumbled up within him; he had lost the thread of his own thoughts. He recalled Moscow, he recalled how " it " had descended upon him then like a sudden hurricane. He felt suffocated: ecstasy—but a desolate, hopeless ecstasy—choked and rent his breast. Not for anything in the world would he have consented that the words uttered by Irína should not really have been uttered by her. . . But what then? All the same, those words could not alter the resolution he had already taken. As before, it did not waver, but held firmly like an anchor which has been cast. Litvínoff had lost the thread of his thoughts . . . yes; but his will remained with him still, and he gave himself orders as he would have given them to a strange man, his subordinate. He rang the bell for a waiter, ordered his bill to be brought, engaged a seat in the evening omnibus: he deliberately cut off all his roads. " Even if I die there afterward," he kept repeating, as he had done during the preceding sleepless night; this phrase was particularly to his taste.—" Even if I die there afterward," he repeated, as he slowly paced to and fro in his chamber, only closing his eyes and ceasing to breathe from time to time involuntarily when those words, those words of Irína invaded his soul, and seared it as with fire. " Evidently, one does not love twice," he thought: " another life has entered into yours, you have admitted it—you cannot rid yourself of that poison to the end, you cannot break those threads! Just so; but what does that prove? Happiness. . . Is that possible? You love her, let us assume . . . and she . . . she loves you. . ."

But at this point he was again compelled to take himself in hand. As a wayfarer, in a dark night, who descries ahead of him a tiny light and fears to lose his road, does not remove his eyes from it for an instant, so also Litvínoff unremittingly concentrated the full force of his attention upon one point, upon one goal. To present himself to his affianced bride, and even not actually to his bride (he tried not to think of her), but in the room of the Heidelberg hotel—that is what stood before him steadfastly, as his guiding light. What was to come afterward he did not know, and did not wish to know. . . . One thing was indubitable: he would not turn back. " Even if I die there," he repeated for the tenth time, and glanced at his watch.

A quarter past six! How long he still had to wait! Again he strode back and forth. The sun was declining to its setting, the sky was glowing red over the trees, and a crimson twilight fell through the narrow windows into his darkening room. All at once it seemed to Litvínoff as though the door had been opened softly and swiftly behind him, and as swiftly closed again. . . He turned round; by the door, enveloped in a black mantilla, stood a woman. . .

" Irína! " he cried, and clasped his hands. . . She raised her head, and fell upon his breast.

Two hours later he was seated on his divan. His trunk stood in a corner, open and empty, and on the table, amid articles scattered there in confusion, lay a letter from Tatyána which Litvínoff had just received. She wrote him that she had decided to hasten her departure from Dresden, as her aunt's health was entirely restored, and that if no obstacles intervened they would both arrive in Baden at twelve o'clock on the following day, and hoped that he would meet them at the railway station. Litvínoff had engaged apartments for them in the same hotel where he was stopping.

That same evening he sent a note to Irína, and on the following morning he received an answer from her. " A day sooner or a day later,"—she wrote, " it was inevitable. I repeat to thee what I said last night: my life is in thy hands, do with me as thou wilt. I do not wish to put any restraint upon thy freedom, but thou must know that, in case of necessity, I will abandon everything, and will follow thee to the ends of the earth. We shall see each other to-morrow, shall we not? Thy Irína."

The last two words were written in a large, bold, decided chirography.

XVIII

AMONG the persons who assembled, on the 18th of August, about twelve o'clock, on the platform of the railway station was Litvínoff. Not long before he had met Irína. She was sitting in an open carriage with her husband and another person, a gentleman already elderly. She had seen Litvínoff, and he had perceived it: something dark had flitted across her eyes, but she immediately concealed herself from him with her parasol.

A strange change had taken place in him since the preceding day—in his whole exterior, in his movements, in the expression of his face; and he himself felt that he was another man. His self-confidence had vanished, his composure had vanished also, along with his self-respect; nothing was left of his former spiritual state. Recent ineffaceable impressions had shut out everything else. A certain unprecedented sensation, strong, sweet—and malign, had made its appearance; a mysterious guest had made his way into the sanctuary, and had taken possession of it, and had lain down therein silently, but at full length, as master of the new domicile. Litvínoff no longer felt ashamed, he was afraid—and, at the same time, a desperate hardihood was kindled within him; this mixture of conflicting feelings is familiar to captives, to the conquered; it is not unknown also to the thief, after he has robbed a church. But Litvínoff had been conquered—conquered suddenly; . . . and what had become of his honour?

The train was a few minutes late. Litvínoff's languor passed into torturing anguish: he could not stand still in one place, and, deathly pale, he squeezed and forced his way among the people. "My God," he thought, "if I might have just one more day. . ." His first glance at Tánya, Tánya's first glance . . . that was what alarmed him, that was what he must get through with as speedily as possible. . . And afterward? Afterward—come what might! . . . He no longer arrived at any decisions, he no longer answered for himself. His phrase of yesterday flashed painfully through his head. . . And that is how he is meeting Tánya. . .

A prolonged whistle resounded at last, a dull roar, which momentarily increased, became audible, and rolling slowly from behind the road-gates, the locomotive made its appearance. The crowd advanced to meet it, and Litvínoff advanced after it, dragging his feet like a condemned man. Faces, ladies' hats, began to show themselves from the carriages, in one small window a white handkerchief began to gleam. . . Kapitólina Márkovna was waving it. . . It was over; she had seen Litvínoff, and he had recognised her. The train came to a standstill, Litvínoff rushed to the door and opened it: Tatyána was standing by the side of her aunt, and smiling brightly, offered him her hand.

He helped them both to alight, uttered a few courteous words, incomplete and obscure, and immediately began to bustle about, began to collect their tickets, their travelling-bags, their plaids, ran off to hunt up a porter, called a carriage; other people were bustling about around him, and he rejoiced at their presence, their noise and their shouts. Tatyána stepped a little to one side, and without ceasing to smile, calmly awaited the conclusion of his hasty preparations. Kapitólina Márkovna, on the contrary, could not stand still; she would not believe that she had at last got to Baden. She suddenly cried out: " And the umbrellas? Tánya, where are the umbrellas?" not noticing that she was holding them firmly under her arm; then she began to bid a loud and prolonged farewell to another lady, whose acquaintance she had made during the journey from Heidelberg to Baden. The lady was none other than Madame Sukhántchikoff, already known to us. She had betaken herself to Heidelberg to worship Gubaryóff, and had returned with " instructions." Kapitólina Márkovna wore a decidedly queer striped mantle, and a round travelling-hat, in the shape of a mushroom, from be-

neath which her closely-clipped white hair stuck
out in disarray; short of stature and gaunt, she
had got very red with the journey, and was talking in Russian, with a shrill and chanting voice.
. . People noticed her immediately.

At last Litvínoff seated her and Tatyána in a
carriage, and placed himself opposite them. The
horses started off. Inquiries began, hands were
shaken afresh, there were mutual smiles, greetings. . . Litvínoff breathed freely: the first moments had passed off successfully. Evidently,
nothing about him had struck or disturbed
Tánya: she looked at him as clearly and confid-
ingly, she blushed as prettily, she laughed as
good-naturedly as ever. At last he made up his
mind to look at her, not fleetingly and super-
ficially, but directly and intently: up to that time
his own eyes had not obeyed him. Involuntary
emotion clutched his heart: the tranquil expression of that honest, open countenance found echo
within him in bitter reproach. " Here—thou hast
come hither, poor girl,"—he thought:—" thou,
whom I so waited for and longed for, with whom
I wished to pass my life until its end—thou hast
come, and thou hast trusted me . . . but I . . .
but I . . ." Litvínoff dropped his head; but
Kapitólina Márkovna gave him no opportunity
for meditation; she showered questions upon him.

" What is that building with the pillars?
Where do they gamble? Who is that coming?

Tánya, Tánya, look, what crinolines! And who
is that yonder? They must be chiefly French
people from Paris here? Only I imagine everything is frightfully dear. Akh, with what a
splendid, clever woman I have made acquaintance! You know her, Grigóry Mikhaílovitch;
she told me that she had met you at a certain Russian's, also a wonderfully clever person. She
promised to call on us. How she does abuse all
these aristocrats—it's simply marvellous! What
gentleman is that with the white moustache? The
King of Prussia? Tánya, Tánya, look, that is
the King of Prussia! No? it isn't the King of
Prussia? The Ambassador from Holland? I
can't hear, the wheels rumble so. Akh, what magnificent trees!"

"Yes, aunty, magnificent,"—assented Tánya:
—"and how green and cheerful everything is
here! Is n't it, Grigóry Mikhaílovitch?"

"It is cheerful . . ." he answered her, through
his teeth.

The carriage stopped at last in front of the
hotel. Litvínoff escorted the two travellers to
the rooms reserved for them, promised to look in
in the course of an hour, and returned to his own
room. The spell, which had subsided for a moment, immediately took possession of him as soon
as he entered it. Here in this room Irína had
reigned since the preceding day; everything
spoke of her, the very air seemed to have pre-

served mysterious traces of her visit. . . Again
Litvínoff felt that he was her slave. He pulled
forth her handkerchief, which he had hidden in
his breast, pressed his lips to it, and burning mem-
ories, like delicate poison, diffused themselves
through his veins. He understood that there was
no turning back now, no choice; the painful emotion aroused in him by Tatyána melted like snow
in the fire, and repentance died within him . . .
died—so that even the agitation within him was
allayed, and the possibility of dissimulation,
which presented itself to his mind, did not revolt
him. . . Love, Irína's love—that was what had
now become his righteousness, his law, his conscience. . . The prudent, sensible Litvínoff did
not even reflect how he was to extricate himself
from a situation the horror and indecency of
which he felt lightly and in an indirect manner,
as it were.

An hour had not elapsed when a waiter presented himself to Litvínoff, sent by the newly-
arrived ladies: they requested him to be so good
as to come to them in their sitting-room. He followed their emissary, and found them already
dressed, and with their hats on. Both expressed
a desire to set off at once to inspect Baden, seeing
that the weather was very fine indeed. Kapitólina Márkovna, in particular, was fairly burning with impatience; she was even somewhat
vexed to learn that the hour for the fashionable

gathering in front of the Konversationshaus had
not yet arrived. Litvínoff gave her his arm, and
the official promenade began. Tatyána walked
by the side of her aunt, and gazed about her with
calm curiosity; Kapitólina Márkovna continued
her interrogatories. The sight of the roulette,
of the stately croupiers, whom she would certainly—had she met them in any other place,—
have taken for Cabinet Ministers, of their
brisk little shovels, of the golden and silver
heaps on the green cloth, of the gambling old
women and painted courtesans put Kapitólina
Márkovna into a state akin to dumb rapture;
she totally forgot that she ought to feel indig-
nant—and only stared, and stared, with all her
eyes, quivering, from time to time, with every
fresh exclamation. . . The buzzing of the ivory
ball in the depths of the roulette penetrated to the
very marrow of her bones—and only when she
found herself in the open air did she gain sufficient command over herself to designate the
game of chance, with a profound sigh, as an im-
moral invention of aristocratism. A fixed, malicious smile made its appearance on Litvínoff's
lips; he talked abruptly and indolently, as though
he were vexed or bored. . . But now he turned to
Tatyána, and was seized with secret discomfiture:
she was gazing attentively at him with an expression as though she were asking herself what
sort of an impression was being aroused within

her? He made haste to nod his head at her; she replied to him in the same way, and again looked at him inquiringly, not without a certain effort, as though he stood a great deal further away from her than he did in reality. Litvínoff led his ladies away from the Konversationshaus, and avoiding "the Russian tree," under which his fellow-countrymen were already encamped, took his way to Lichtenthaler Avenue. No sooner had he entered the avenue than he descried I;ína from afar.

She was walking toward him with her husband and Potúgin. Litvínoff turned pale as a sheet, but did not retard his pace, and when he came on a level with her he made her a silent bow. And she bowed to him, pleasantly but coldly, and scrutinising Tatyána with a swift glance, she slipped past. . . Ratmíroff raised his hat very high, Potúgin mumbled something.

" Who is that lady? "—suddenly inquired Tatyána. Up to that moment she had hardly opened her lips.

" That lady? "—repeated Litvínoff.—" That lady? She is a certain Madame Ratmíroff."

" A Russian? "

" Yes."

" Did you make her acquaintance here? "

" No; I have known her this long time."

" How beautiful she is! "

" Did you notice her toilette? "—put in Kapi-

tólina Márkovna.—" Ten families might be fed
for a whole year for the money which her laces
alone are worth. Was that her husband walking
with her? "—she inquired of Litvínoff.

" Yes."

" He must be frightfully rich."

" Really, I do not know; I do not think so."

" And what is his rank? "

" That of general."

" What eyes she has! "—remarked Tatyána:—
" and the expression of them is so strange: both
thoughtful and penetrating. . . I have never
seen such eyes."

Litvínoff made no reply; it seemed to him that
he again felt on his face Tatyána's questioning
glance, but he was mistaken: she was looking under her feet at the sand of the path.

" Good heavens! Who is that monster? "—
suddenly exclaimed Kapitólina Márkovna, pointing with her finger at a low *char-à-bancs,* in
which, boldly lolling, lay a ruddy-haired, snub-
nosed woman, in an unusually rich costume and
lilac stockings.

" That monster! Goodness, that is the famous
Mademoiselle Cora."

" Who? "

" Mademoiselle Cora . . . a Parisian . . . .
celebrity."

" What? that pug-dog? Why, she is extremely
ugly! "

"Evidently, that is no hindrance." Kapitólina Márkovna simply flung out her hands with
amazement.

"Well, your Baden!"—she ejaculated at last.
—"But may we sit down on this bench? I feel
rather fatigued."

"Of course you may, Kapitólina Márkovna. . .
That's what the benches are placed here for."

"Well, the Lord only knows! They say that
off there, in Paris, benches stand on the boule-
vards, also, but it is not proper to sit on them."

Litvínoff made no reply to Kapitólina Márkovna. Only at that very moment did he reflect
that a couple of paces distant was the very spot
where he had had with Irína the explanation
which had settled everything. Then he recol-
lected that to-day he had noticed on her cheek a
tiny red spot. . .

Kapitólina Márkovna sank down on the bench,
Tatyána seated herself beside her, Litvínoff remained on the path; between him and Tatyána
—or did it only seem so to him?—something had
taken place . . . something unconscious and
gradual.

"Akh, she is queer, she is queer,"—ejaculated
Kapitólina Márkovna compassionately, shaking
her head.—"Now, if you were to sell *her* toilette,
you could feed not ten, but a hundred families.
Did you see the diamonds on her red hair under
her hat? Diamonds by daylight, hey?"

"Her hair is not red,"—remarked Litvínoff;
—"she dyes it to a reddish hue; that's the fashion
now."

Again Kapitólina Márkovna threw her hands
apart in amazement, and even fell into meditation.

"Well,"—she said at last,—"we have n't
gone to such scandalous lengths in Dresden yet.
Because, after all, it is further from Paris.
You think so too, don't you, Grigóry Mikhaílitch?"

"I?"—replied Litvínoff, and said to himself:
"What the deuce is she talking about?"—"I?
Of course . . . of course. . ."

But here hurried footsteps became audible, and
Potúgin approached the bench.

"How do you do, Grigóry Mikhaílovitch,"—
he said, smiling, and nodding his head.

Litvínoff immediately caught him by the arm.

"Good afternoon, good afternoon, Sozónt
Ivánitch. I think I met you just now, with . . .
just now, in the avenue."

"Yes, it was I."

Potúgin bowed respectfully to the ladies as
they sat.

"Permit me to introduce you, Sozónt Ivánitch. My good friends, and relatives, have only
just arrived in Baden. Potúgin, Sozónt Ivánitch, a fellow-countryman, also a visitor to
Baden."

Both ladies rose slightly. Potúgin repeated his salutes.

" It is a regular rout here," began Kapitólina Márkovna, in a thin little voice; the kindly old maid was easily abashed, but she tried her best to keep up her dignity:—" every one regards it as a pleasant duty to come here."

" Baden really is a very agreeable place,"— replied Potúgin, casting a sidelong glance at Tatyána;—" a very agreeable place is Baden."

" Yes; only too aristocratic, so far as I can judge. She and I have been living in Dresden this long time . . . it is a very interesting town; but it is, most decidedly, a rout here."

" She has taken a fancy to that word," thought Potúgin.—" Your observation is perfectly just," —he said aloud:—" On the other hand, nature is wonderful here, and the situation is such as is rarely to be found. Your companion must particularly appreciate it. Do you not, madame? "— he added, this time addressing himself directly to Tatyána.

Tatyána raised her large, clear eyes to Potúgin. She seemed rather perplexed as to what was wanted of her, and why Litvínoff had introduced her, on that first day of her arrival, to that strange man, who had, however, a clever and amiable face, and who looked at her in a courteous and friendly manner.

"Yes,"—she said, at last,—"it is very pretty here."

"You ought to visit the old château,"—went on Potúgin;—"in particular, I recommend you to go to Iburg."

"The Saxon Switzerland,"—began Kapitólina Márkovna.

A blast of notes from trumpets rolled down the avenue: it was the Prussian military band from Rastadt (in 1862 Rastadt was still a federate fortress) beginning its weekly concert in the pavilion. Kapitólina Márkovna instantly rose.

"Music!"—she said:—"the music at the *à la Conversation!* . . . we must go there. It must be three o'clock now, is it not? Society is beginning to assemble now?"

"Yes,"—replied Potúgin;—"this is the most fashionable hour for society, and the music is very fine."

"Well, then we must not delay. Tánya, let us go."

"Will you permit me to accompany you?"—inquired Potúgin, to the no small astonishment of Litvínoff: it could not enter his head that Irína had sent Potúgin.

Kapitólina Márkovna grinned.

"With the greatest pleasure, monsieur . . . monsieur. . ."

"Potúgin,"—prompted he, and offered her his arm.

Litvínoff gave his to Tatyána, and both couples directed their steps toward the Konversationshaus.

Potúgin continued to argue with Kapitólina Márkovna. But Litvínoff walked along without uttering a word, and merely laughed a couple of times, without any cause whatever, and lightly pressed Tatyána's arm. There was falsehood in those pressures, to which she did not respond, and Litvínoff was conscious of the falsehood. They did not express mutual confidence in the close union of two souls which had given themselves to each other, as before; they were now taking the place—for the time being—of the words which he could not invent. That speechless something, which had begun between the two, grew and strengthened. Again Tatyána gazed attentively, almost intently, at him.

The same state of affairs continued in front of the Konversationshaus, at the little table, around which all four seated themselves, with this sole difference that Litvínoff's silence appeared more comprehensible under the bustling turmoil of the crowd, and the thunder and crash of the band. Kapitólina Márkovna was quite beside herself, as the saying is; Potúgin was hardly able to humour her, and satisfy her curiosity. Luckily for him, the gaunt figure of Madame Sukhántchikoff and her ever-restless eyes suddenly made their appearance in the throng. Kapitólina Márkovna instantly recognised her, called her up to the table, made her sit down—and a hurricane of words ensued.

Potúgin turned to Tatyána and began to converse with her in a soft and quiet voice, with a caressing expression on his slightly inclined countenance; and she, to her own surprise, answered him lightly and without constraint; she found it agreeable to chat with this stranger, whom she did not know, while Litvínoff continued, as before, to sit motionless, with the same fixed and malicious smile on his lips.

The hour for dinner arrived at last. The band ceased to play, the crowd began to thin out. Kapitólina Márkovna bade a sympathetic farewell to Madame Sukhántchikoff. She had conceived an immense respect for her, although she told her niece afterward that she was an extremely spiteful person; but, on the other hand, she knew everything about everybody! And sewing-machines ought, really, to be introduced as soon as the wedding was celebrated. Potúgin bowed himself off: Litvínoff took his ladies home. As they entered the hotel, a note was handed to him: he stepped aside, and hastily tore off the envelope. On a small scrap of vellum paper stood the following words, scribbled in pencil: "Come to me this evening, for a moment, at seven o'clock, I beg of you. Irína." Litvínoff thrust the paper into his pocket, and as he turned round he smiled again . . . . at whom? why? Tatyána was standing with her back to him.

The dinner took place at the general table. Litvínoff sat between Kapitólina Márkovna and Tatyána, and having grown rather strangely vivacious, chatted, narrated anecdotes, poured out wine for himself and for the ladies. He bore himself with so much freedom of manner that a French infantry officer from Strassburg, with a goatee and moustache *à la* Napoleon III, who sat opposite, found it possible to join in the conversation, and even wound up with a toast *à la santé des belles moscovites!* After dinner Litvínoff escorted the two ladies to their room, and after standing for a short time by the window, with frowning brows, he suddenly announced that he must absent himself for a little while on business, but would return, without fail, later in the evening. Tatyána said nothing, turned pale, and dropped her eyes. Kapitólina Márkovna had a habit of taking a nap after dinner; Tatyána knew that Litvínoff was aware of this habit of her aunt's: she had expected that he would take advantage of it, that he would remain, as he had not yet been alone with her, had not talked frankly with her, since their arrival. And here he was going off! How was she to understand that? And, altogether, his whole conduct in the course of the day . . . .

Litvínoff made haste to depart, without await-

ing any objections; Kapitólina Márkovna lay
down on the divan and, after sighing and drawing a couple of deep breaths, fell into an untrou-
bled sleep; but Tatyána went away to a corner
and seated herself in an arm-chair, with her arms
tightly folded on her breast.

XIX

Litvínoff briskly ascended the stairs of the Hotel de l'Europe. . . A young girl of thirteen, with a cunning little Kalmýk face, who, evidently, was lying in wait for him, stopped him, saying to him in Russian, "This way, please; Irína Pávlovna will be here directly." He glanced at her with surprise. She smiled, repeated, "If you please, if you please," and led him into a small room which was opposite Irína's bedroom, and filled with travelling coffers and trunks, then immediately vanished, closing the door softly behind her. Litvínoff had not succeeded in taking a survey when the same door swiftly opened and Irína made her appearance, in a pink ball-gown, with pearls in her hair and on her neck. She fairly flung herself at him, seized him by both hands, and remained speechless for several moments; her eyes beamed and her bosom heaved, as though she had been running up a hill.

"I could not receive . . . . you there,"—she began, in a hurried whisper;—" we are going immediately to a formal dinner, but I felt that it was imperatively necessary that I should see you. . . . That was your betrothed, of course, with whom I met you to-day?"

" Yes, that *was* my betrothed,"—said Litví-noff, laying special emphasis on the word " was."

" Exactly, and so I wished to see you for a moment, in order to tell you that you must consider yourself entirely free, that all that which took place yesterday ought not, in the least, to alter your decision. . . ."

" Irína! "—exclaimed Litvínoff:—" why dost thou say this? "

He spoke the words in a loud voice. . . . Boundless passion rang out in them. For a moment Irína involuntarily closed her eyes.

" Oh, my dear one! "—she went on, in a still softer whisper, but with uncontrollable impulsiveness:—" thou dost not know how I love thee, but yesterday I only paid my debt, I expiated a fault of the past. . . Akh! I could not give thee my youth, as I would have liked to do, but I imposed no obligations upon thee, I did not release thee from any promise, my darling! Do as thou wilt: thou art free as air; thou art in no wise bound; understand that! Understand it! "

" But I cannot live without thee, Irína,"—Litvínoff interrupted her, now in a whisper.—" I am thine forever and forever, since yesterday. . . . . Only at thy feet can I breathe. . . ."

He tremblingly pressed himself against her arms. Irína gazed at his bowed head.

" Well, then, thou must know,"—she said,— " that I am ready for anything, that I will regret

nobody and nothing. As thou dost decide, so
shall it be. I also am thine forever . . . . . .
thine."

Some one knocked cautiously at the door.
Irína bent over, whispered once more, "Thine.
. . . . Farewell!" Litvínoff felt her breath on
his hair, and the touch of her lips. When he
straightened himself up she was no longer in the
room, only her gown was to be heard rustling in
the corridor, and Ratmíroff's voice was audible
in the distance, *"Eh bien? Vous ne venez
pas?"*

Litvínoff sat down on a tall trunk and covered
his face. A feminine odour, delicate and fresh,
was wafted over him. Irína had held his hands
in her hands. "This is too much . . . . too
much," he said to himself. The young girl entered the room, and smiling again in response to
his troubled glance, she said:

"Please go, sir, while . . . . ."

He rose and left the hotel. An immediate return home was not to be thought of: he must recover his senses. His heart was beating slowly
and unevenly; the earth seemed to be moving
faintly under his feet. Litvínoff again directed
his steps to Lichtenthal Avenue. He comprehended that the decisive moment had arrived,
that it had become impossible to delay any longer,
to dissimulate, to turn aside, that an explanation
with Tatyána was inevitable; he pictured to him-

self how she was sitting there without moving and waiting for him . . . he foresaw what he would say to her; but how was he to set about it, how was he to begin? He had renounced all his regular, well-arranged, orderly future: he knew that he meant to fling himself headlong into the whirlpool, into which it was not proper to glance; . . . but this did not disturb him. That affair was ended, and how was he to present himself before his judge? And even if his judge were to meet him, as it were an angel with a flaming sword: it would be easier for his guilty heart. . . . but otherwise, he himself would be obliged to drive the dagger home. . . . Horrible! But turn back, renounce that other, take advantage of the liberty which was promised him, which was recognised as his right . . . No! It would be better to die! No, he would none of that shameful liberty; . . . but he would abase himself in the dust, and in order that those eyes might incline with love . . . .

" Grigóry Mikhaílitch! "—said a mournful voice, and a hand was laid heavily on Litvínoff.

He glanced round, not without alarm, and beheld Potúgin.

" Excuse me, Grigóry Mikhaílitch,"—began the latter, with his customary grimace;—" perhaps I startled you, but, catching a glimpse of you from afar, I thought . . . However, if you do not feel like talking to me . . . ."

" On the contrary, I am very glad,"—muttered Litvínoff through his teeth.

Potúgin walked along by his side.

" It is a beautiful evening,"—he began:—" so warm! Have you been walking long? "

" No, not long."

" But why do I ask? I saw you come out of the Hotel de l'Europe."

" So you have been following me? "

" Yes."

" Have you anything to say to me? "

" Yes, "—repeated Potúgin in a barely audible voice.

Litvínoff halted and gazed at his unbidden companion. His face was pale, his eyes were roving; ancient, long-past grief seemed to start forth upon his distorted features.

" What, precisely, is it that you wish to say to me? "—said Litvínoff slowly, and again moved onward.

" Permit me . . . I will tell you at once. If it is all the same to you,—let us sit down on this bench here. It will be more convenient."

" But it is something private,"—said Litvínoff, as he sat down beside him. " You do not seem like yourself, Sozónt Ivánitch."

" Yes, I 'm all right; and there is nothing private about it. In fact, I wished to inform you . . . of the impression which your betrothed has produced on me . . . for she is your betrothed bride,

I believe? . . . Well, in a word, that young girl to whom you introduced me to-day: I must say that never, in the whole course of my life, have I met so sympathetic a person. She—has a heart of gold, a truly angelic soul."

Potúgin uttered all these words with the same bitter and afflicted aspect, so that even Litvínoff could not fail to observe the contradiction between the expression of his face and his remarks.

" You have judged Tatyána Petróvna with entire justice,"—began Litvínoff;—" although I am bound to feel astonished, in the first place, that you are acquainted with my relations to her, and, in the second place, that you have so speedily divined her. She really has an angelic soul; but allow me to inquire if that is what you wished to talk to me about? "

" She cannot be divined at once,"—responded Potúgin, as though avoiding the last question:— " one must look into her eyes. She deserves every possible happiness on earth, and enviable is the lot of that man whose fate it shall be to procure her that happiness! We must wish that he will prove worthy of such a fate."

Litvínoff frowned slightly.

" Excuse me, Sozónt Ivánitch,"—he said:—" I must confess that I find your conversation decidedly original. . . . I should like to know: does the hint which your words contain refer to me? "

Potúgin did not immediately reply to Litvínoff; evidently, he was struggling with himself.

"Grigóry Mikhaílitch,"—he began at last,
—"either I am entirely mistaken in you, or you
are in a condition to hear the truth, from whom-
soever it may come, and under whatsoever un-
sightly cover it may present itself. I just told
you that I had seen whence you came."

"Well, yes—from the Hotel de l'Europe.
And what of that?"

"Of course I know whom you saw there!"

"What?"

"You saw Madame Ratmíroff."

"Well, yes; I was with her. What more?"

"What more? . . . You are the affianced husband of Tatyána Petróvna; you have had a meeting with Madame Ratmíroff, whom you love
. . . . and who loves you."

Litvínoff instantly rose from the bench; the
blood flew to his head.

"What's that?"—he said at last, in a wrath-
ful, choking voice:—"is this an insipid jest, or
spying? Be so good as to explain yourself."

Potúgin cast a dejected glance at him.

"Akh! Do not take offence at my words, Grigóry Mikhaílitch; you cannot insult me. It
was not for that that I began this conversation
with you, and I am in no mood for jesting now."

"Possibly, possibly. I am ready to believe in
the purity of your intentions; but, nevertheless,

I shall permit myself to ask you, by what right do you meddle with my private affairs, with the heart-life of a stranger, and on what grounds do you set forth your . . . . fiction, with so much self-confidence, for the truth?"

"My fiction! If I had invented that you would not have got angry! and as for my right, I have never yet heard of a man putting to himself the question: whether he had the right to stretch forth a hand to a drowning person."

"I thank you humbly for your solicitude," retorted Litvínoff angrily,—"only I do not stand in the slightest need of it, and all these phrases about perdition prepared by fashionable ladies for inexperienced youths, about the immorality of the highest society and so forth, I regard as merely phrases, and even, in a certain sense, I despise them; and therefore, I must request you not to inconvenience your saving right hand, and allow me to drown in all quietness."

Again Potúgin raised his eyes to Litvínoff. He was breathing heavily, his lips were twitching.

"Well, look at me, young man,"—he burst out at last, and he smote himself on the breast:—"do I look like an ordinary, self-complacent moralist, a preacher? Cannot you understand that, out of mere sympathy for you, no matter how strong that might be, I would never have uttered a word, would not have given you the right to reproach me for that which I hate more than anything else

—for indiscretion, for intrusiveness? Do not you see that the matter here is of a totally different nature—that before you is a man who has been crushed, ruined, definitively annihilated by the very same feeling, from the consequences of which he would like to save you, and . . . . for the very same woman!"

Litvínoff retreated a pace.

" Is it possible! what have you said. . . . You . . . you . . . Sozónt Ivánitch? But Madame Byélsky . . . that child . . . ."

" Akh, do not question me . . . trust me! That dark, terrible story I will not tell you. I hardly knew Madame Byélsky; the child is not mine, but I took entire charge of her . . . . because . . . . because *she* wished it, because it was necessary for *her*. Why should I be here, in your repulsive Baden? And, in conclusion, do you suppose, could you, for one moment, have imagined that I had made up my mind to warn you out of sympathy? I am sorry for that kind, good young girl, your betrothed; but, however, what business have I with your future, with both of you? . . . But I fear for her . . . for her."

" You do me much honour, Mr. Potúgin,"— began Litvínoff,—" but since, according to your words, we are both in the same situation, why do not you read the same sort of exhortations to yourself. And ought not I to attribute your fears to another sentiment?"

" That is, to jealousy, you mean to say? Ekh, young man, young man, you ought to be ashamed to shuffle and shift; you ought to be ashamed not to understand what bitter woe now speaks through my mouth! No, you and I are not in the same situation! I, I—am an old, ridiculous, utterly harmless eccentric fellow . . . but you! But what is the use of talking? Not for one second would you consent to take upon yourself the rôle which I am playing, and playing with gratitude! And jealousy? The man who has not a single drop of hope is not jealous, and this would not be the first time that I have had occasion to experience that emotion. I am only terrified . . . terrified for her, understand that. And could I foresee, when she sent me to you, that the feeling of guilt, which she admitted to be hers, would lead her so far? "

" But permit me, Sozónt Ivánitch, you seem to know . . . "

" I know nothing, and I know everything. I know,"—he added, and turned his head away.— " I know where she was last night. But she is not to be restrained now: like a stone that has been hurled, she must roll to the bottom. I should be a still greater fool if I were to imagine that my words would immediately arrest you . . . you, to whom such a woman . . . . But enough on that score. I could not restrain myself, that is my sole excuse. Yes, and, in conclusion, how was I to

know, and why should I not make the attempt?
Perhaps you will think better of it, perhaps some
word of mine will fall into your soul. You will
not wish to ruin her and yourself, and that innocent, lovely creature. . . Akh, be not angry, do
not stamp your foot! Why should I be afraid—
why should I stand on ceremony? It is not jealousy which is speaking in me now, nor irritation.
. . I am ready to fall at your feet, to entreat
you. . . But farewell. Have no fear: all this
will remain a secret. I have wished your good."

Potúgin strode along the avenue, and soon disappeared in the already descending gloom. . . .
Litvínoff did not detain him.

" A terrible, dark story,"—Potúgin had said to
Litvínoff, and had not been willing to narrate it.
. . . . And we will touch upon it in a couple of
words only.

Eight years previous to this time he had happened to be temporarily ordered by his Ministry
to Count Reisenbach. The affair took place in
the summer. Potúgin had been in the habit of
driving out to his villa with documents, and spent
whole days in this manner. Irína was then living
with the Count. She never disdained persons of
inferior positions, at all events, she never shunned
them, and the Countess had repeatedly scolded
her for her superfluous Moscow familiarity. Irína
speedily divined the clever man in this humble
official, clothed in uniform, in a coat buttoned to

the throat. She chatted with him frequently and gladly . . . and he . . . he fell in love with her, passionately, profoundly, secretly. . . Secretly! *He* thought so.

The summer passed. The Count ceased to require an outside assistant. Potúgin lost sight of Irína, but could not forget her. Three years later he quite unexpectedly received an invitation from one of his acquaintances, a lady of mediocre standing. This lady was somewhat embarrassed, at first, to express her meaning, but after having extracted from him an oath that he would maintain the greatest secrecy in regard to everything which he should hear, she proposed to him . . . that he should marry a certain young girl who occupied a prominent position in society, and for whom marriage had become indispensable. The lady could hardly make up her mind to hint at the principal in the affair, and then and there offered Potúgin money . . . a great deal of money. Potúgin did not take offence,—amazement overwhelmed his feeling of wrath,—but, as a matter of course, he gave a downright refusal. Then the lady handed him a note addressed to him—from Irína. " You are a noble, kind man," she wrote,—" and I know that you will do anything for me; I ask this sacrifice of you. You will save a being who is dear to me. In saving her, you will save me also. . . Do not ask . . . how. I could not have brought myself to apply to any one with such a request, but I do stretch out my hands to you, and say: ' Do this for my sake.' " Potúgin reflected, and said that, in fact, he was ready to do a great deal for Irína Pávlovna, but would like to hear her wish from her own lips. The meeting took place that same evening: it did not last long, and no one knew about it, except the lady. Irína was no longer living at Count Reisenbach's.

" Why did you think of me, in particular? "— Potúgin asked her.

She was on the point of enlarging upon his fine qualities, but suddenly paused. . .

" No,"—she said,—" I must tell you the truth. I knew—I know that you love me: this is why I decided upon it. . . . " And thereupon she told him everything.

Eliza Byélsky was an orphan; her relatives did not like her, and were counting upon her inheritance . . . ruin stared her in the face. By saving her, Irína really was rendering a service to the man who was the cause of it all, and who had now come to stand very close to her, Irína. . . Potúgin gazed silently and long at Irína, and consented. She fell to weeping, and all in tears, flung herself on his neck. And he also began to weep . . . but their tears were different. Everything was already prepared for a secret marriage, a powerful hand had swept aside all obstacles. . . But illness ensued . . . and a daughter was born, and the mother—poisoned herself. What was to be done with the child? Potúgin took it under his charge from the same hands, from the hands of Irína.

A terrible, dark story. . . Let us pass on, reader, let us pass on!

Over an hour more elapsed before Litvínoff made up his mind to return to his hotel. He was already drawing near to it, when he suddenly heard footsteps behind him. Some one appeared to be persistently following him, and walking faster when he accelerated his pace. As he came under a street-lamp, Litvínoff glanced round, and recognised General Ratmíroff. In a white necktie, and an elegant overcoat thrown open on the breast, with a row of tiny stars and crosses on a golden chain, in the buttonhole of his evening coat, the general was returning from the dinner alone. His glance, directly and boldly riveted upon Litvínoff, expressed such scorn and such hatred, his whole figure breathed forth such an importunate challenge, that Litvínoff considered it his duty to advance to meet him, summoning his courage to advance to meet that " row." But, on coming alongside of Litvínoff, the general's face instantly underwent a change: again his wonted playful elegance made its appearance, and his hand, in its pale lilac glove, raised his shining hat on high. Litvínoff silently took off his, and each went his way.

"Assuredly, he has noticed something!"—thought Litvínoff. "If only . . . it were any other person!" thought the general.

Tatyána was playing picquet with her aunt, when Litvínoff entered their room.

"Well, you are a nice one, my dear fellow!"—exclaimed Kapitólina Márkovna, and flung her cards on the table:—"on the very first day you have disappeared, and for the entire evening! Here we have been waiting and waiting for you, scolding and scolding. . ."

"I have not said anything, aunty,"—remarked Tatyána.

"Well, everybody knows what a submissive creature you are! Shame on you, my dear sir! And a betrothed bridegroom, to boot!"

Litvínoff excused himself, after a fashion, and seated himself at the table.

"Why have you stopped playing?"—he asked, after a brief silence.

"That's just the point! She and I play cards out of ennui when there is nothing to do . . . . but now you have come."

"If you would like to listen to the evening concert,"—said Litvínoff,—"I will take you with great pleasure."

Kapitólina Márkovna looked at her niece.

"Let us go, aunty, I am ready,"—said the latter,—"but would it not be better to remain at home?"

" The very thing! Let us drink tea, in our own Moscow fashion, with a samovár; and let 's have a good talk. We have n't yet had a thoroughly good chat."

Litvínoff ordered tea to be brought, but they did not succeed in having a good talk. He experienced an incessant gnawing of conscience; no matter what he said, it always seemed to him as though he were lying, and that Tatyána divined it. But, in the meanwhile, no change was perceptible in her; she bore herself with as little constraint as ever . . . . only, her glance never once rested on Litvínoff, but slipped over him in a condescending and timid sort of way—and she was paler than usual.

Kapitólina Márkovna asked her whether she had not a headache?

At first Tatyána was on the point of answering " No," but changed her mind, and said: " Yes, a little."

" It is from the journey,"—said Litvínoff, and fairly blushed with shame.

" It is from the journey,"—repeated Tatyána, and again her glance glided over him.

" You must rest, Tánetchka."

" I shall go to bed soon, aunty."

On the table lay the " Guide des Voyageurs "; Litvínoff began to read aloud the description of the environs of Baden.

" All that is so,"—Kapitólina Márkovna interrupted him,—" but one thing we must not forget. They say that linen is very cheap here, so we might buy some for the trousseau."

Tatyána dropped her eyes.

" There is plenty of time, aunty. You never think of yourself. But you certainly must have a new gown made. You see how finely dressed every one is here."

" Eh, my darling! Why should I? What sort of a fashionable figure-plate should I make? It would be all right if I were as beautiful as that acquaintance of yours, Grigóry Mikhaílitch— what in the world is her name?"

" What acquaintance?"

" Why, the one we met to-day."

" Ah, that one!"—said Litvínoff, with simulated indifference, and again he felt odious and ashamed. " No!" he said to himself, " things cannot go on in this way!"

He was sitting by the side of his betrothed, and a few inches away from her, in his pocket, was Irína's handkerchief.

Kapitólina Márkovna went into the next room for a moment.

" Tánya . . . ."—said Litvínoff, with an effort. He called her by that name for the first time that day.

She turned toward him.

" I . . . . have something important to say to you."

" Ah! Really? When? Immediately? "

" No, to-morrow."

" Ah! To-morrow. Well, very good."

Boundless pity immediately filled Litvínoff's soul. He took Tatyána's hand and kissed it submissively, like a guilty man; her heart contracted silently, and that kiss did not make her rejoice.

That night, at two o'clock, Kapitólina Márkovna, who slept in the same room with her niece, suddenly raised her head and listened.

" Tánya! "—she said:—" are you crying? "

Tatyána did not immediately reply.

" No, aunty,"—her gentle little voice made itself heard;—" I have a cold in the head."

XX

" WHY did I say that? " thought Litvínoff, on the following morning, as he sat in front of the window in his own room. He shrugged his shoulders with vexation: he had said it to Tatyána precisely for the purpose of cutting off all retreat from himself. On the window-sill lay a note from Irína: she summoned him to her at eleven o'clock. Potúgin's words incessantly recurred to his memory; then they rushed past with an ominous, though feeble, rather subterranean roar; he waxed angry, and could not, in any way, rid himself of them. Some one knocked at the door.

" *Wer da?* "—inquired Litvínoff.

" Ah! You are at home! Open! "—rang out Bindásoff's hoarse bass voice.

The handle of the door rattled.

Litvínoff turned pale with wrath.

" I am not at home,"—he said sharply.

" Why are n't you at home? What sort of a jest is this? "

" I tell you—I am not at home; take yourself off."

" That 's amiable of you! And I came to borrow money,"—growled Bindásoff.

But he withdrew, clacking his heels, as usual.

Litvínoff almost rushed out after him, so great was his desire to break the neck of that disgusting, insolent fellow. The events of the last few days had deranged his nerves: a little more, and he would have wept. He drank a glass of cold water, locked all the drawers in the furniture, without knowing why he did so, and went to Tatyána.

He found her alone—Kapitólina Márkovna had betaken herself to the shops to make purchases. Tatyána was sitting on the divan, and holding a book with both hands; she was not reading it, and even hardly knew what book it was. She did not stir, but her heart was beating violently in her breast, and the white collar round her neck quivered perceptibly and regularly.

Litvínoff was disconcerted . . . but he sat down beside her, bade her good morning, and smiled; and she smiled silently at him. She had bowed to him when he entered, bowed politely, not in a friendly manner—and had not looked at him. He offered her his hand; she gave him her cold fingers, immediately disentangled them, and returned to her book. Litvínoff felt that to begin the conversation with trivial subjects would be equivalent to offering Tatyána an affront; according to her wont, she demanded nothing, but everything in her said: " I am waiting, I am waiting. . ." He must fulfil his promise. But, although he had thought of nothing else almost all night, he had not prepared even the first introductory words, and positively did not know how to break that cruel silence.

" Tánya,"—he began at last,—" I told you yesterday that I have something important to communicate to you " (in Dresden, when he was alone with her, he had begun to address her as " thou," but now such a thing was not to be thought of). " I am ready, only, I beg you in advance, not to blame me, and to feel assured that my feelings for you . . . ."

He halted. He had lost his breath. Still Tatyána never moved, nor did she glance at him: she merely grasped her book more firmly than before.

" Between us,"—went on Litvínoff, without completing the speech he had begun,—" between us there has always been perfect frankness; I respect you too much to resort to double dealing with you; I want to prove to you that I prize the loftiness and freedom of your soul, and although I . . although, of course . . . ."

" Grigóry Mikhaílitch,"—began Tatyána in an even voice, and her whole face became overspread with a death-like pallor,—" I will come to your assistance: you have ceased to love me, and you do not know how to tell me that."

Litvínoff involuntarily shuddered.

" Why? "—he said, almost inaudibly,—" why

should you think that? . . . I really do not understand. . ."

" Well, is it not the truth? Is it not the truth? tell me! tell me! "

Tatyána turned her whole body toward Litvínoff; her face, with its hair thrown back, approached his face, and her eyes, which had not looked at him for so long, fairly devoured his eyes.

" Is it not true? "—she repeated.

He said nothing, did not utter a single sound. He could not have lied at that moment, even if he had known that she would believe him, and that his lie would save her; he was not even capable of enduring her gaze. Litvínoff said nothing, but she no longer needed an answer; she read the answer in his silence, in those guilty, downcast eyes, —and threw herself back, and dropped her book. . . . She had still doubted, up to that moment, and Litvínoff understood this; he understood that she still doubted—and how repulsive, actually repulsive, was everything that he had done!

He threw himself on his knees before her.

" Tánya! "—he exclaimed:—"if I had known how painful it would be to me to behold you in this situation, how frightful it would be to me to think that it is I . . . . I! My heart is lacerated; I do not know myself; I have lost myself and thee, and everything. . . . Everything is ruined, Tánya, everything! Could I have foreseen that I

. . I would deal such a blow to thee, my best friend, my guardian angel! . . . Could I have foreseen that thou and I would meet, would pass such a day as yesterday! . . ."

Tatyána tried to rise and withdraw. He detained her by the hem of her gown.

" No; listen to me for another minute. Thou seest, I am kneeling before thee. But I have not come to ask forgiveness,—thou canst not and must not forgive me; I have come to tell thee that thy friend has gone to destruction, that he is falling into the abyss, and does not wish to drag thee down with him. . . . But save me . . . no! even thou canst not save me. I myself would have repulsed thee. . . . I have perished, Tánya, I have perished irrevocably! "

Tatyána looked at Litvínoff.

" You have perished! "—she said, as though she did not fully understand him.—" You have perished? "

" Yes, Tánya, I have perished. All that is past, all that is dear, all that has heretofore constituted my life,—has perished for me; everything is ruined, everything is torn away, and I know not what awaits me in the future. Thou didst tell me immediately that I had ceased to love thee. . . No, Tánya, I have not ceased to love thee, but another, a terrible, irresistible feeling has descended upon me, has flooded me. I resisted it as long as I was able. . . . "

Tatyána rose; her brows were contracted, her pale face had darkened. Litvínoff also rose.

" You have fallen in love with another woman,"—she began,—" and I divine who she is. .. We met her yesterday, did we not? Very well! I know now what remains for me to do. As you yourself say that this feeling is unalterable in you . . ." (Tatyána paused for an instant: perhaps she still hoped that Litvínoff would not let this last word pass without a reply, but he said nothing) " all there is left for me to do is to give you back . . . your word." Litvínoff bent his head, as though submissively accepting a merited blow.

" You have a right to be angry with me,"—he said,—" you have a perfect right to reproach me with pusillanimity . . . with deceit."

Again Tatyána looked at him.

" I have not reproached you, Litvínoff; I do not accuse you. I agree with you: the very bitterest truth is better than what went on yesterday. What a life ours would have been under present circumstances! "

" What a life mine will be under present circumstances! " echoed painfully in Litvínoff's soul.

Tatyána approached the door of the bedroom.

" I beg that you will leave me alone for a time, Grigóry Mikhaílitch,—we shall meet again, we shall talk together again. All this has been

so unexpected. I must collect my forces . . . .
leave me . . . spare my pride. We shall see each
other again."

And having said these words, Tatyána hastily
left the room and locked the door after her.

Litvínoff went out into the street as though
confused, stunned; something dark and heavy
had taken root in the very depths of his heart; a
man who has cut another man's throat must experience a similar sensation, and, at the same time,
he felt relieved, as though he had at last cast off
a hateful burden. Tatyána's magnanimity annihilated him; he was vividly conscious of all that
he had lost . . . and what then? Vexation was
mingled with his repentance; he longed for
Irína, as the sole refuge left him,—and was
angry with her. For some time past, and with
every succeeding day, Litvínoff's feelings had
been becoming more and more powerful and
complex; this complication tortured, irritated
him; he felt lost in this chaos. He thirsted for
one thing: to come out, at last, on a road, on any
road whatever, if only he might no longer whirl
around in this unintelligible twilight. Positive
people, like Litvínoff, ought not to get carried away by passion; it destroys the very meaning of their lives. . . But nature asks no questions
about logic, our human logic; she has her own,
which we do not understand and do not recognise
until it rolls over us, like a wheel.

After parting from Tatyána, Litvínoff held
one thought firmly in his mind: to see Irína; and
he set out for her abode. But the general was
at home,—at least, so the porter told him,—and
he did not care to enter; he did not feel himself
in a condition to dissimulate, and strolled off to
the Konversationshaus. Litvínoff's incapacity
for dissimulation was experienced that day by
Voroshíloff and Pishtchálkin, who chanced to
encounter him: he fairly told one of them point-
blank that he was as empty as a tambourine; the
other, that he was tiresome enough to make a man
swoon; it was a good thing that Bindásoff did
not turn up: a "grosser Scandal" certainly
would have ensued. Both young men were
amazed; Voroshíloff even asked himself whether
his honour as an officer did not demand repara-
tion?—but, like Gógol's lieutenant Pirogóff, he
soothed himself in the café with bread and butter.
Litvínoff caught a distant glimpse of Kapitólina
Márkovna, busily running from shop to shop in
her motley mantle. . . He felt ashamed before
the kind, ridiculous, noble old woman. Then he
recalled Potúgin and their conversation of the
preceding day. . . . But now some influence was
breathing upon him, something impalpable and
indubitable; had the exhalation emanated from
a falling shadow, it could not have been more
intangible. But he immediately felt that Irína
was approaching. And in fact, she appeared at

a distance of a few paces, arm in arm with another lady; their eyes instantly met. Irína, in all probability, noticed something unusual in the expression of Litvínoff's face; she halted in front of a shop, in which a mass of tiny wooden clocks of Schwarzwald manufacture were on sale, summoned him to her by a movement of her head, and pointing out one of these clocks to him, and requesting him to admire the pretty dial-plate, with a painted cuckoo at the top, she said, not in a whisper, but in her ordinary voice, as though completing a phrase which had been begun—which attracts less attention from strangers:

" Come an hour hence, I shall be at home and alone."

But at this point, that squire of dames, Monsieur Verdier, fluttered up to her, and began to go into ecstasies over the *feuille morte* tint of her gown, over her low-crowned Spanish hat, which was pulled down to her very eyebrows. . . Litvínoff vanished in the crowd.

XXI

" Grigóry,"—said Irína to him, two hours later, as she sat beside him on the couch and laid both her hands on his shoulders.—" What is the matter with thee? Tell me now, quickly, while we are alone."

" With me? "—said Litvínoff.—" I am happy, happy, that is what is the matter with me."

Irína dropped her eyes, smiled, sighed.

" That is not an answer to my question, my dear one. "

Litvínoff reflected.

" Well, then, thou must know . . . since thou imperatively demandest it " (Irína opened her eyes very widely, and drew back a little): " I have to-day told my betrothed everything."

" What dost thou mean by everything? Didst thou mention my name? "

" Irína, for God's sake, how could such a thought enter thy head! that I . . . ."

Litvínoff actually clasped his hands.

" Well, forgive me . . . . forgive me. What didst thou say? "

" I told her that I no longer loved her."

" Did she ask why? "

"I did not conceal from her the fact that I loved another, and that we must part."

"Well . . . and how about her? Did she consent?"

"Akh, Irína, what a girl she is! She is all self-sacrifice, all nobility!"

"I believe it, I believe it . . however, there was nothing else left for her to do."

"And not a single reproach, not a single bitter word to me, to the man who has spoiled her whole life, who has deceived her, pitilessly abandoned her. . ."

Irína inspected her finger-nails.

"Tell me, Grigóry, did she love thee?"

"Yes, Irína, she did love me."

Irína said nothing, but smoothed her gown.

"I must confess,"—she began,—"that I do not quite understand why thou hast taken it into thy head to have an explanation with her."

"How is it that thou dost not understand it, Irína! Is it possible that thou wouldst have wished to have me lie, dissimulate before her—before that pure soul? Or didst thou assume . . . ."

"I assumed nothing," interrupted Irína.—"I must admit that I have thought very little about her. . . I cannot think of two persons at the same time."

"That is, thou intendest to say . . ."

"Well, and what then? Is she going away, that pure soul?"—interrupted Irína again.

a more pitiful rôle: the rôle of a man who does not know what is going on in his own soul!"

It was now Litvínoff's turn to draw himself up.

"Irína,"—he began.

But she suddenly pressed both palms to her brow, and flinging herself on his breast, with a convulsive impulse, embraced him with unfeminine force.

"Forgive me, forgive me,"—she said in a trembling voice,—"forgive me, Grigóry! Thou seest how spoiled I am, how hateful, jealous, wicked I am! Thou seest how I need thy help, thy indulgence! Yes, save me, tear me out of this abyss before I perish utterly! Yes, let us flee, let us flee from these people, from this society, into some distant, free, beautiful land! Perhaps thy Irína will become, at last, more worthy of the sacrifices which thou art making for her! Be not angry with me, my dearest,—and understand that I will do everything which thou commandest; I will go anywhere, whithersoever thou leadest me!"

Litvínoff's heart was completely upset. Irína pressed more violently than ever to him with her supple young body. He bent over her disheveled, perfumed locks, and in an intoxication of gratitude and rapture, hardly ventured to caress them with his hand, hardly touched them with his lips.

"Irína, Irína,"—he kept repeating,—"my angel. . ."

She suddenly raised her head, listened. . . "Those are my husband's footsteps . . he has gone into his own room,"—she whispered, and hastily moving away, she seated herself in an arm-chair. Litvínoff was on the point of rising. . . "Where art thou going?" she continued in the same whisper:—"remain; he suspects thee, as it is. Or art thou afraid of him?"—She never took her eyes from the door.—"Yes, it is he; he will come hither immediately. Tell me something, converse with me."—Litvínoff could not at once recover himself, and remained silent.— "Are not you going to the theatre to-morrow?" —she said aloud.—"They are playing ' Le Verre d'Eau,' a stale old piece, and Plessy is frightfully affected. . . I feel as though I were in a fever," —she added, lowering her voice,—we cannot go on like this; we must think it over carefully. I must warn thee that he has all my money; *mais j'ai mes bijoux.* Let us go to Spain, shall we?" —Again she raised her voice.—"Why is it that all actresses get fat? There is Madeleine Brohan, for example. . Do say something; don't sit there dumb like that. My head is whirling. But thou must have no doubts of me. . . I will let thee know where thou must come to-morrow. Only, it was unnecessary for thee to tell that young lady. . . . *Ah! mais c'est charmant!*"—

she suddenly exclaimed, and with a nervous laugh she tore off the border of her handkerchief.

" May I come in? "—inquired Ratmíroff, from the adjoining room.

" Yes . . . . yes."

The door opened, and the general appeared on the threshold. He scowled at the sight of Litvínoff, but saluted him, that is to say, he swayed the upper part of his body.

" I did not know that thou hadst a visitor,"— he said:—" *je vous demande pardon de mon indiscretion.* And does Baden still amuse you, Monsieur . . . . Litvínoff? "

Ratmíroff always pronounced Litvínoff's surname with hestitation, as though he had forgotten it every time, and could not immediately recall it. . . By this means, and by raising his hat in an exaggerated manner, he meant to sting him.

" I do not find myself bored here, Monsieur *le general.*"

" Really? But I have grown horribly tired of Baden. We are going away shortly, are we not, Irína Pávlovna? *Assez de Bade comme ça.* Moreover, luckily for you, I have won five hundred francs to-day."

Irína coquettishly held out her hand.

" Where are they? Please give them to me. For pin-money."

" I have them . . . I have them. . . . But are you going already, M'sieu' . . . Litvínoff? "

" Yes, sir, I am going, as you see."

Again Ratmíroff swayed his body.

" Farewell until another pleasant meeting!"

" Good-bye, Grigóry Mikhaílovitch,"—said Irína.—" And I shall keep my promise."

" What promise? if I may be so curious as to inquire? "—asked her husband.

Irína smiled.

" No—that is . . . a matter between ourselves. *C'est àpropos du voyage . . . où il vous plaira.* Art thou acquainted with Staël's works? "

" Ah! of course, of course I am. Very pretty pictures. . ."

Ratmíroff appeared to be on good terms with his wife: he addressed her as " thou."

XXII

" 'Tis better not to think about it," Litvínoff kept
repeating to himself, as he strode along the street,
and became conscious that the turmoil within him
was rising once more. " The matter is settled.
She will keep her promise, and all I have to do
is to take all the necessary measures. . . But she
seems to doubt." . . . He shook his head. His
own intentions presented themselves to him in an
odd light; there was a touch of strangeness and
improbability about them. It is not possible to
dwell long upon one and the same set of thoughts;
they gradually shift their places, like bits of glass
in a kaleidoscope . . . . and the first one knows,
the figures before his eyes are totally different.
A sensation of profound weariness overpowered
Litvínoff. . . He longed to rest for an hour. . .
But Tánya? He gave a start, and without reflecting further, submissively wended his way
home, and the only thing which occurred to him
was that to-day he was being tossed from one
woman to another, like a ball. . . It mattered
not: he had been compelled to make an end of it.
He entered the hotel, and in the same submissive
manner, without hesitation or delay, he betook
himself to Tatyána.

He was met by Kapitólina Márkovna. With his first glance at her, he recognised the fact that she knew everything: the poor spinster's eyes were swollen with tears, and her reddened face, framed in rumpled white hair, expressed alarm and the pain of indignation, of burning and boundless amazement. She darted toward Litvínoff, but instantly paused, and biting her quivering lips, she gazed at him, as though she wished to entreat him, and slay him, and convince herself that all this was a dream, madness, an impossible affair, was it not?

" Here, you . . you have come, you have come," she began. . . The door leading into the adjoining room instantly flew open—and Tatyána, pale to transparency, entered with a light step.

She softly embraced her aunt with one arm, and made her sit down by her side.

"Do you sit down also Grigóry Mikháilitch," —she said to Litvínoff, who was standing, as though bewildered, near the door.—" I am very glad to see you again. I have communicated your decision, our mutual decision, to aunty; she shares it entirely, and approves of it. . . Without mutual love there can be no happiness; mutual respect alone is not sufficient " (at the word "respect" Litvínoff involuntarily cast down his eyes), " and it is better to part beforehand, than to repent afterward. Is n't that true, aunty? "

"Yes, of course,"—began Kapitólina Márkovna,—"of course, Tániusha, the man who does not know how to value you . . . who has made up his mind . . ."

"Aunty, aunty,"—Tatyána interrupted her, —"remember what you promised me. You yourself have always said to me: 'the truth, the truth before everything, and—liberty.' Well, and truth is not always sweet, neither is liberty; otherwise, wherein would our merit lie?"

She kissed Kapitólina Márkovna tenderly on her white hair, and turning to Litvínoff she went on:

"My aunt and I have decided to leave Baden. . . I think it will be easier so for all of us."

"When do you think of going?"—said Litvínoff, in a dull voice. He recalled that Irína had said the very same words to him not long before.

Kapitólina Márkovna was on the point of starting forward, but Tatyána restrained her, touching her lightly on the shoulder.

"Probably soon, very soon."

"And will you permit me to inquire whither you intend to go?" asked Litvínoff in the same voice as before.

"First to Dresden, then, probably, to Russia."

"But what do you want to know that for now, Grigóry Mikhaílitch?" . . exclaimed Kapitólina Márkovna.

"Aunty, aunty," interposed Tatyána again. A brief silence ensued.

"Tatyána Petróvna,"—began Litvínoff,— "you understand what a torturingly—painful and sorrowful feeling I must be experiencing at this moment. . . ."

Tatyána rose.

"Grigóry Mikhaílitch,"—she said,—"let us not talk about that. . . . Please, I entreat you, for your own sake as well as for mine. I cannot recognise you since yesterday, and I can very well imagine that you must be suffering now. But what is the use of talking, what is the use of irritating . . . ." (She paused: it was evident that she wished to wait until her rising emotion was allayed, to swallow the tears which were already welling up; and in this she succeeded.) "What is the use of irritating the wound which it is impossible to heal? Let us leave that to time. But now I have a request to make of you, Grigóry Mikhaílitch: I will give you a letter presently; be so good as to post that letter yourself, it is of considerable importance, and aunty and I have no time now. . . . I shall be very much obliged to you. Wait a moment. . . I will return immediately. . . ."

On the threshold of the door Tatyána cast an apprehensive glance at Kapitólina Márkovna; but the latter was sitting in so dignified and decorous an attitude, with such a severe expression on her frowning brow and tightly-compressed lips, that Tatyána only nodded to her, and left the room.

But the door had barely closed behind her, when all expression of dignity and severity instantaneously vanished from the face of Kapitólina Márkovna: she rose, rushed up to Litvínoff on tiptoe, and bending double, and striving to look into his eyes, she began to speak in a hurried, tearful whisper:

"O Lord my God,"—said she,—"Grigóry Mikhaílitch, what is the meaning of this: is it a dream? *You* reject Tánya, you have ceased to love her, you have betrayed your word! You are doing this, Grigóry Mikhaílitch, you, in whom we all had trusted as in a wall of stone! You? You? Thou, Grísha? . . ." Kapitólina Márkovna paused.—"Why, you are killing her, Grigóry Mikhaílitch,"—she went on, without awaiting an answer, and her tears fairly streamed, in tiny drops, down her cheeks.—"You need not regard the fact that she is keeping up her courage, for you know what her disposition is! She never complains; she never pities herself, so others must pity her! Here she is now, persuading me: 'Aunty, we must maintain our dignity!' but who cares about dignity, when I foresee death, death. . . ." Tatyána made a noise with a chair in the adjoining room.—"Yes, I foresee death,"—resumed the old woman, in a still softer voice.—

" And what can have happened? Have you been
bewitched? It was not so very long ago, was it,
that you were writing her the tenderest sort of
letters? Yes, and in conclusion, can an honest
man behave in this manner? I, as you know, am
a woman wholly devoid of prejudices, *esprit fort,*
and I have given Tánya the same sort of education—she, also, has a free spirit. . . ."

" Aunty!" rang out Tatyána's voice from the
next room.

"But your word of honour,—this is duty,
Grigóry Mikhaílitch. Especially for people with
your—with our principles! If we do not recognise duty, what is left to us? That must not be
violated—in this way, at one's own caprice, without considering what is to be the result on others!
This is dishonest . . . yes, it is a crime; what sort
of freedom is this?"

" Aunty, come here, please,"—rang out again.

" In a minute, my darling, in a minute. . ."
Kapitólina Márkovna seized Litvínoff by the
hand.—" I see you are angry, Grigóry Mikhaílitch. . ." (" I? I am angry?" he tried to ex-
claim, but his tongue was benumbed.) " I do not
wish to make you angry—O Lord! am I in any
mood for that? On the contrary, I wish to entreat
you: change your mind while still there is time;
do not destroy her, do not destroy your own
happiness; she will trust you again, Grigóry
Mikhaílitch, she will trust you again; nothing

is lost yet; for she loves you as no one ever will
love you! Abandon this hateful Baden-Baden,
let us go away together, only get away from under this spell, and, the chief thing of all, have
pity, have pity. . ."

"But aunty,"—said Tatyána, with a trace of
impatience in her voice.

But Kapitólina Márkovna did not obey her.

"Only say yes,"—she persisted to Litvínoff,
—"and I will arrange all the rest. . . Come, at
least nod your head at me! nod your head, just
once, like this!" Litvínoff felt as though he
would gladly have died at that moment; but he
did not utter the word "yes," and he did not nod
his head.

Tatyána made her appearance, letter in hand.
Kapitólina Márkovna instantly sprang away
from Litvínoff, and turning her face aside, bent
low over the table, as though she were inspecting
the bills and papers which lay upon it.

Tatyána approached Litvínoff.

"Here,"—said she,—"this is the letter of
which I spoke to you. . . You will go immediately to the post-office, will you not?"

Litvínoff raised his eyes. . . Before him, in
very truth, stood his judge. Tatyána seemed
to him taller, more stately; her face, beaming
with unprecedented beauty, had become magnifi-
cently petrified, as in a statue; her bosom did
not rise and fall, and her gown, uniform in hue,

and close-fitting, fell, like a chiton, in the long, straight folds of marble fabrics, to her feet, which it concealed. Tatyána was gazing straight before her, at Litvínoff only, and her glance, also smooth and cold, was the glance of a statue. In it he read his sentence; he bowed, took the letter from the hand which was immovably outstretched toward him and silently departed.

Kapitólina Márkovna flew at Tatyána, but the latter repulsed her embrace, and dropped her eyes; a flush overspread her face, and with the words, " Come, as quickly as possible now! " she returned to the bedroom; Kapitólina Márkovna followed her, with drooping head.

On the letter intrusted to Litvínoff by Tatyána stood the address of one of her friends in Dresden, a German, who let out small, furnished apartments. Litvínoff dropped the letter into the post-box, and it seemed to him that, along with that little scrap of paper, he had laid all his past, his whole life, in the grave. He went out of the town, and roamed, for a long time, along the narrow paths among the vineyards; he could not rid himself of an incessant feeling of scorn for himself, which beset him like the buzzing of an importunate summer fly: he certainly had played a far from enviable part in this last interview. . . . And when he returned to the hotel and, a little while later, inquired about his ladies, he was informed that immediately after his departure they had ordered themselves to be driven to the railway station, and had set off, with the mail-train, no one knew whither. Their things had been packed and their bills paid since the morning. Tatyána had requested Litvínoff to take the letter to the post-office, evidently with a view to getting him out of the way. He tried to question the door-porter: " Had not the ladies left a note for him? " but the porter replied in the negative, and even manifested surprise; it was plain that this sudden departure from rooms engaged for a week struck him as strange and suspicious. Litvínoff turned his back on him, and locked himself up in his own room.

He did not leave it until the following day; during the greater part of the night he sat at the table, writing and tearing up what he had written. . . Daylight had already begun to dawn when he finished his work,—which was a letter to Irína.

XXIII

THIS is what the letter to Irína contained:

"My betrothed bride went away yesterday: we shall never see each other again. . . I do not even know with certainty where she will live. She carried away with her everything which hitherto had seemed to be desirable and precious; all my purposes, plans, intentions, vanished along with her; my very labours have disappeared, my prolonged toil has been turned to naught, all my occupations have lost their sense and application; all this is dead; my *ego*, my former *ego*, died and was buried with yesterday. I feel that plainly, I see, I know it. . . And I do not complain, in the least, of that. It is not for the purpose of complaining that I have begun to discuss this with thee. . . Have I any cause to complain, when thou lovest me, Irína? I only want to tell thee, that out of all this dead past, out of all these beginnings and hopes—which have turned to smoke and dust—only one living, invincible thing remains: my love for thee. Save for this love, I have nothing left; it would not be enough to call it my sole treasure; I am all in this love, this love is the whole of me; in it is my future, my vocation, my holy things, my fatherland! Thou knowest me, Irína, thou knowest that set phrases are foreign and abhorrent to me, and however forcible may be the words wherewith I strive to express my feeling, thou wilt not doubt their sincerity, thou wilt not consider them exaggerated. It is not a boy, who is stammering out ill-considered vows before thee, in a burst of momentary enthusiasm, it is a man, already tried by the years, who simply and straightforwardly, almost with terror, is expressing that which he has recognised to be the indubitable truth. Yes, thy love has taken the place of everything else with me—everything, everything! Judge for thyself: can I leave *all* this in the hands of another man, can I permit him to dispose of thee? Thou, thou wilt belong to him, all my being, my heart's blood, will belong to him,—and I myself . . . Where am I? What am I? I am to stand on one side, as a looker-on . . . . a looker-on at my own life! No, this is impossible, impossible! To share, to share by stealth in that without which it is not worth while, without which it is impossible to *breathe* . . . that is a lie and death. I know how great is the sacrifice I require of thee, without having any right so to do; and what can give one a right to a sacrifice? But I do not take this step from egoism: an egoist would find it easier and more tranquil not to raise this question at all. Yes, my demands are heavy, and I shall not be surprised if they frighten thee.—The people with whom thou must live are hateful to me, society oppresses thee; but hast thou the strength to abandon that same society, to trample under foot the crown wherewith it has crowned thee, to arouse against thee public opinion, the opinion of those hateful people? Ask thyself, Irína; do not take upon thyself a burden greater than thou canst bear. .— I do not mean to reproach thee, but remember: once before thou hast failed to resist the charm. I can give thee so little in exchange for what thou wilt lose!

Hearken to my last word: if thou dost not feel thyself in a condition to leave everything and follow me to-morrow, to-day,—thou seest how boldly I speak, how little I spare myself,—if the uncertainty of the future, and estrangement, and isolation, and public censure alarm thee, if thou canst not trust thyself, in a word—tell me so frankly and without delay, and I will go away; I will go away, with a harrowed soul, but I will thank thee for thy truthfulness. But if thou, my most beautiful, my radiant empress, hast really come to love such a petty, obscure man as I, and art really ready to share his lot,—well, then give me thy hand, and we will set forth together on our different road! Only, thou must know this: my resolution is firm: either all, or nothing! This is madness . . . but I cannot do otherwise, I cannot, Irína! I love thee too mightily.

" Thy G. L."

This letter did not please Litvínoff himself very much. It did not quite faithfully and accurately express what he wished to say; awkward expressions, by turns magniloquent and bookish, occurred in it, and when it was finished it was no better than many of the other letters which he had torn up; but it happened to be the last one, and after all, the chief thing had been said; and weary, exhausted, Litvínoff did not feel himself capable of extracting anything else from his head. Moreover, he did not possess the skill to set forth his whole thought in literary form, and, like all persons who are not accustomed to this, he worried over the style. His first letter had, probably, been the best: it had poured forth burning hot from his heart. At any rate, Litvínoff despatched his epistle to Irína.

She replied with a brief note:

"Come to me to-day," she wrote to him; "*he* has gone off for the whole day. Thy letter has agitated me extremely. I keep thinking, thinking . . . and my head is dizzy with my thoughts. I am greatly distressed, but thou lovest me, and I am happy.

"Thy I."

She was sitting in her boudoir when Litvínoff presented himself to her. He was ushered in by the same thirteen-year-old girl who had kept watch for him on the staircase the day before. On the table, in front of Irína, stood an open, semicircular pasteboard box filled with laces; she was abstractedly turning them over with one hand; in the other she held Litvínoff's letter. She had only just stopped crying: her eyelashes were wet, and her eyelids were swollen; the traces of tears which had not been wiped away were visible on her cheeks. Litvínoff halted on the threshold: she had not observed his entrance.

"Thou art weeping?" he said in amazement.

She started, passed her hand over her hair, and smiled.

"Why art thou weeping?"—repeated Litvínoff. She silently pointed to the letter.

" So thou art crying over that . . ." he said, haltingly.

" Come here, sit down,"—she said,—" give me thy hand. Well, yes, I have been crying. . . . Why does that surprise thee? Is *this* easy? " Again she pointed at the letter. Litvínoff sat down.

" I know that it is not easy, Irína; I say the same thing to thee in my letter. . . I understand thy position. But if thou believest in the significance of thy love for me, if my words have convinced thee, thou must also understand what I now feel at the sight of thy tears. I have come hither like a condemned man, but I am waiting: what will be announced to me? Death or life? Thy answer will decide everything. Only, do not look at me with such eyes. . . . They remind me of the eyes of days gone by, the Moscow eyes."

Irína suddenly blushed and turned away, as though she herself were conscious of something improper in her gaze.

" Why dost thou say that, Grigóry? Art not thou ashamed of thyself? Thou wishest to know my answer . . . . but canst thou doubt it? Thy letter, my friend, has set me to thinking. Thou writest here that my love has replaced all else for thee, that even thy former occupations must now remain without application; but I ask thee: Can a man live by love alone? Will it not pall on him in the end, will not he long for activity, and will not he upbraid that which has alienated him from it? That is the thought which terrifies me; that is what I fear, and not that which thou hast proposed."

Litvínoff gazed attentively at Irína, and Irína gazed attentively at him as though each of them was desirous of penetrating further and more profoundly into the soul of the other, further and more profoundly than the spoken word can attain, or reveal.

" There is no necessity for thy fearing that,"— began Litvínoff.—" I must have expressed myself badly.—" Boredom? Inactivity? With the new forces which thy love will give me? Oh, Irína, believe me, thy love is all the world to me, and I myself cannot now foresee all that may develop from it!"

Irína became thoughtful.

" But where are we to go? "—she whispered.

" Where? We will talk about that hereafter. But, of course . . . of course, thou consentest . . . thou consentest, Irína? "

She looked at him.—" And thou wilt be happy? "

" Oh, Irína! "

" Thou wilt regret nothing? Never? "

She bent over the box of laces, and again began to sort them over.

" Be not angry with me, my dearest, if I busy myself with this nonsense at such a moment. . .

I am obliged to go to a ball, given by a certain lady. These rags have been sent to me, and I must make my selection to-day. Akh! I am terribly distressed!"—she suddenly exclaimed, and laid her face against the edge of the box. . . Again tears dropped from her eyes. . . She turned away: the tears might fall on the lace.

"Irína, thou art weeping again,"—began Litvínoff, anxiously.

"Well, yes, I am,"—assented Irína.—"Akh, Grigóry, do not torture me, do not torture thyself!... Let us be free people! What is the harm if I do cry? Yes, and do I understand myself why these tears flow? Thou knowest, thou hast heard my decision, thou art convinced that it is unalterable, that I consent to . . . how was it thou didst word it? . . to everything or nothing . . . what more? Let us be free! Why these mutual chains? Thou and I are alone now. Thou lovest me, I love thee; have we nothing better to do than to extort our opinions from each other? Look at me; I have not tried to present myself in a fine light before thee, not by so much as a single word have I hinted at the fact, that it may not be so easy for me to trample under foot my conjugal duties. . . But I do not deceive myself, I know that I am a criminal, and that *he* has a right to kill me. Well, and what of that! Let us be free, I say. The day is ours—eternity is ours."

She rose from her chair, and looked down upon

Litvínoff, smiling faintly, and narrowing her eyelids, and with her arm, bare to the elbow, sweeping back a long lock of hair, upon which sparkled two or three tears. A rich lace shoulder-cape slipped from the table and fell on the floor, at Irína's feet. She trod upon it with scorn.— "Do not I please thee to-day? Have I grown ugly since yesterday? Tell me, hast thou often beheld a more beautiful arm? And my hair? Tell me, dost thou love me?"

She seized him with both arms, pressed his head to her breast; her comb rattled and fell, and her loosened hair flowed over him in a soft, perfumed flood.

XXIV

LITVÍNOFF paced to and fro in his room at the hotel, with thoughtfully drooping head. It now behoved him to pass from theory to practice, to seek the means and the road for a flight, for an emigration to unknown lands. . . But, strange to say, he was not meditating about these means and roads so much as on the point,—had the resolution on which he had so obstinately insisted been actually, indubitably taken? Had the final, irrevocable word been uttered? But, surely, Irína had said to him at parting: "Act, act, and when everything is ready, thou hast only to inform me." It was settled! Away with all doubts. . . He must proceed. And Litvínoff had proceeded—so far—to meditation. First of all, there was the question of money. Litvínoff had on hand one thousand three hundred and thirty-eight gulden—in French money two thousand eight hundred and fifty-eight francs; it was an insignificant sum, but sufficient for their first necessities, and so he must write at once to his father to send him as much as possible: he might sell a forest, a bit of land. . . But under what pretext? . . . Well, a pretext would be found. Irína

had spoken, it is true, of her *bijoux,* but it was not
proper to take that into consideration; who knows
but they might serve for a rainy day. In addition, among his assets was a fine Geneva half-
chronometer watch, for which he might get . . say,
four hundred francs. Litvínoff betook himself
to his bankers, and turned the conversation, in a
roundabout way, on the subject whether it would
be possible, in case of need, to borrow money.
But the bankers in Baden are an experienced
and cautious folk, and in reply to such roundabout hints immediately assume a decrepit, languid mien, precisely like that of a field-flower
whose stem has been severed by the scythe; several of them, however, laugh cheerfully and
boldly in your face, as though they appreciate
your innocent jest. Litvínoff, to his own mortifi-
cation, even tried his luck at roulette, even—oh,
the ignominy!—placed a thaler on thirty num-
bers, corresponding to the number of his years.
He did this with a view to augmenting and
rounding out his capital; and, in fact, if he did
not augment, he did round out his capital, by
losing the extra twenty-eight gulden. The
second question was, also, of no little importance:
A passport. But a passport is not so obligatory
for a woman, and there are countries where it is
not required at all. Belgium, for example, or
England; and, in conclusion, a passport which
was not Russian might be obtained. Litvínoff

reflected very seriously on all these things. His resolution was strong, without the slightest trace of wavering; but in the meantime, contrary to his will, against his will, something the reverse of serious, something almost comic, passed through, leaked through his meditations, as though his enterprise itself were a matter of jest, and no one had ever eloped with any one in reality, but only in comedies and romances, and, possibly, somewhere in the provincial tracts, in some Tchukhlóm or Syzrán district, where, according to the statement of one traveller, people even vomit with tedium at times. At this point it recurred to Litvínoff's memory how one of his friends, cornet Batzóff, on the retired list, had carried off a merchant's daughter in a post-sledge with sleigh-bells, having preliminarily got her parents, and even the bride herself, intoxicated, and how it had afterward turned out that he had been cheated, and almost killed outright, to boot. Litvínoff waxed extremely wroth with himself for such inappropriate recollections, and then, recalling Tatyána, her sudden departure, all that woe and suffering and shame, he became but too profoundly conscious that the deed which he was contemplating was of anything but a facetious nature, and that he had been in the right when he had said to Irína that no other issue was left, for his own honour's sake. . . And again, at this mere name, something burning momentarily enveloped him with a sweet anguish, then died away around his heart.

The trampling of a horse's hoofs resounded behind him. . . He stepped aside . . Irína had overtaken him on horseback; by her side rode the fat general. She recognised Litvínoff, nodded her head to him, and giving her horse a blow on the withers with her whip, started it into a gallop, then suddenly urged it onward at full speed. Her dark veil floated in the wind. . .

"*Pas si vite! Nom de Dieu! pas si vite!*"— shouted the general, and galloped after her.

XXV

ON the following morning, Litvínoff had just
returned home from his bankers, with whom he
had had another conference about the playful
unsteadiness of our rate of exchange, and the best
method of sending money abroad, when the door-
porter handed him a letter. He recognised
Irína's handwriting, and without breaking the
seal—an evil premonition awoke in him, God only
knows why—he went off to his own room. This
is what he read (the letter was written in French):

" MY DEAREST! I have been thinking all night about
thy proposition. . . I will not deceive thee. Thou hast
been frank with me, and I will be frank: I *cannot* elope
with thee, I *have not the strength* to do it. I feel how
culpable I am toward thee; my second fault is greater
than the first—I despise myself, my cowardice; I over-
whelm myself with reproaches, but I cannot change
myself. In vain do I demonstrate to myself that I
have ruined thy happiness, that thou now hast a right
to regard me merely as a frivolous coquette, that I
offered myself, that I myself gave thee a solemn promise. . . I am horrified; I feel hatred toward myself, but
I cannot act otherwise—I cannot, I cannot. I do not
seek to justify myself; I will not tell thee that I myself

274

was carried away . . . . all that signifies nothing; but I do wish to tell thee, and to repeat it, and repeat it yet again: I am thine, thine forever, do with me as thou wilt, when thou wilt: without resistance or calculation, I am thine. . . But flee, abandon everything. . . no! no! no! I entreated thee to save me. I myself hoped to obliterate everything, to consume everything, as in the fire . . . but evidently, there is no salvation for me; evidently, the poison has penetrated too deeply within me; evidently, it is not possible to breathe this atmosphere for a space of many years with impunity! I have wavered long whether I ought to write thee this letter; it is terrible to me to reflect what decision thou wilt arrive at; I trust only in thy love for me. But I have considered that it would be dishonest on my part not to tell thee the truth—the more so as thou hast, perhaps, already begun to take the first measures for the accomplishment of our intention. Akh! it was very beautiful, but impossible of fulfilment! Oh, my friend, regard me as a weak, frivolous woman; despise me, but do not desert me, do not desert thy Irína! . . . I have not the strength to abandon this society, but neither can I live in it without thee. We shall soon return to Petersburg; do thou come thither; dwell there; we will find occupation for thee; thy past labours shall not be wasted; thou shalt find a profitable application for them . . . only live near me, only love me as I am, with all my weaknesses and vices, and understand fully that no one's heart will ever be so tenderly devoted to thee as the heart of thy Irína. Come quickly to me; I shall not have a minute's peace until I see thee.

"Thine, thine, thine, I."

SMOKE

The blood beat like a hammer in Litvínoff's head, and then slowly and heavily retreated to his heart, and became as cold within him as a stone. He read over Irína's letter, and, as on that other occasion in Moscow, fell fainting on the divan, and remained there motionless. A dark abyss had suddenly surrounded him on all sides, and he stared despairingly, bereft of reason, into the gloom. Thus, once more betrayal, or no, worse than betrayal—a lie and trivialities... And life was shattered; everything had been torn up by the roots, utterly, and the only thing to which he might have clung—that last support—was shattered into fragments also! "Follow us to Petersburg,"—he repeated with a bitter, inward laugh: " we will find occupation for thee there " . . . " Will they promote me to be head clerk of a department, I wonder? And who is *we?* That is where her past spoke out! There lies the secret, repulsive thing, which I do not know, but which she would like to obliterate, and burn as in the fire! That is that world of intrigues, of secret relations, of scandals of Byélskys and Dólskys. . . And what a future! what a splendid rôle awaits me! To live near her, to visit her, to share with her the vicious melancholy of a fashionable lady whom society oppresses and bores, though she cannot exist outside its circle, to be her domestic friend, and, of course, the friend of His Excellency also . . . until . . .

until her whim is past, and the plebeian friend loses his piquancy, and that same fat general or Mr. Fínikoff replaces him,—that is both possible and agreeable, and, if you like, profitable . . . she speaks of a profitable application of my talents?—but that design is impossible of realisation, impossible of realisation! . . ." In Litvínoff's soul there arose something in the nature of the momentary gusts of wind which precede a thunderstorm—sudden, wild outbursts. . . Every expression in Irína's letter aroused his indignation; the very assurances as to the immutability of her feelings affronted him. " Things cannot remain like this,"—he exclaimed at last,—" I will not permit her to play so pitilessly with my life. . ."

Litvínoff sprang up, seized his hat. But what was there to be done? Fly to her? Reply to her letter? He halted, and his arms sank by his sides.

Yes: what was there to be done?

Had he not himself proposed to her that fatal choice? It had not turned out as he had wished. . . every choice is subject to that misfortune. She had changed her decision, it is true; she herself had been the first to declare that she would abandon everything and follow him—that was true also. But neither did she deny her guilt, she called herself, in plain terms, a weak woman; she had not meant to deceive him, she had been de-

ceived in herself. . . . . What retort was there
to make? At all events, she was not dissimulat-
ing, not dealing doubly with him . . . she was
frank with him, pitilessly frank. Nothing had
forced her to state her intentions on the spot,
nothing had prevented her soothing him with
promises, putting off everything, leaving everything in uncertainty, until their very departure
. . . her departure with her husband for Italy!
But she had ruined his life, she had ruined two
lives! . . . Was not that enough?

But toward Tatyána she was not to blame;
he was to blame, he alone, Litvínoff, and he
had no right to shake off from himself the
responsibility for that which his fault had
imposed, like an iron yoke, upon him. . . .
All that was so; but what remained to be done
now?

Again he flung himself on the divan, and
again, darkly, leaving no trace, with devouring
swiftness . . . the moments flitted past. . .

"And why not obey her?"—flashed through
his mind. "She loves me, she is mine—and in
our very attraction for each other, in that passion which, after the lapse of so many years, has
broken out and made its way forth to the sur-
face with such violence, is there not something
inevitable, irresistible as the law of nature? Live
in Petersburg . . . but shall I be the first man
who finds himself in such a position? Yes, and

where could she and I have found a refuge?..."
And he fell into thought, and the image of
Irína, in that aspect in which it had forever im-
printed itself on his most recent recollections,
softly presented itself before him. . . .

But not for long... He recovered himself, and
with a fresh outburst of indignation, he thrust
away from him both those recollections, and that
enchanting image.

" Thou art giving me to drink of that golden
cup,"—he exclaimed,—" but there is poison in
thy beverage, and thy white wings are soiled
with filth. . . Away! To remain here with thee,
after having . . . driven away, driven away my
betrothed bride . . . would be a dishonourable, a
dishonourable act!" He clenched his fists bitterly, and another face, with the imprint of
suffering and set features, with speechless reproach in the farewell glance, surged up from
the depths. . .

And for a long time Litvínoff tormented
himself in this manner; for a long time, like a
critically sick man, his tortured thoughts tossed
from side to side. . . At last he calmed down; at
last he reached a decision. From the very first
moment he had foreseen what that decision
would be . . . it presented itself to him, at first,
as a remote, barely-perceptible spot in the midst
of the whirlwind and the gloom of his internal
conflict; then it began to come nearer and nearer,

and ended by cutting into his heart with a cold, sharp blade.

Again Litvínoff dragged his trunk forth from the corner; again, without haste, and even with a certain dull carefulness, he packed all his things, rang for a servant, paid his bill, and despatched a note in Russian, to Irína, which ran as follows:

"I do not know whether you are more to blame with respect to me now than you were in days gone by; but I do know that the present blow is much the stronger. . . This is the end. You say to me: 'I cannot'; and I repeat the same to you: I cannot . . . do what you wish. I cannot, and I will not. Do not answer me. You are not in a position to give me the only answer which I would accept. I am going away to-morrow, early, by the first train. Farewell; may you be happy. . . Probably we shall not meet again."

Litvínoff did not leave his room until night-fall; God knows whether he was expecting anything! About seven o'clock in the evening, a lady in a black mantle, with a veil over her face, walked twice past the entrance of his hotel. After stepping a little to one side, and casting a glance at some point in the distance, she suddenly made a decisive movement, and for the third time directed her steps toward the entrance. . .

"Whither are you going, Irína Pávlovna?"
—rang out a constrained voice behind her.

She turned round with convulsive swiftness. .
Potúgin rushed up to her.

She halted, reflected, and fairly flung herself
at him, thrust her arm in his, and drew him
aside.

"Take me away, take me away,"—she kept
repeating, panting.

"What is the matter with you, Irína Pávlovna?"—he murmured, in amazement.

"Take me away,"—she repeated with redoubled force,—"if you do not wish to have me
remain forever . . . . there!"

Potúgin bowed his head submissively, and
both walked rapidly away.

Early on the following morning Litvínoff
was entirely ready for his journey, when there
came into his room . . . that same Potúgin.

He silently approached him, and silently
shook his hand. Litvínoff, also, said nothing.
Both wore long faces, and both endeavoured in
vain to smile.

"I have come to wish you a prosperous journey,"—Potúgin said, at last.

"And how did you know that I was going
away to-day?"—inquired Litvínoff.

Potúgin gazed around him, on the floor. . .
"It became known to me . . . as you see. Our
last conversation finally took such a strange turn.

. . I did not wish to part from you without expressing to you my sincere sympathy."

"Do you sympathise with me now, when I am going away?"

Potúgin gazed mournfully at Litvínoff.—"Ekh, Grigóry Mikhaílitch, Grigóry Mikhaílitch,"—he began, with a short sigh,—"we are in no frame of mind for that now, we are in no mood for subtleties and disputes. Here you are, so far as I am able to judge, decidedly indifferent to our national literature, and therefore, perhaps, you have no conception of Váska Busláeff?"

"Of whom?"

"Of Váska Busláeff, the dashing hero of Nóvgorod . . . in the Collection of Kirshá Daníleff."

"What Busláeff?"—ejaculated Litvínoff, somewhat dazed by the sudden turn which the conversation had taken.—"I don't know."

"Well, no matter. See here, this is what I wished to call to your attention. Váska Busláeff, after he has dragged his Nóvgorodians off to Jerusalem on a pilgrimage, and there, to their horror, has bathed naked in the holy river Jordan, for he believed 'neither in bell-clang, nor in dream, nor in the croaking of birds,'—that logical Váska Busláeff ascends Mount Tabor, and on the crest of that mountain, lies a huge stone, across which all sorts of people have tried, in vain, to leap. . . . Váska wishes to try his luck also. And on his way up the mountain he encounters a skull, human bones; he kicks it. Well, and the head says to him: 'Why dost thou kick? I have known how to live; I know also how to wallow in the dust—and the same thing shall happen unto thee.'[1] And in fact Váska leaps across the stone, and would have got clear over had not he caught his heel, and cracked his skull. And here I must remark, by the way, that it would not be a bad thing if my friends, the Slavyanophils, who are great hands at kicking all sorts of death's-heads and rotten folks, would ponder over this epic song."

"But what is your object in saying all this?"—interrupted Litvínoff impatiently at last.— "I must go, excuse me. . . ."

"My object is,"—replied Potúgin, and his eyes beamed with a friendly feeling which Litvínoff had never expected from him,—"to keep you from repulsing the dead human skull; and perchance, in return for your goodness, you will succeed in leaping across the fatal stone. I will not detain you any longer, only you must permit me to embrace you in farewell."

"I shall not even attempt to leap across,"—said Litvínoff, as he exchanged the threefold kiss with Potúgin. And to the sorrowful emotion,

[1] The version which I have given, "Vasíly Busláevitch," in "The Epic Songs of Russia" (Charles Scribner's Sons), is from a slightly different original to the one here quoted.—TRANSLATOR.

which filled his soul to overflowing, there was added, for an instant, compassion for another poor wretch. But he must go, he must go. . . He flung himself about the room.

" I will carry something for you, if you like." —Potúgin offered his services.

" No, thanks, don't trouble yourself; I will manage alone. . . ." He put on his hat, took his bag in his hand.—" So you say,"—he inquired, as he was standing on the threshold,—" that you have seen her? "

" Yes, I have seen her."

" Well . . and what of her? "

Potúgin made no answer for a while.—" She expected you last night. . . and will expect you to-day."

" Ah! Well, then tell her. . . No, it is not necessary, nothing is necessary. Farewell, . . . Farewell! "

" Farewell, Grigóry Mikhaílitch. . . . Let me say one word more to you. You will have time to hear me out: the train does not leave for half an hour yet. You are returning to Russia. . . You will . . . in course of time . . . become active there. . . Permit an old failure—for I, alas! am a failure, and nothing else—to give you a parting bit of advice. On every occasion, when you are obliged to enter upon an undertaking, ask yourself: are you serving civilisation,—in the exact and strict sense of the word,—are you furthering

one of its ideas; is your labour of that pedagog-
ical, European character, which alone is profitable and fruitful in our day, in our country? If
so—advance boldly: you are on the right road,
and your affair is an honourable one! Glory to
God! You are not alone now. You will not be
'a sower of the desert': hard workers . . . .
pioneers . . . have already sprung up among us.
. . But you do not care to hear about that now.—
Good-bye, do not forget me!"

Litvínoff descended the stairs at a run, flung
himself into a carriage, and drove to the railway
station, without casting a single glance at the
town where so much of his own life was being
left behind. . . He seemed to be yielding to a bil-
low: it seized him, swept him onward, and he
firmly resolved not to resist its impulse . . . he renounced every other manifestation of will.

He was already entering the railway carriage.
"Grigóry Mikhaílovitch . . . Grigóry . . ." he
heard a beseeching whisper behind him. He
shuddered. . . Could it be Irína? Exactly that:
it was she. Wrapped in her maid's shawl, with a
travelling hat on her unkempt locks, she was
standing on the platform and gazing at him with
dimmed eyes. "Turn back, turn back, I have
come for thee!" said those eyes. And what,
what all, did not they promise! She did not
move; she had not the strength to add a single
word; everything about her, even the disorder of

her garments, everything seemed to be entreating mercy. . . .

Litvínoff could hardly stand on his feet, could hardly refrain from rushing to her. . . . But the wave to which he had yielded himself asserted its power. . . He sprang into the carriage, and, turning round, he motioned Irína to a place beside him. She understood him. The time was not past. Only one step, one movement, and two lives forever united would have sped forth into the unknown distance. . . While she hesitated a loud whistle rang out, and the train started.

Litvínoff flung himself back, and Irína walked tottering to a bench and sank down upon it, to the extreme amazement of an ex-diplomat who had accidentally wandered into the station. He was only slightly acquainted with Irína, but took a great interest in her, and perceiving that she was lying as though unconscious, he thought that she had had "*une attaque de nerfs,*" and consequently regarded it as his duty, the duty *d'un galant chevalier,* to go to her assistance. But his amazement assumed far greater proportions when, at the first word he addressed to her, she suddenly rose, repulsed the offered arm, and, rushing forth into the street, in a few moments vanished in the milky cloud of mist, which is so characteristic of the Black Forest climate in the early days of autumn.

XXVI

WE once chanced to enter the cottage of a peasant woman who had just lost her only, fervently-loved son, and to our no small surprise, we found her entirely composed, almost cheerful.—"Let her alone!" said her husband, whom this surprise did not escape:—"she is hardened just now."—In the same way Litvínoff "was hardened." The same sort of composure came upon him during the first hours of his journey. Utterly annihilated, and hopelessly unhappy, he nevertheless was at rest, at rest after the turmoils and tortures of the preceding week, after all the blows which, one after the other, had descended upon his head. They had shaken him all the more violently because he was not created for such tempests. He no longer had any hope of anything now, and tried not to remember—most of all, not to remember. He was going to Russia . . . he must take refuge somewhere! but he no longer made any plans which personally concerned himself. He did not recognise himself; he did not understand his proceedings; it was exactly as though he had lost his real " I," and, altogether, he felt very little interest in that " I." Sometimes it seemed to him as though

he were carrying his own corpse, and only the
bitter convulsions of an incurable spiritual malady, which ran through him now and then,
reminded him that he was still endowed with life.
At times it seemed incomprehensible to him how
a man—a man!—could permit a woman, love,
. . . . to exercise such influence over him. . . . .
" A shameful weakness! " he whispered, and
shook out his cloak, and settled himself more
squarely in his seat, as much as to say, There
now, old things are done with, let us start on
something new . . . . A minute later, and he
merely smiled bitterly and felt amazed at himself. He took to gazing out of the window.
The day was grey and damp; there was no rain,
but the fog held on, and low-lying clouds veiled
the sky. The wind was blowing in the contrary
direction to the course of the train; whitish
clouds of steam, now alone, now mingled with
other, darker clouds of smoke, swept, in an end-
less series, past the window beside which
Litvínoff sat. He began to watch the steam,
the smoke. Incessantly whirling, rising and
falling, twisting and catching at the grass, at
the bushes, playing pranks, as it were, lengthen-
ing and melting, puff followed puff . . . . they
were constantly changing, and yet remained the
same . . . . a monotonous, hurried, tiresome game!
Sometimes the wind changed, the road made a
turn—the whole mass suddenly disappeared,

and immediately became visible through the opposite window; then, once more, the huge trail flung itself over, and once more veiled from Litvínoff the wide view of the Rhine Valley. He gazed and gazed, and a strange reflection occurred to him. . . He was alone in the carriage; there was no one to interfere with him.—" Smoke, smoke,"—he repeated several times in succession; and suddenly everything appeared to him to be smoke—everything, his own life, everything pertaining to men, especially everything Russian. Everything is smoke and steam, —he thought;—everything seems to be constantly undergoing change; everywhere there are new forms, phenomenon follows phenomenon, but in reality everything is exactly alike; everything is hurrying, hastening somewhither—and everything vanishes without leaving a trace, without having attained to any end whatever; another breeze has begun to blow—and everything has been flung to the other side, and there, again, is the same incessant, agitated—and useless game. He recalled many things which had taken place, with much sound and clatter, before his eyes during the last few years . . . . " smoke,"—he murmured,—" smoke "; he recalled the heated disputes, shovings and shouts at Gubaryóff's, and at the houses of other persons, of high and of low degree, of prominent people, and of people who had lagged behind, of old people and of young . . . " smoke "—he repeated,—" smoke and steam "; he recalled, in conclusion, the famous picnic also; and other judgments and speeches of other statesmen also recurred to his mind—and even everything which Potúgin had preached . . . . " smoke, smoke, and nothing more." But his own aspirations and feelings and efforts and dreams? He merely waved his hand in renunciation of them.

And in the meantime the train was dashing on, dashing on Rastadt, Karlsruhe and Bruchsal had long since been left behind; the mountains on the right side of the road were retreating, receding into the distance, then advanced again, but were not so lofty now, and were more sparsely covered with forests. . . The train made a sharp turn to one side—and behold, there was Heidelberg. The railway carriages rolled up under the shed of the station; the cries of pedlars, selling every sort of thing, even Russian newspapers, resounded; the travellers fidgeted in their seats, emerged on the platform. But Litvínoff did not leave his corner, and continued to sit with bowed head. Suddenly some one called him by name; he raised his eyes; Bindásoff's ugly face thrust itself through the window, and behind him—or did it only seem so to him?—no, it was a fact: they were all faces from Baden, familiar faces: there was Madame Sukhántchikoff, there was Voroshíloff, and there was Bambáeff, all of them advancing toward him—and Bindásoff was roaring:

" And where is Pishtchálkin? We have been waiting for him; but never mind, crawl out, soaker, we 're all going to Gubaryóff's."

" Yes, my dear fellow, and besides, Gubaryóff is waiting for us," Bambáeff confirmed his statement, as he stepped forward:—" get out."

Litvínoff would have flown into a rage had it not been for that dead weight which lay upon his heart. He glanced at Bindásoff, and turned silently away.

" I tell you, Gubaryóff is here,"—cried Madame Sukhántchikoff, her eyes almost starting from their sockets.

Litvínoff did not stir.

" Yes, listen, Litvínoff," began Bambáeff, at last. " Not only is Gubaryóff here, but there is a whole phalanx of the most splendid, the cleverest young men, Russians,—and all are devoting themselves to the natural sciences, all cherish the most noble convictions! Do stop, on their account, for goodness' sake. Here, for example, is a certain . . . ekh! I 've forgotten his name! but he 's simply a genius! "

" Come, let him alone, let him alone, Rostisláff Ardaliónitch! "—interposed Madame Sukhántchikoff,—" let him alone! you see what sort of a man he is; and all his tribe are of the same sort. He has an aunt: at first I thought her a sensible woman, but day before yesterday I travelled hither in her company—she had only just arrived in Baden, and lo and behold! back she flies,—well, sir, I travelled with her, and I began to question her. . . If you will believe me, not one word could I get out of the haughty creature. The disgusting aristocrat!"

Poor Kapitólina Márkovna—an aristocrat! Did she ever expect such a disgrace?

But Litvínoff still held his peace, and turned away, and pulled his cap down over his eyes. At last the train started.

"Come, say something by way of farewell, you man of stone!"—shouted Bambáeff.

"You can't go off like this!"

"Trash! simpleton!"—roared out Bindásoff. The carriages rolled more and more rapidly, and he could revile with impunity.—"Miser! Mollusc! Drunken bummer!"

Whether Bindásoff invented this last epithet on the spur of the moment, or whether it had reached him from other hands, at all events it evidently afforded great pleasure to the extremely noble young men who were studying the natural sciences, for a few days later it made its appearance in the Russian periodical sheet, which was published at that time in Heidelberg, under the title: *À tout venant je crache!* or "If God does n't desert you, the pigs won't eat you." [1] [2]

---

[1] "Him whom God helps, nobody can harm."—TRANSLATOR.
[2] An historical fact.

But Litvínoff kept repeating his former word: smoke, smoke, smoke! Here now, he thought, there are now more than a hundred Russian students in Heidelberg; all are studying chemistry, physics, physiology—they will not even listen to anything else . . . but let five or six years elapse, and there will not be fifteen men in the courses of those same celebrated professors . . . the wind will change, the smoke will rush to the other side . . . smoke . . . smoke . . . smoke! [1]

Toward nightfall he passed Kassel. Together with the twilight, an intolerable anguish descended like a vulture upon him, and, nestling in the corner of the railway carriage, he began to weep. For a long time his tears flowed without relieving his heart, but torturing him in a caustic, bitter way; and, at that same time, in one of the hostelries of Kassel, on her bed, in a burning fever, lay Tatyána; Kapitólina Márkovna sat beside her.

" Tánya,"—she said,—" for God's sake, allow me to send a telegram to Grigóry Mikhaílovitch; do let me, Tánya! "

" No, aunty,"—she answered,—" it is not necessary; do not feel alarmed. Give me some water; this will soon pass off."

And, in fact, a week later her health mended, and the two friends resumed their journey.

[1] Litvínoff's presentiment was fulfilled. In 1866, there were thirteen Russian students in the summer term, and twelve in the winter term, at Heidelberg.

XXVII

Without halting either in Petersburg or in Moscow, Litvínoff returned to his estate. He was frightened when he saw his father, so greatly enfeebled and aged had the latter become. The old man rejoiced at the sight of his son, as much as a man can rejoice whose life is drawing to a close; he immediately transferred to him all his affairs, which were in great confusion, and after creaking on a few weeks longer, departed from the arena of earth. Litvínoff was left alone in his ancient wing of the manor-house, and with a heavy heart, without hope, without zeal and without money, he began to farm the estate. Farming an estate in Russia is a cheerless affair, only too well known to many persons; we will not enlarge on the point of how bitter it seemed to Litvínoff. As a matter of course, there could be no question of reforms and innovations; the application of the knowledge which he had acquired abroad was deferred for an indefinite period; want compelled him to worry on from day to day, to consent to all sorts of compromises,—both material and moral. New ideas won their way badly, old ones had lost their force; the ignorant clashed with the dishonest; his whole deranged

existence was in constant motion, like a quaking
bog, and only the great word " liberty " moved,
like the spirit of God, over the waters. Patience
was required, first of all, and not passive but
active, persistent patience, not devoid, at times,
of tact, not devoid of guile . . . . which Litvínoff,
in his actual spiritual state, found doubly difficult. He had very little desire left to live. . .
Whence could he summon a desire to bestir himself and work?

But a year passed, then a second, the third was
beginning. The grand thought was gradually
being realised, was being transformed into flesh
and blood: a sprout was putting forth from the
seed that had been sown; and its enemies, either
open or secret, could no longer trample it under
foot. Litvínoff himself, although he had ended
by giving up the greater part of his land to the
peasants, on the rotation-of-crops system, that
is to say, had returned to the wretched, primitive methods of farming, yet had some success: he re-established the factory, set up a tiny
farm with five hired labourers,—he had as many
as forty, at different times,—paid off the principal part of the debts. . . And his spirit grew
firm within him; again he began to resemble the
Litvínoff of former days. The painful, deeply-
concealed feeling, it is true, never left him, and
he had grown sedate beyond his years, had
shut himself up in his narrow circle, had broken

off all his previous connections . . . . but the deathlike indifference had vanished, and again he moved about among the living, and behaved like a living man. The last traces of the witchery which had taken possession of him had vanished also: everything which had taken place at Baden presented itself to him as in a dream. . And Irína? She, also, had paled and disappeared, and it was only in a confused way that Litvínoff was conscious of something terrible beneath the mist in which her image had gradually become enveloped. News of Tatyána reached him from time to time; he knew that she and her aunt had settled on her little estate, about two hundred versts from him, were living quietly and receiving hardly any guests,—and, for the rest, were composed and well.—But one day, one beautiful May day, he was sitting in his study, and indifferently turning over the leaves of the last number of a Petersburg journal: a servant entered and announced the arrival of his aged uncle. This uncle was the first cousin of Kapitólina Márkovna, and had recently visited her. He had purchased an estate in Litvínoff's neighbourhood, and was on his way thither. He spent a whole day with his nephew, and told him a great deal about Tatyána's manner of life. On the day after his departure, Litvínoff sent her a letter, the first since their parting. He requested permission to renew the acquaintance, by letter at least, and also desired to know whether he must forever abandon the thought of seeing her some day? Not without agitation did he await the reply . . . and a reply arrived at last. Tatyána made a friendly response to his question. " If you should take a fancy to visit us," she said in conclusion, " come, we shall be glad to see you: they say that weak people feel more comfortable together than apart." Kapitólina Márkovna sent her compliments. Litvínoff was as happy as a child; his heart had not beaten so cheerfully for a long time. And he suddenly felt relieved and bright. . . Exactly as when the sun rises and drives away the shades of night, a light zephyr flits with the sun's rays over the face of the reviving earth. All that day Litvínoff did nothing but smile, even when he made the rounds of his farm and issued his orders. He immediately began to make preparations for the journey, and two weeks later he set off to Tatyána.

XXVIII

HE travelled rather slowly along the country
roads, without any particular adventures: only
once the tire on one of the hind wheels broke; a
blacksmith welded and welded it, cursed it and
himself, and then threw up the job; luckily, it
turned out that one can travel very well indeed
in our country even with a broken tire, especially
on a " soft " road, that is to say, in the mud. On
the other hand, Litvínoff had two or three decidedly curious encounters. At one posting-
station he found a meeting of justices of the
peace, and among their number, Pishtchálkin,
who produced upon him the impression of being
a Solon or a Solomon: such lofty wisdom did his
speech breathe forth, with such unbounded respect did both landed proprietors and peasants
bear themselves toward him: . . . and in his appearance, also, Pishtchálkin had begun to resemble a sage of olden days: his hair had receded
from his temples, and his face, which had grown
fuller, had become completely petrified into a sort
of majestic jelly of virtue unhampered by anything whatsoever. He congratulated Litvínoff on
his arrival " in my own district—if I may make
so bold as to use so ambitious an expression,"—

and thereupon, instantly sank into a paroxysm of well-intentioned emotions. But he did succeed in imparting one piece of news, namely, concerning Voroshíloff. That paladin of the gilded classes had again entered the military service, and had already managed to deliver a lecture to the officers of his regiment on " Buddhism," or " dynamism," or something of that sort. . . . . Pishtchálkin could not remember exactly what. At the next posting-station they did not harness Litvínoff's horses for a long time; the affair happened at daybreak,—and he was dozing as he sat in his calash. A voice which struck him as familiar awakened him: he opened his eyes. . .

Heavens! was it not Mr. Gubaryóff who was standing there in a grey round jacket and flapping sleeping-trousers, and swearing, on the porch of the posting-cottage? . . . No, it was not Mr. Gubaryóff. . . But what a startling resemblance! . . . . Only, this gentleman's mouth was wider and fuller of teeth, and the gaze of his dismal eyes was still fiercer, his nose was bigger, and his beard thicker, and his whole aspect was heavier and more repulsive.

" The sca-aoundrels, the sca-aoundrels! "—he was repeating, slowly and viciously stretching his wolfish mouth very wide:—" the damned peasantry. . . . Here you see it . . . . . . this lauded liberty . . . . and you can't get any horses . . . the sca-aoundrels! "

" The sca-aoundrels, the sca-aoundrels! "—
another voice here made itself heard inside the
house, and on the porch there presented himself,
—also in a grey round jacket and flapping sleeping-trousers,—presented himself, this time actually and indubitably, the genuine Mr. Gubaryóff himself, Stepán Nikoláevitch Gubaryóff.
" The damned peasantry! "—he continued, in
imitation of his brother (it appeared that the
first gentleman was his elder brother, the
" Danteist " [1] of the old school, who managed his
estate.) —" They ought to be flogged, that 's what
they ought; flogged on their snouts, that 's the
sort of liberty they need—flogged on their teeth.
. . They talk about . . . forsooth, ... about the
mayor of the district! . . . I 'll give it to them!
. . . Yes, and where 's that M'sieu' Roston? . . .
What does he superintend? . . . It 's his business, the cursed sluggard . . . not to reduce one
to anxiety. . . . . "

" But I have repeatedly told you, brother,"—
put in the elder Gubaryóff,—" that he was
not fit for anything, a regular sluggard! Only
you, for old acquaintance' sake. . . . M'sieu'
Roston, M'sieu' Roston! . . . . What has become of you? "

" Roston! Roston! "—shouted the younger,
the great Gubaryóff.—" Come, brother Dore-
medónt Nikoláitch, call him well! "

[1] A term applied to cruel serf-owners.—TRANSLATOR.

" That 's precisely what I am doing, brother Stepán Nikoláitch.—Monsieur Roston!"

" Here I am, here I am, here I am!"—a precipitate voice made itself heard, and from round the corner of the cottage sprang forth—Bambáeff.

Litvínoff fairly cried aloud in amazement. On the ill-starred enthusiast mournfully dangled a hussar jacket abbreviated by wear, with rents in the sleeves; his features were not so much altered as pinched and wizened; his extremely uneasy little eyes expressed slavish terror and hungry subserviency; but his dyed moustache bristled up above his full lips as of old. The Gubaryóff brothers set to work instantly and simultaneously to berate him from the elevation of the porch; he halted in front of them, below, in the mud, and, with his back meekly bowed, endeavoured to placate them with a timid smile, crumpling his cap in his red fingers, shifting from one foot to the other, and muttering that the horses would make their appearance immediately. . . But the brothers did not cease, until the younger, at last, let his eyes fall on Litvínoff. Whether he recognised him, whether he felt ashamed in the presence of a stranger, at all events, he suddenly turned on his heel, in bear-like fashion, and, gnawing his beard, hobbled into the posting-cottage; his brother instantly became mute, and turning round, in bear-like fashion also, followed in his footsteps. The great Gubaryóff, evidently, had not lost his influence in his own country either.

Bambáeff was on the point of following softly after the brothers... Litvínoff called him by name. He glanced round, took another look, and, recognising Litvínoff, fairly precipitated himself at him, with outstretched arms; but when he had rushed up to the carriage, and grasped the door, he fell against it with his breast and burst into a flood of tears.

"Stop, do stop, Bambáeff,"—Litvínoff said again and again, bending over him and touching him on the shoulder.

But he continued to sob.—"This .... this .... this is what I have come to ..." he murmured, sobbing.

"Bambáeff!"—thundered the brothers inside the cottage.

Bambáeff raised his head and hastily wiped away his tears.

"Good morning, my dear fellow,"—he whispered,—"good morning and good-bye! .... you hear, they are calling me."

"But how in the world do you come to be here?"—inquired Litvínoff:—"and what is the meaning of all this? I thought they called you a Frenchman..."

"I am their ... their house-steward, their butler,"—replied Bambáeff, and jerked his finger in the direction of the cottage.—" And I came to be a Frenchman by chance, by way of a jest. What can a man do, brother? When there is nothing to eat, you see, and you have spent your last penny, you put your neck into the noose, willy-nilly. You don't feel like being ambitious."

" But has *he* been long in Russia? And how did he part from his former comrades?"

" Ekh, brother! All that is over now. . . The weather has changed, you know. . . . He simply pitched Madame Sukhántchikoff, Matryóna Kuzmínitchna, out, neck and crop. She went off to Portugal, out of grief."

" Went to Portugal? What nonsense is this?"

" Yes, brother, to Portugal, with two Matryónovtzys."

" With whom?"

" With the Matryónovtzys: that's what the adherents of her faction are called."

" Has Matryóna Kuzmínitchna a faction, and is it numerous?"

" Why, it consists of just those two men. But *he* returned here nearly six months ago. Then others got into trouble, but he's all right. He lives in the country with his brother, and you just ought to hear now . . . ."

" Bambáeff!"

" Immediately, Stepán Nikoláitch, immediately. But thou, my dear fellow, art blooming, thou art enjoying thyself! Well, God be thanked! Where art thou bound for now?— Why, I never thought, I never foresaw that. . . . Dost thou remember Baden? Ekh, that was living! By the way, dost thou remember Bindásoff also? Just imagine, he is dead. He obtained a position in the excise office, and got into a fight in a dram-shop; and they smashed his skull with a billiard-cue. Yes, yes, hard times have come upon us! But I still say: Russia, what a land this Russia is! Look even at that pair of geese: surely, in all Europe, there is nothing like them! Real Arzamás fowls!"

And after paying this parting tribute to his ineradicable necessity to go into raptures, Bambáeff ran into the station-cottage, where his name was again being uttered, not without a few emphatic epithets.

Toward the end of that day, Litvínoff drove up to Tatyána's village. The little house, wherein dwelt his former betrothed, stood on a hill, above a small river, in the centre of a garden which had been newly laid out. The little house was new also, only just built, and was visible from afar, across river and meadow. It revealed itself to Litvínoff at a distance of two versts with its pointed partial upper story and row of windows, which gleamed brightly in the rays of the evening sun. From the time he quitted the last station, he had begun to experience a secret agitation; but at this point downright consternation seized upon him, joyous consternation, not unmingled with a certain alarm. " How will they receive me? "—he thought,—" how shall I present myself? " . . . In order to divert his thoughts somewhat he began to chat with the postilion, a peasant of the steppes, with a grey beard, but who had charged him for thirty versts, when, in reality, the distance was not twenty-five. He asked him: Did he know the Shestóff ladies?

" The Shestóffs, do you mean? Of course I know them! Kind ladies they are, there's no denying that! And they heal us poor folks too. I'm telling you the truth. Regular women doctors! Folks go to them from the whole county. That's so. They just crawl there in hordes. No sooner does any one fall ill, or cut himself, or anything else, than he immediately hastens to them, and they immediately apply a fomentation, or powders, or a plaster,—and that's the end of it: it helps. But don't dare to offer gifts of gratitude; we don't consent to that, say they; we don't do it for money. They've set up a school, too. . . . Well, but that doesn't amount to anything."

While the postilion was talking, Litvínoff never took his eyes from the little house. . . Now a woman in white came out on the balcony, stood, and stood, and then vanished. . . . " Can it be she?" His heart fairly leapt within him. "Faster! Faster!" he shouted to the postilion: the latter whipped up his horses. A few moments more . . . and the calash rolled in through the open gates. . . And on the porch Kapitólina Márkovna was already standing, and, quite beside herself, was clapping her hands and screaming: "I recognised him, I was the first to recognise him! 'T is he! 't is he!—I recognised him!"

Litvínoff sprang out of the calash, without giving the groom who came running up a chance to open the door, and hastily embracing Kapitólina Márkovna, rushed into the house, through the ante-room, into the salon. . . . Before him, all covered with confusion, stood Tatyána. She glanced at him with her kind, affectionate eyes (she had grown a little thinner, but it became her), and offered him her hand. But he did not take the hand, he fell on his knees before her. She had not in the least expected this, and did not know what to say, what to do.—The tears rushed to her eyes. She was startled, but her whole countenance beamed with joy. . . . "Grigóry Mikhaílitch, what is this, Grigóry Mikhaílitch?" she said . . . but he continued to kiss the hem of her garment . . . and with emotion he recalled how he had lain on his knees before her, in the same manner, at Baden. . . . . . But then —and now!

"Tánya,"—he repeated, over and over again,
—"Tánya! hast thou forgiven me, Tánya?"

"Aunty, aunty, what is this?"—Tatyána
appealed to Kapitólina Márkovna, who entered
at the moment.

"Do not hinder him, do not hinder him,
Tánya,"—replied the kind old woman.—"Thou
seest he has confessed his wrong."

But it is time to make an ending; and besides,
there is nothing more to add; the reader will
divine the outcome for himself. . . . But what
of Irína?

She is just as charming as ever, in spite of
her thirty years. Innumerable young men fall in
love with her, and even more would fall in love
with her, if . . . . if . . . . Reader, will not you
consent to be transported with us, for a few moments, to Petersburg, to one of the most prominent buildings there? Behold: before you lies
a spacious room, furnished, we will not say
"richly,"—that is too vulgar an expression,—but
imposingly, in a stately, impressive style. Do
you feel a certain tremor of servility? You must
know: you have entered a temple, a temple con-
secrated to the loftiest decorum, to virtue overflowing with love—in a word, to unearthly virtue.
A certain mysterious, actually mysterious silence
receives you into its embrace. The velvet por-
tières, the velvet curtains at the windows, the soft,

thick carpet on the floor, all seem destined and
designed to soothe and soften all harsh sounds
and violent emotions. Carefully-shaded lamps
inspire dignified feelings; a decorous perfume
is disseminated in the close atmosphere; the very
samovár on the table is hissing in a repressed and
modest way. The mistress of the house, an important personage in Petersburg society, is talking in a barely audible tone; she always speaks
in that way, as though there were a very critically
ill, almost dying person in the room. The other
ladies, in imitation of her, barely whisper; but
to-day, her sister, who is pouring tea, is moving
her lips with entire absence of sound, so that the
young man who is sitting before her, and has
accidentally got into the temple of decorum, is
even perplexed to know what she wants of him,
and she rustles at him, for the sixth time:
"*Voulez vous une tasse de thé?*" In the corner,
young, good-looking men are to be seen; mild
deference beams in their glances; tranquilly
mild, although insinuating, is the expression of
their faces; a multitude of tokens of distinction
glitter mildly on their breasts. The conversation
which is in progress is mild also; it touches upon
spiritual and patriotic subjects, *The Mysterious
Drop* by F. M. Glínka, the mission to the East,
the monasteries and brotherhoods of White Russia. From time to time, treading noiselessly
over the soft carpet, liveried lackeys pass to and

fro; their huge calves, clothed in tightly-fitting silk stockings, quiver calmly at every step; the respectful quiver of their stout muscles only intensifies the general impression of magnificence, benevolence, devoutness. . . It is a temple! It is a temple!

" Have you seen Madame Ratmíroff to-day? " —asks a personage gently.

" I met her to-day at Lise's," replies the mistress of the house, like an æolian harp:—" I feel sorry for her. . . She has an embittered mind . . . . *elle n'a pas la foi*."

" Yes, yes,"—repeats the personage;—" I remember that Peter Ivánitch said that of her, and it was very truly said—he said *qu'elle a . . . qu'elle a* an embittered mind."

" *Elle n'a pas la foi—*" the voice of the hostess dies away in the air, like the smoke of incense. —" *C'est une ame égarée.* She has an embittered mind."

" She has an embittered mind,"—repeats her sister, with her lips alone.

And that is why all the young men, without exception, do not fall in love with Irína. . . They are afraid of her . . . they are afraid of her " embittered mind."

That is the form which the current phrase about her has assumed; in that phrase, as in every phrase, there is a grain of truth. And it is not the young men alone who fear her; the older men, and persons of high rank, and even personages, fear her also. No one is capable of noting so accurately and delicately the ridiculous or the petty side of a character, no one possesses such a gift for pitilessly branding it with an unforgettable word. . . . And that word burns all the more painfully, because it proceeds from a fragrant, exquisitely beautiful mouth. . . . It would be difficult to say what is taking place within that soul; but rumour does not bestow upon any one of her adorers the title of the favoured suitor.

Irína's husband is advancing rapidly along that road which the French call the road of honours. The fat general is overtaking him; the condescending one is being left behind. And in that same town where Irína dwells, dwells also our friend, Sozónt Potúgin: he rarely sees her, and she has no particular need for maintaining relations with him. . . The little girl who was intrusted to his guardianship died not long ago.